Cloda adult and

childr with her

husba has two grown-up children.

*Also by Clodagh Chapman*

Jack In The Green

*And under the name Clodagh Gibson Jarvie*

The Web

# The Night Before Dark

Clodagh Chapman

HEADLINE

First published in Great Britain in 1988
by Judy Piatkus (Publishers) Ltd

First published in paperback in Great Britain in 1989
by HEADLINE BOOK PUBLISHING PLC



ISBN 0 7472 3217 2

Printed and bound in Great Britain by
Collins, Glasgow

HEADLINE BOOK PUBLISHING PLC
Headline House
79 Great Titchfield Street
London W1P 7FN

# The Night Before Dark

# Prologue

For the fourth day in succession the tall, red-haired man was the last member of the public to leave the archives search room.

'I'm sorry – last again.' He pushed his notes together and smiled at the clerk. He looked as though he held the lid of his emotions tight down on some simmering excitement.

The clerk saw that as well as the notes from his research he had a bundle of estate agents' literature which he sorted out and stowed, with the notes, into a music case – not a brief case. That at least was original. The clerk had become quite an expert on briefcases of many kinds and conditions.

'Did you find what you were looking for?' she asked.

'Oh, yes. It all fits into place, you know, eventually.' The man laughed, aquamarine eyes twinkling happily, and went out, walking with a loose-limbed gait which in a woman would have been described as coltish.

The clerk sighed. Now she must tidy up, close and lock the main doors behind her, say good night to the watchman, and go home. The start of the weekend, with a Sunday drive planned, she and her boy-friend walking in the April woods – not many bluebells in Suffolk, though – and going home laden with branches of silver and gold catkins. But that must wait. She gave old Sid a hand with loading his trolley with documents to be returned to the strongroom. Then she took the visitors' book back to her desk to lock it in the drawer, glancing at the open page.

M.J. Carne was the name of the red-haired man, and he had put the purpose of his visit as "family research", and then a London address.

The clerk wondered briefly at his interest in a remote rural parish. Although obviously excited by the results of his research, he had betrayed irritated frustration that a quantity of the relevant documents were in fact missing. 'It happens,' the clerk said apologetically, and the man had sighed, and then said, smiling: 'Imagine the load of paper you'd be lumbered with if everyone thought of keeping everything they considered remotely interesting to future researchers!'

She had been able to tell him that the Registers of the parish he was researching were still housed at the parish church, and was pleased to see the look of excitement return. Now she smiled at the memory and locked the drawer.

Meanwhile, M.J. Carne walked whistling cheerfully through the Ipswich streets.

# *Part One*

# Georgina

The photograph was blurred, romantic, and showed the house after a heavy fall of snow. The white of the steep-pitched thatched roofs merged into the white of the sky. The surrounding garden was featureless, the backdrop of wintry trees unreal.

> period house of character
> the historic fifteenth-century house contains many features:
> exposed timbers
> two crown-posts and a wealth of panelling
> well-appointed kitchen with Aga and dining area
> Walk-in larder, pantry and rear hall
> three reception rooms, five bedrooms and serviceable attics
> bathroom containing low-level suite
> upstairs toilet and downstairs lobby with toilet
> airing cupboard
> self-contained "granny flat" in east wing
> eleven acres of land including mature garden, orchards, mixed woodland
> barn, stabling, cart shed and garage for two cars
> in good order
> easy access

'Right – ' Sam opened the road atlas – 'We'll see it after we've looked at the "residence of historic charm" at Mellis.'

'Mellis,' Dinah repeated. 'Nice. It has a honeyed sound – hives in the garden.'

Sam laughed. 'Hives? I leave that sort of thing to my parents.' He paused, picturing his parents in the "granny flat". 'Mellis does sound attractive, but it's further from Ipswich than Monks Hempstall is. I think we'd better look at it, though.'

The house at Mellis was still occupied, wealthily. Swimming pool in the garden and ponies in a paddock. No bee hives.

Pooks Hall at Outwood Green, Monks Hempstall, was empty. The garden was overgrown and the drive green with weeds.

'This is it,' Dinah said. 'It's as though it has been expecting us. I can imagine just how it looks upstairs without even going up.'

They stood in the beamed hall, looking up the dog-leg staircase down which sunbeams slanted, motes of brilliant light swirling.

'Yes,' Sam nodded.

His offer was accepted.

'What are we going to do with the granny flat?' Sam asked on the day the contracts were exchanged.

'Oh, I've got plans – don't worry,' Dinah grinned.

Sam started to speak but Dinah interrupted. 'When shall we take the children to see the house?'

The weeks passed, somehow, without any other members of the family seeing Pooks Hall.

Georgina, however, might be said to be there already in spirit. Convinced by its name alone that it was a magic place, she had made an immediate connection with the Rudyard Kipling stories.

'If Puck can be at Pooks *Hill*,' she said, 'why can't he be at Pooks *Hall*?'

The summer moved towards autumn. Harvest time, late this year, came and went.

It was Michaelmas.

'Why Michaelmas? Why did we have to wait?' Dinah had been impatient. 'It was empty for years, after all, and it's not as if it was a farm.'

'The farmer at Outwood Green was renting the buildings from the syndicate.'

'Oh, of course.'

In the cloudless sky a high distant drone proclaimed the unseen aircraft. Just visible in the blue against the sun's glare larks were soaring and singing, and swallows swooped and darted both high and low. In a small tree near the house a multitude of starlings chattered and whistled, all talking at once, none pausing to listen. Pigeons crooned in the woods, and a collared dove planed over the house with a startling, weirdly raucous cry.

Leaning out of a top floor window, the thick thatch of the roof arched like an eyebrow above the casement, Sam and Dinah Warner looked out over the yard and farm buildings.

They could hear the sound of a baler at work, the regular whirr and throb of the tractor engine and the rhymthic rattle and thud of the baler mechanism, where two fields of golden stubble away they stitched their neat line of oblong bales.

Somewhere over the horizon straw was being burned, not baled, and the smell of smoke was in the air.

'Sunday work,' Sam remarked. 'Perhaps the weather's going to break.'

'Oh, I hope not!' Then, hearing only the sounds from the field, the sounds of insects and birds, Dinah said, 'Where are the children?'

Sam sighed, closed the window. He was in the mood for making love, here and now, the bright sky at the window and the house an empty shell beneath them.

He followed Dinah as she clattered down the stairs and through the house, through the strata of centuries, and out to the garden.

He pointed. 'Down the orchard.'

They saw movement, a touch of fox-red, and low to the ground a glint of white-blond hair which was Simon.

'We'll have to get a dog,' Sam said as he and Dinah sat on the grass in the sun. 'Georgina wants one, anyway – a border collie like Priscilla's – or perhaps if *they* came . . .' He paused, then went on quickly. 'We can train it to round up the children. We are going to have more children, aren't we?'

Dinah knew why Sam had paused. *He's thinking of getting his parents to live in the flat.* She sighed. *It's not that I'm not very fond of them.* Then she shook her head and smiled, narrowing her eyes against the sun.

'The week you tutored at Summer School,' she said, 'I missed my period, *and* again.'

Sam turned to her quickly, a huge smile lighting his usually rather serious face. 'Are you sure?'

'Of course I'm sure,' Dinah laughed. 'I conceive at the drop of a hat! When I miss even one period I'm sure. First miss, Georgina. Second miss, Simon.' She reached out and touched Sam's face. 'Third time lucky, anyhow. Twins would be nice.' She stretched her arms wide. 'Oh, I love this place! Big enough to live *and* work in – big enough for a family. It's going to be a good life!'

Sam rolled towards her and put his head on her knees, looking up at her face, upside down against the sky, haloed in light hair and sunshine. His hands moved, one to her breast, the other to capture one of hers which he put to his lips.

After a while Dinah said, 'We ought to be unpacking those boxes we brought, it'll soon be lunch time.'

Sam sat up, pulling a folded Ordnance Survey map out from under him. He unfolded it and they located Monks Hempstall and Outwood Green, and then Pooks Hall itself.

'What are those lines?' Dinah indicated ruled lines pencilled in, cobwebbing the map they had borrowed from one of Sam's Open University students. 'Look, some of them intersect – converge – right *here*. Are they anything to do with the Maths or Technology courses?'

Sam laughed. 'I don't think for a moment that either maths or technology were in Annabel's mind when she ruled this network – don't you recognise them? They're ley-lines — or more precisely in this part of the country, moat alignments.'

'Of course! *The Old Straight Track.*' Dinah glanced back at the house. 'There aren't any natural landmarks like peaks and passes or great lumps of stone so the old routes were marked out with water. And we've an ancient dried moat here.'

Sam pushed his fingers through the hair at the back of Dinah's neck. 'Annabel is into that sort of thing. Mystery-history and the occult.' He grimaced. 'There's even a rumour that she belongs to a coven.'

There was a pause. Dinah opened her mouth to say something flippant, like "I suppose there are a lot of covens round here", but she said instead, 'Funny the way the estate agents both denied having sent us the stuff on this house.'

Sam shrugged. 'The left hand not knowing what the right hand is up to, I should think.'

'Well, I'm glad, anyway, whoever sent it to us.' Dinah looked at the house again. 'Maybe the agents thought it was really too big for us.' Then she added hastily, 'There's a load of mistletoe on some of the trees in the orchards – did you notice? That makes it all the more magical, doesn't it?' She laughed. 'Perhaps we'd better get your Annabel over to test how magic – or how haunted it is here.'

Sam, laughing, said, '*My* Annabel? Hardly. Seeing her at tutorials is enough. She's nice but a rather powerful personality! Why do you think I changed my Summer School week?'

Sam saw Dinah bite her lip. He had frequently reassured her that the Summer School jokes were, as far as he was concerned, a puerile fantasy – but how can you know what another person actually *wants* to believe? He folded the map.

'I must go to the Records Office and find out all I can about the house, about Outwood Green and Monks Hempstall,' Dinah was saying. 'We could meet for lunch, but I should have to be home to meet Georgina from school. Oh – Simon! Children – little kids – aren't allowed among the archives.'

'Well, we know the solution to that,' Sam began, and Dinah pretended not to hear.

'We must find out, there should be plenty of documents. Sometimes I really do wish that I were psychic! I'd love to tune in to the people who lived here.'

Sam demurred.

'I'm against trying to find spy-holes in time.'

They knew already that not many people had actually lived at Pooks Hall since records were kept. They knew that in the late eighteenth-century the owner had built the barns and stables, and drained and partially filled in the moat. After this there was a hiatus until the holding of deeds became mandatory. At that date Pooks Hall was empty, owned by a farmer in the next parish.

Sam recapitulated: 'And then recently there were only transients.' And Dinah added, 'The Army during the war, and then those last people who put in the plumbing and electricity and then emigrated! They must have been mad – all that work and expense. The re-thatching alone, for heaven's sake!' She shook her head. 'I'd have stayed.'

'Then we shouldn't have been here.'

Dinah grimaced. 'True. Anyway, I've decided that I'll have the east wing, the granny flat – ghastly expression – as my own self-contained studio and workshop. There's even enough space, just, for me to run small residental courses. Maybe I'll even build another floor loom.'

Sam sighed. 'Shades of William Morris – we'll have to rename this place Kelmscott-in-Suffolk! Still, I guess that leaves me the rest of the house – me and the kids.'

They both laughed, then stopped, listening.

Across the heat-hazed trees beyond the garden and the orchards their laughter was echoed, mimicked, startling and eerie.

A shadow passed overhead. It was only a bird, but for the blink of an eye the sun over Dinah was obscured, leaving her in shadow with the sunshine all about her.

'The kids – yes.' Dinah shivered convulsively as the small shadow passed. 'Where have they got to now, I wonder?'

To the south of Pooks Hall the bank and ditch bordering the old domain was marked by a tall hedge of laden hazels. One side of the hedge was orchard – rough grass, ancient apple and pear trees, greengages, all laced with trailing bramble thickets. Beyond the hazel hedge was a spreading tangle of mixed woodland known for centuries as Mongwodes, or Mongwoods, most of which now belonged to Sam Warner.

The two children stood peering through the small forest of hazel stems into the dark, the secret, the rustling and whispering woodland.

There was a bright, vibrant look to everything.

Georgina's freckled face was flushed and damp, tense with concentration. She was staring, staring, wondering how she came to be in this place. She knew perfectly well *where* she was. She simply did not remember the journey from the house, just that call and a feeling of fear, anger. She shook her head, and the brief shimmering in the air stopped.

Relieved, she returned to the idea she had been developing in the car coming to Pooks Hall this morning, her worn copy of Kipling's *Puck of Pook's Hill* clutched in her lap.

She wondered if Puck would really appear, whether she would know him – or whether, maybe, he'd have to get used to her and Simon first.

She was hot. She dropped her cardigan as she peeled it off, and rubbed a sticky hand across her wet brow. Simon was looking up at her with anxious eyes.

Aged four to Georgina's eleven, it was not only the years which separated him from her today.

In his trusting, easily bruised mind Georgina today was not the same as the Georgie of all his other days. On the hot and hurried walk through wild gardens and tangled orchards to reach this spot on the edge of the great dark forest, Georgina had been mean and spiteful, had refused to hold his hand or pick him up. She hadn't even stopped to help him when he had got caught in brambles and cried for her as the thorns made his legs bleed.

Ready tears surged into his eyes at the memory. He heaved a great sigh, then flinched as Georgina turned.

But now she smiled and dropped to one knee, crooned over his tears, and, spitting on her fingers, tried to soothe the bramble scratches.

'Georgie?' Simon rubbed his eyes and grinned.

'I'm Una now, and you are Dan – we've come to meet Puck, at the edge of the wood.'

'What's a puck?'

'Puck – it's one of his names. He's Robin Goodfellow, the fairy. He's magic.' Georgina stood up, peering through the hazel thicket again. 'What else is out there in the woods?' She murmured. 'Pheasants? Deer? Badgers and foxes for sure.'

'Mice?' Simon entered the game.

'Oh, yes, mice and voles.'

'Rabbits.' Simon was on familiar ground now. 'Rabbits and edge-ogs and dinosaurs!'

Georgina laughed, and deep in the wood another wilder laugh sounded, and both children held their breath.

The air seemed to be humming. Simon thought there must be armies of insects buzzing round them, all about, but he couldn't see them.

The laughter came again, and Simon relaxed. Laughter was nice, wasn't it? Nice, and not frightening.

'It's only a yaffle laughing – a green woodpecker,' Georgina whispered. And then said, as though surprised, 'Or is it a woodsprite? But they don't laugh, that's the wetbird that laughs.' She put a hand to her head. *Woodsprite? Wetbird?* The words had come into her head from nowhere.

Words and images, strange and yet at once familiar, streamed through her mind. She felt as though the sides of her head were wide open to the sky and wind, a whole new world of bright images and words.

'Woodsprite's the spotted one.' The sound of her own voice surprised her. 'Yaffle's green. The wetbird . . . But it's so hot – no rain-clouds anywhere.'

The humming grew louder. A bird fluttered noisily somewhere out of sight in the trees. A woodpecker? Simon glanced apprehensively into the woods, afraid of seeing green or spotted things like dinosaurs advancing through the green tangle: *pecking* – pecking at the trees – maybe coming to peck *him*. He reached out a hand to Georgina.

At that moment a cock pheasant chose to rocket from the floor of the hazel thicket almost at the children's feet, bursting upwards, an explosion of colour and noise.

Simon gave a shriek, clutching Georgina's hand as he watched the bird clatter up through the branches to the sky.

Georgina was holding her breath, squeezing Simon's hand – and not looking at the pheasant's progress. Fear, like her fingers closed on Simon's, was squeezing her heart as she stared at the old man who was standing quite close, watching her.

'Puck?' She whispered, lips dry and trembling. But she knew he was not Puck. And then, in the shimmering air, as though seeing the world through water, Georgina felt herself moving *towards* the figure standing in the wood, almost knowing who he was.

Simon clutched her with both hands now. 'Georgie – Georgie – *wait*!' His wail cut through the humming sound.

Everything was suddenly bright and clear and the air stilled. As though released from a spell, Georgina spun Simon round to head with him back across the orchard – away from the woods.

Simon twisted his head to look back. 'Who – was it? Who – ?' His words jerked out stupidly as he ran, stumbling.

Neither child understood the terrible feeling which had pushed out of the wood at them – despair, hopelessness, guilt – all they recognised was terror.

At last they stopped running and stood, panting. Simon looked at Georgina and she stared back at him, dishevelled and scared. But he thought that she looked like his Georgie again, and he ventured a grin, feeling the fear going away. Georgina tugged at the tangled ends of her hair, unable to return Simon's smile. She kept on feeling today as though she had been somehow *waking up* in different places. What had happened to her, and to time and place which seemed to be moving about, and even disappearing? She had vague memories, like dreams, and her alarm increased when Simon next spoke.

'Was it that man who laughed? Who was he, Georgie?'

'No-one. *No-one* – there wasn't anyone!' And she swooped on Simon, a mousing owl, pinching him with cruel claws. 'You dew craze me, Willum!'

Each caught in their own fear they plodded on across the tussocky grass, and as they approached the house Georgina slowed her pace. She didn't know why – she was not afraid of ghosts, believing Dinah when she had said they were "just echoes" – but she dreaded entering the house. She recalled how excited she had been about the move, being allowed to have *two* rooms of her own, but now she wanted none of it, and she could not understand why.

The sun flashed on a window and Georgina gasped.

'Ah, here you both are. The call of the stomach!' Sam laughed at them out of the window and across the intervening spaces of sunshine. He regarded the two children, his step-daughter and his son. 'Stick around,' he called. 'We're about to have the great picnic!'

Simon suddenly bent low to the ground, jack-knifing his sturdy little body. For an instant a lizard, only the length of his index finger, had been on a bare patch of earth near to his dusty sandals. Then it was gone. 'A little, little dinosaur I saw!' he exclaimed, delight in his voice.

In the noon quiet the sound of the tractor and baler had ceased and the birds were almost silent.

'What was that, Si? What did you see?' Georgina asked.

Simon stood grinning, hugging himself, dimples appearing low on his cheeks. 'I saw a tiny, little, *little* dinosaur!' He made his fingers shape it, show its size.

Georgina nodded, not knowing about the lizard. 'If you imagine them very, very small – then they can't hurt you, can they?' she said.

'That man – shall we make *him* all little and small so he doesn't scare us?'

Georgina turned on him sharply. 'What? *What* man?'

Simon put his hands up in front of him as though defending himself. He shook his head, silently.

Georgina sat cross-legged, Simon beside her, on the grass in the partially shaded dominion of the large hawthorn on the edge of the lawn. She licked her lips, extending her exploring tongue to taste the sweet-sour rim of apple-juice dewing the downy skin round her mouth.

Suddenly she had an unbidden and horrid vision of herself like a jigsaw puzzle, strange boundaries drawing areas of herself apart or together, and – even worse – gaps where no Georgina was at all. In fright and revulsion she gave a convulsive shudder.

Dinah saw Georgina's movement. 'Goose walked over your grave, Georgina, love?'

Glad of the familiarity of the words, Georgina was able to grin at her mother.

Dinah had been angry a moment ago, accusing Georgina of being rotten to Simon. 'But I'm never rotten to Si – I love him!' Georgina simply was not aware that she had been teasing Simon, or indeed had said anything to him. She licked her lips again. The picnic looked good and she was hungry.

And now Dinah was asking her to go to the house and fetch the bag with the bread in it which had been left behind.

'Georgie,' Dinah prompted.

Suddenly Georgina was looking straight at her, aquamarine eyes very bright, almost fevered.

'Send Simon,' Georgina said. 'Why does it always have to be me?'

'He's too small, for goodness sake! Oh, come on, Georgina. It's your picnic too, you know.'

'I'm hungry,' Simon began to nag. 'I want my roll and butter and cheese, Mum. Where's the bread? I'm hungry!'

'Oh, shut up, you! Go and get it yourself if you want it so badly,' Georgina snapped at him.

Sam had been opening a bottle of white wine. Now he looked up sharply, the cork half drawn. He looked at Dinah where she knelt, knife and fork poised to portion out the helpings of terrine, frowning over her task, a stray lock of hair over her brow.

Georgina had inherited her red hair and green-blue eyes from her father. Dinah was mousey fair, with smoky hazel eyes and the classic oval face reproduced in Simon.

Now she looked up again, smiling as she accepted a glass of wine from Sam. 'Come on, Georgina, go and fetch that bag,' she coaxed.

'Where – '

'You know where it is, I told you. In the big kitchen.' She glanced at Simon. 'Yes, Si, in a moment. I know you want a roll – I know you're hungry, so are we all!'

'Why don't – ' Georgina began.

'Georgie – ' Sam warned, at a loss to understand today's strange change in the usually gentle and amenable Georgina.

'I can't go there,' Georgina said.

'What do you mean?' Dinah was puzzled.

'Mummy, that *smell*!' Georgina, remembering why she didn't want to go into the house, grimaced tellingly, clutching her hands over her stomach.

'Smell?' Sam asked quickly. 'What smell? Where?'

Georgina jerked her head towards the house.

Up the slope of the tattered once-lawn Pooks Hall stood against the blue summer sky, the amber-coloured clay walls, age-silvered timbers and hay-coloured thatch looking as though the house – like the trees and the grass – had grown out of the soil.

Georgina was twisting her hands in her lap. 'I can't stand that horrid-horrible-*putrid* stink in the house. It makes me sick!'

Dinah put out a hand to Sam and he grasped her fingers. Georgina was not a child who lied. Romancing, yes, but not lying. Also, she was not a timid child. And here was Georgina apparently both scared and lying – and such a preposterous lie!

'What do you suppose it smells of, then? None of *us* smelled anything in the house,' Dinah said. 'And you were only *in* the house a couple of minutes.'

Georgina threw her a glance opaque in its hinting of the unspeakable, the unknowable. She muttered that she didn't know.

'Well, if you don't know, how can you –' Sam began, smiling.

'Then you can find out,' Dinah said, not smiling. 'You just do as I ask you – it's not unreasonable – and go and fetch that bag.'

Dinah stood up as she spoke and Georgina, shocked at the sudden movement, put a hand to her mouth, tilting her head back to see her mother against the sky above her, looking so much taller than usual – Pooks Hall behind her, like a cutout against the blue.

In confusion she scrambled to her feet, and a great dragonfly darted, wings rustling, across her line of vision as she turned towards the house to hide her tears.

'Whatever got into her?' Sam watched Georgina as she trudged, diminishing, towards the house.

'Heat, excitement, who knows?' Dinah said. 'I just wish she hadn't started stirring Simon up.' She paused, then spoke reluctantly, 'I wonder – is she worried that we haven't definitely decided about the east wing?'

'She's tremendously attached to my parents, Di,' Sam said, eager but cautious. 'I think it's a good scheme. The place is really too large. And think, love, anyway – Priscilla and Dad in the flat, on call – help in the garden, resident child-minders.'

'But I *do* want to use those rooms,' Dinah sighed, 'and I really don't want to live in a communal situation – or an extended family.'

'But it's self-contained, you wouldn't –'

'But we *would*, darling, how could we not!' She tried to laugh. 'There'd be the dogs, and the goats.'

'But –'

'But nothing, Sam. I had enough mother-in-law with

Martin's – ' Dinah began irritably, flushing hotly. Then she stopped and guiltily she thought: *How can I compare Priscilla with that awful harpy?* Martin was the rather unlikely only son of "my late husband, the Brigadier" Crane and the daughter of a rear-Admiral, and she, when the elder Crane died, made the younger the centre of her life. Like a spider, she almost consumed him in her possessive love. Dinah turned as Georgina joined them breathlessly.

The meal proceeded, Sam and Dinah determined to enjoy it in spite of the incessant bickering of the two children. 'Just ignore them,' Sam said.

'But they're *never* like this!'

'Well, never or not, they're like it now.' Sam poured the last of the wine. 'Where *do* they get that language?'

'It's Georgina, she's really winding Si up – *and* me!' Dinah glared at the children, now messily battling over the last of the yogurt. 'Don't be so foul, Georgie, let him have it!'

Georgina did, but in this case a sharp slap as well as the plastic container. Simon howled.

Georgina turned her back. She stared through the russet silken web of her hair, seeing prisms slanting across the sunshine, meshing her vision of the rose-jungled garden. She sat straight-backed, cross-legged, her knees demurely covered by the skirt of the Laura Ashley print pinafore dress she wore over her Snoopy tee-shirt.

After a while she pushed her hair off her face and turned round.

' – think about what?' Dinah was saying.

'Oh, hell, nothing.' Sam lit a cigarette.

'"Nothing will come of nothing, think again!"' Dinah said, and Georgina, not knowing that it was a quotation, thought, *What a funny thing to say.*

Dinah continued: 'How would you feel if it were *my* parents?'

'Well, I suppose – but, shit, Dinah, you know they'd never leave Bath for a place out in the sticks like this! And, darling, Priscilla – you know she'd help with the kids, especially with the new baby coming.'

'Sam, let's forget it. Let's at least get settled in.'

'And you'll fill those rooms with your gear before we've had time to discuss it any further.'

'We've discussed it,' Dinah said.

'You sounded just like your mother then.'

Dinah stood up. 'And what's wrong with that?'

Sam shrugged, also standing.

'It's not as if I was sounding like your father!' Dinah spoke without thinking, felt her cheeks flush, then pale.

The afternoon seemed to hold its breath. For a moment it seemed to Dinah that Sam had actually reached across and slapped her face – a blow which Sam seemed to feel his hand delivering.

Georgina, shocked, put her hands over her ears. But the voices were still there, and the pictures, breaking in again. They were dreamlike, unfamiliar, and yet something in her recognised them, the violence, the pain.

Then the moment ended, and the flat echo of the undelivered blow bounced away out of their several imaginations.

The picnic was over.

'What in hell's got into Georgina today?' Dinah complained as she helped Sam into the house with the last box from the back of the estate car. 'Plaguing the life out of Simon when she's usually so good with him.'

'Too good, you sometimes say! Shall we struggle upstairs with this or unpack it here?'

'Oh, here,' Dinah straightened up and wiped her forehead with the back of one hand. 'Yes,' she mused, 'my little Martha stereotype.' Georgina had, from babyhood, been almost alarmingly a "a little mother" of a child – weeping over every slain bird or hedgehog on the road, brooding, breathy and starry-eyed, into every perambulator she saw. When Simon was born, far from being jealous, Georgina seemed to achieve some sort of fulfilment. Now Dinah wondered again at today's sudden change in her. 'I hope she isn't sickening for something.'

'A touch of liberation, perhaps?' Sam grinned, then said: 'Di, how old is Georgie?'

'What? You know how old she is! Eleven – eleven and a quarter. What . . . oh, I see what you mean. The dreaded premenstrual tension.' Dinah looked thoughtful, and felt the approach of her thirty-fifth birthday due a week before Georgina's twelfth. She suddenly turned round, sniffing the air, dog-like.

Only the expected smells of wood, dust, dry emptiness and the summer air through the open windows and doors.

Sam looked at her and nodded. 'I wondered, too, how she got that idea about the smell.'

Together they gathered up empty boxes and took to the cars those needed for tomorrow – tomorrow, when the move would be accomplished, and Pooks Hall became truly their home.

The sun slanted across the tops of the trees. The tractor and baler still panted and thumped between Pooks Hall and the village, and the birds were active in both flight and song.

Sam and Dinah walked through the house again to the door out to the garden.

'It's ours,' Sam sighed happily, and stretched.

'For good!' Dinah put her arms round him and squeezed, smiling up at him. He must have been as blond as Simon as a child, but his eyes were blue, not hazel. Simon would grow to be tall like Sam. Dinah smiled to herself at the thought of Simon taller than herself, looking down at her. 'Where'd he get to?' she wondered, and stepped out into the late sun, across the grass towards the old rose garden. 'Ah, here he comes.'

Simon was coming up through the garden from the direction of the walled garden and the orchards. He stumped through the hummocky long grass, hampered by the slow descent of his trousers. Dinah felt a sentimental twinge as she imagined his rear view, small pale buttocks visible over the empty trouser seat. But Simon's hands – little suppliant paws – were in a begging attitude at his chest, and his features appeared smudged, liquified, adrift in tears, a small muddle of a face.

Some way after him came Georgina, her cardigan like a shawl across her shoulders. She was muttering, shaking her head, looking over her shoulder from time to time.

Dinah called out and started to move towards the children and Simon turned at the sound of her voice. He began to wail loudly, his mouth too large for his face.

Sam, watching them from the doorway, heard Simon's wailing and saw Dinah's reaction: her quickening steps as she moved towards the little boy, Simon pointing at Georgina, Dinah's frown of annoyance before she stooped to Simon, arms outstretched.

'Hey there Georgie girl! What on earth are you up to?' Sam sang out to her.

Georgina stopped in her tracks with a strange birdlike shriek. For a moment she almost cringed, one elbow crooked out towards Sam, her arm protecting her face.

Surprised and puzzled, Sam strode down the three shallow, worn stone steps on to the weed grown path. Suddenly he felt at a loss.

Georgina now stood slackly staring, her hands hanging at her sides. 'Another one gone,' she said, her voice and accent unfamiliar, and glanced back the way she had come. 'More room!' She gave a wry little laugh, then pulled the cardigan off her shoulders. 'That's hully stoovy.' She rubbed a hand over her perspiring face and pushed back her damp hair. 'Stoovy – een't as loike that stink'll goo.'

'What?' Sam stared. 'What did you say?'

Georgina's unawakened face seemed to sag and set into a heavy, lumpish look. She moved her shoulders as though stiff from weariness, then twisted an arm round to scratch her back, dull eyes still looking towards Sam. He felt for a moment as though cold water trickled down his spine.

'Georgina?' He whispered.

'Dunno,' she muttered, and then Dinah was with them, her expression stormy, Simon in her arms.

Georgina looked then as if she had just wakened out of deep sleep, her eyes still not in focus, mind not yet tuned.

'What did you *do* to him?' Dinah was demanding angrily.

Georgina's face flushed redder than the heat had made it, but to Sam the child's face appared her own again – sharpish, with that charming fox-cub prettiness that suited her hair.

'I didn't do anything to him – I wasn't even *with* him – I don't know where he was!' Georgina protested. Her eyes filled with tears and she bit her lip. 'Honestly,' she said.

'Oh, well.' Dinah shifted Simon to the other shoulder and he quietened, hitching his breath and making small sounds, like a whimpering puppy. 'We'd better lock up and get moving. We're all tired, and tomorrow's going to be a big day.'

'I'll go across to Mum and Dad's,' Sam said, following them into the house. 'Come on in, Georgie, I want to put some things away then lock up.'

But Georgina, face suddenly pale, shook her head. 'I'll meet you at the car.' And she backed away from Sam's outstretched hand.

In the house, recalling the earlier scene with his step-daughter, Sam prowled swiftly through all the downstairs rooms – except the east wing flat – checking for nauseating smells. Nothing. He muttered 'Bees in her bonnet', and joined the rest of the family in the yard after locking the main door behind him. Georgina and Simon were standing with their backs to one another.

'Can I go in your car, Sam?' Georgina turned to him.

Feeling a surge of warmth and relief at this approach after her earlier rebuff, he was about to say of course – that his parents would love to see her – when Dinah said sharply: 'No, you'll come with me. Sam'll stay to supper there, I know, and it'll be too late for you. Come on.'

'They'll be disappointed – I mean about this place,' he said.

Dinah stared.

'Oh, Sam, you didn't *tell* them about it, did you?' She grimaced. 'Oh, god! Now there'll be a great thing about me not wanting them here. It'll be all my fault, of course!'

'I'm sorry, darling. I just mentioned it – it seemed – ' He paused, clearing his throat. 'I'll make it right, and I won't be late.'

'Oh, you will,' Dinah muttered, 'You always are! Come on, kids, in you get. Buckle Simon in, will you, Georgina? We must get along home. Home!' She stopped, looking around. 'This'll be home after tomorrow!'

But a sense of irritation still irked her as she watched Sam drive out of the yard in a swirl of dust, and Dinah opened the door of the Volvo estate and flounced into her seat.

'Oh, bugger!' she whispered venomously as she sat down hard on the buckle of the seat belt.

A titter behind her: Georgina.

Whispering and giggling – then a sharp yell of anger.

'*Quiet*!' Dinah glared ahead, not looking at the house again as she turned the car and headed down the drive.

She tried to concentrate her mind on the future, all the things that needed to be done. She tried without success to ignore the sounds behind her – sounds of children over-excited and out of control, becoming sillier and sillier. Georgina had an ear for word play and she was juggling with words now, between gusts of her own and Simon's laughter.

'Can't you simmer down, you two?' Dinah complained. 'Georgie, I don't want Si to laugh himself sick. Play some quiet game.'

Dinah tried to shut the noise out, a quiet game seemed impossible, but at least they were not fighting. She grinned a little bleakly, thinking of Sam speeding towards the smallholding, towards the low flint house in the forest near Elveden. She visualised the welcome there, the good meal, the talk – about Pooks Hall, of course. She felt herself growing increasingly tense, and eased her foot off the throttle, loosening her clenched hands, sweating on the wheel. Annoyance at feeling so unusually wound up made her tension increase. It was almost as she used to feel with Martin.

Suddenly in the rear-view mirror Dinah's vision was disturbed by flailing arms as Simon lurched in his harness trying to reach Georgina, just out of reach. The game had turned into a battle.

Dinah swore as she turned the car off the slip road up to the dual carriageway. The sun was in her eyes now, and her sunglasses, she knew, were in Sam's car.

A screech of rage from Simon.

'Leave him alone, Georgina. That's *enough*, both of you!' Dinah scowled into the mirror. 'Can't you sit still, Georgie?'

She had unbuckled her harness and was clambering back into the rear of the car behind the seat.

'Can't you smell it?' Georgina complained. 'Si's gone and peed himself and he *stinks*! I can't sit next to him – stinks and smells all day, horrible smells!'

A sound like a shot.

All forward vision was cut off by the granulation of the windscreen. In the mirror were the children's faces, slack with terror, eyes and mouths agape.

Dinah raised a fist to break a hole in the windscreen's blindness.

All this in the space of a heartbeat, Dinah's feet trampling clutch and brake pedals as she felt the car leaving her control.

Something vast and dark thrust through the sightlessness ahead and Dinah screamed as she saw Georgina flying forwards past her shoulder, Georgina hurtling to meet the dark.

At Elveden Sam was easily persuaded to join his parents for supper. He told them something of the day at Pooks Hall – but being who he was, and preferring to avoid unnecessary unpleasantness, he said nothing about the uncharacteristic behaviour of the children, or about Dinah's apparently uncompromising attitude towards the fate of the "granny flat". Anyhow, he had resolved to work on Dinah a bit more about that. So he put off telling Priscilla and Talbot that Dinah wanted to use the flat herself, and he avoided even thinking of their disappointment if Dinah remained adamant.

A hazy, reddish moon had risen and the stars were pricking the clear sky when he set off for the last night at the cottage at Snailwell. Sam frowned as he drove, impatient with other road-users, impatient with himself. *Congenitally lazy, that's Sam Warner,* he thought. *Avoid unnecessary exertion, avoid trouble at all costs.* And yet it was he who had hammered on about the subject of the east wing today.

As he approached Snailwell he was thinking of the move tomorrow. They could stand the expense of the larger house. The cottage had sold above their expectations, and Sam was now teaching full-time at the Suffolk College. Also his travelling expenses would be substantially cut by living nearer to Ipswich.

Pooks Hall. He thought about the house again, about tomorrow. He must take Georgina to her old school for her last day there, and then pack as much as possible into his one day off. Then later either he or Dinah would fetch Georgie and she would join her little half-brother in their new home.

Home . . . But what had gone wrong there today? Sam recalled the winding up of tension, the irritations. *Oh, hell – and these last couple of years've been so much more relaxed.*

Sam had known Dinah for eight years, since before her divorce, and he had loved both her and Georgina on sight. He had been grateful for Dinah's disintegrating marriage, for her turning to him, and their marriage had given her happiness – given her Simon, as well – and had saved Sam from perhaps becoming too indolent and easy-going. Sam at thirty-eight appeared younger than his younger brother. But if Sam lacked the drive that had surged David into success and brought wealth and an apparently assured future in computers, Sam also lacked the hypertension, high volume of material responsibilities and high alcohol intake. Teaching, some research and travelling, and Dinah and the children were Sam's ingredients for a good life.

The Police were waiting at the door of the dark cottage in Snailwell.

After the identification Sam was allowed to see Simon and Dinah.

He moved automatically. He spoke when addressed, answered questions, and took note of his surroundings with an obsessive concentration and clear perception.

He knew he was awake, that this was now, the present, and happening to him – and yet he felt that he was dreaming. It should be a dream – these things happened to other people, didn't they? – a terrible dream from which he longed to wake.

But you cannot wake up from reality.

Simon was a shrunken and discoloured caricature of the real Simon, but even in his drugged sleep he made typical grimaces – and those new gestures with his hands.

Then Sam saw Dinah.

He was assured that, like Simon, she was very much alive – vital signs good – and that she had had a miraculous escape. Sam stared at the drips tubed into her, and the machine to which she was wired, blipping her vital rhythm across a monitor screen, like some repetitive code.

'She lost a good deal of blood.'

Sam felt that he had just lost most of his. 'Oh, my god – did she miscarry?'

Sam touched Dinah's face with gentle fingers. He sat with her for a while. His head throbbed and his eyes were aching, and he had a sensation of dry nausea.

Images of the children intruded as he sat watching Dinah breathe – the piecing together from a remembered strand of hair, a recalled line of brow or shape of fingernail – the piecing together of a loved person from fragments of mortality.

And Dinah? Sam tried to call her back whole from the glimpses he had now of her battered mortal face, an arm, her hair limp and lustreless.

The Police offered to drive him to Elveden when it seemed that he must leave the hospital. Sam, however, drove himself back to Snailwell.

He spent the remainder of that night packing.

In the empty light of a cool and misty morning smelling of apples and chrysanthemums, Sam stood by an open window and looked only at tragedy and horror – the greater horror being his present shocked emptiness of any emotion, while his thoughts continued to tick over items, like some nightmare shopping list: *Turn off water. Turn off electricity. Keys to the agent. Find out where Martin is. Tell Dinah. Tell Priscilla and Talbot. Tell Dinah's parents. Tell the Aunts, David and Jean. Undertaker. Church.*

The list repeated itself over and over, always stopping at the thought of a funeral – not for Georgina, no funeral, she had to be alive too, like Simon and Dinah! And then he would remember again what it was like when the sheet was turned back, and he would know there was no mistake.

Later he drank scalding hot tea, and then took apart the final set of bookshelves, first packing its contents in boxes.

Sam was still packing the last of the bed linen into an ancient tin trunk borrowed from Talbot, when the sound of the pantechnicon set the neighbourhood dogs barking.

'We can have a dog!' Georgina had said when told about Pooks Hall.

## DEATHS

CRANE, on September 29th, as the result of a tragic accident, Georgina Mary, aged 11 years and 3 months; beloved daughter of Dinah Warner and Martin Crane; dearly loved step-daughter of Sam Warner.

# *Part Two*

# Simon

Dinah tried to open her eyes, but it seemed that her lashes stitched the lids together, or else the lids were weighted. *Weights? Coins?* Reaction to that thought was immediate. Her lids flicked open.

She was staring upwards with eyes not focusing properly and it seemed that she could see only a ceiling directly over her, low and close like a lid. *They think I'm dead – put me in a coffin!*

She gave a muffled scream and moved to break out. But something stuck into her left arm, and was hurting.

She heard sounds out of long ago memories – a curtain was swished along a rail, somewhere a trolley was wheeled along with a delicate jangling of glass.

Dinah panted. Her side hurt. *The children?* Faces in a mirror, mouths open. Georgina flying, flying – *where*?

Dinah flung her right arm out sideways and a glass vase toppled off the table to shatter on the floor. Suddenly she was in the car again, thrusting her bruised right fist again through the deadly opacity of the windscreen.

She saw Georgina hurtling forward past her. *Come here. Come back – I didn't mean it!*

The next time she opened her eyes, the coffin-lid was no longer there above her, Dinah saw just an ordinary ceiling. She seemed to be in a little room made out of curtains. *How pretty – a fourposter bed. Don't much like the design of these curtains though. Always meant to have a fourposter. Dear Sam, he put one in at Pooks Hall for me – a surprise! But where's the canopy? And the tester? And our ceiling isn't like that! Where's the tie beam, the crown-post, the rafters? Where –*

She fretted a little, whimpering. The bed was too narrow for two. *Sam can't have left me! Not him too!* Her head ached fiercely so she closed her eyes again. She could hear other people whispering, murmuring, and light, quick footsteps.

Nurses. Only nurses walked like that.

*Of course, I'm in hospital! What are they doing to me? Where are the children?*

As if in answer Georgina again swooped past her, hair flying, arms flailing, again and again – and again the annihilating impact, the explosion and fragmentation of person, personality. Dinah cried out. She wanted to know.

The footsteps came nearer, the curtains parted. A face, ferret-like but kind, peered at Dinah.

The face blurred and two ferrets smiled brightly. Brisk but gentle hands adjusted the needle in Dinah's strapped arm.

'Can't really see very well,' Dinah whispered.

Then she became aware that she could not *smell* anything at all, and she knew that hospitals always had a very distinctive smell.

'What's wrong with me?' Panic, and a memory recalled with fear. 'I was pregnant.' Dinah struggled to focus on the nurse, who had red hair and freckles.

'I'm afraid you lost it, Mrs Warner. But doctor says you'll be absolutely all right. You're getting on fine – you may not think it but you are.' The nurse cranked a handle behind Dinah's head and the pillow tilted a little more. 'All right?'

A bolt of anger shot through her fear, and faded. 'Where is – ?' Dinah began.

But the nurse was going. At the curtains she turned back. 'You'll really be able to *talk* to your husband today – he will be pleased!'

*Sam's been here and I don't remember? What's been happening? What day is it? Must ask – the children – Simon – they'll wonder where I am –*

That afternoon she discovered that this was her third day in hospital. She still had difficulty with her eyes, still could not smell or taste anything, and she also had a constant headache as well as a sensation of pins and needles in her left arm and leg. The bruising of her face and her cracked ribs only hurt if she moved, or thought about them.

There was activity and a sense of expectancy in the world outside the curtains.

'Nearly opening time,' a woman's voice said, a rough, ginny, humorous voice.

The lights were on in the ward and the curtains were gone from one side of her bed. Dinah could see the sky through the large window, darkly blue, overlaid with reflections from within the ward beyond her curtained privacy. She saw a table with vases of flowers. Reflected in the window she saw a tall, blond man cross the ward towards her curtains.

Then there were two men, the reflection and the actual Sam.

'Oh, Sam.' Dinah held out her right hand. The left merely twitched. Even the pins and needles had gone, leaving arm and hand "asleep".

She remembered, with a shock, that of course she had seen Sam here before.

She recalled him leaning over her, calling her name, sitting by her and holding her hand – her right hand. Perhaps he had held the left as well, but that hand remembered no sensation.

Dinah remembered Sam weeping, his head on the pillow beside hers, weeping in terrible silence. In such a silence now Georgina sped past Dinah's shoulder into oblivion, hands like the fins of a flying fish, translucent against the dark.

'Sam,' Dinah whispered urgently, 'tell me, please.'

Her eyes would not stay in focus. She stared at double outlines.

Sam sat close by the bed. His face had discovered new lines, ageing, maturing, weary lines. Dinah saw all this double, Sam's dear face an etching – all lines.

'Oh, my darling,' he said softly, 'I really think you look more like my Dinah – ' He smiled a crooked smile.

'Sam, tell me.' Her voice was stronger. 'Simon?'

'Still shocked – bruised – cuts on his face. They're healing well. He was allowed home yesterday.'

'Georgina?'

Sam frowned, controlling his features fiercely. 'You know. Di – you *know*! Do I have to tell you again? Listen, darling, Georgie was killed instantly. She's dead. *Georgina is dead*.'

Time had run out. Cruel. How cruel it was for there to be no second chance – and again Dinah saw the road, then the blindness of the ruined windscreen. But now, try as she would, she could remember nothing else – though she knew that she had had another memory and that it was one of Georgina.

'I've lost it,' she whispered. 'I can't see it any more. It was – terrrible – but now I want to remember and see it again, but it's not there and I've lost it!'

'We still have Simon.' Sam was stroking her brow, her cheeks, his fingers light as feathers, 'And I've still got you.'

*Oh, no.* Dinah's thoughts spun. *We haven't GOT anyone – only the responsibility of them, of loving or not loving.* She closed her eyes, afraid that the sudden surge of grief and of guilt must show in her expression. Sam saw none of it. He still stroked her face.

Then Dinah opened her eyes again, frowning with the effort to focus, and Sam eagerly waited.

'Sam,' Dinah began softly, 'forgive me – so guilty. Forgive me!' She paused, the great hole in her emotions at last filling with some sort of grief. 'You see – no – you'll never be able to understand. Oh, God! You see – I never *ever* loved her – I didn't even *like* her!' She choked on the grief and no tears would come. 'I never loved her – ever – even when – and now she's dead – can't even *remember* her – only bits, like her hair.'

Sam tried to comfort her, and did not believe her. *Of course she loved Georgina, we all did. Di's a super mother. We all loved Georgie. This is shock, just shock.*

Dinah spent most of the next day sitting in a chair. Her left arm and leg still felt unreal, asleep, and the headache persisted. The loss of the senses of smell and taste began to obsess her, but this acted as a relief from worrying about memories, or lack of them. She tried to think less of herself and more of Sam when he came in that evening.

'You look so tired, darling, you really needn't come in every day – I understand!' Later, she wanted to be reminded. 'You *did* move into Pooks Hall, didn't you?'

'Everything went as planned, yes,' Sam said.

'And I missed it – I'm sorry.' Dinah paused, bit her lip. 'Sam – where – where are Georgina's things?'

'Packed up – in store.' His voice was flat.

*No trace,* he thought. *Hide it all away. Some people keep everything as it was, even the bed made up ready.*

Sam would not readily forget the nightmare, shared with his mother, of finding and packing up everything of Georgina's. If Dinah wanted to keep anything let her choose, but later. All those bits and pieces of a child's life had to be collected – bird's nest collection, books and toys as well as clothes, little calendars, cards, embroideries, and quantities of artifacts of obscure purpose brought home from school. Stacks of drawings and paintings, recorder and music – that recorder had certainly got on Dinah's nerves, though Georgina had played particularly well, as befitting Martin's daughter. So much – so many *little* things – shells, pebbles, beads, feathers. Sam suddenly wondered if he had done the right thing in packing up all tangible reminders of Georgina, but Priscilla had agreed.

He still could not believe Dinah's extraordinary confession to him about her lack of feeling for her first child.

'Where's Simon sleeping?'

'Well – '

An expression of horror registered then on Dinah's face.

'Who's looking after him?' She felt awash with shame and guilt. 'Why haven't you *told* me? Why haven't I asked you *before*?'

Sam held her hands in his. 'You – don't try to think of everything at once.' He felt her right hand grasping his, the left one limp and passive. 'Priscilla is looking after him, of course.'

'Is he at Elveden then? I thought, didn't you say he was at *home*?'

Sam drew a deep breath. 'Yes.' He spoke slowly. 'When I fetched Simon home I fetched Priscilla and Dad home too. They are all – well – sort of camping in the granny flat. Simon's better sleeping there since he's there all during the day.' He paused. 'It simply seemed the obvious thing to do.'

Silence for a while, then Dinah asked: 'How much does he understand? How is he – now?'

Neither had an answer.

A young man waylaid Sam outside the ward. 'I'm Doctor Redmond.'

They walked out to the vestibule.

'Your wife is progressing well,' the young doctor said. 'Of course we're not satisfied yet about her reflexes.'

'Neither is she,' Sam cut in. 'Nor am I.' He lit a cigarette and after a couple of draws ground it out in a firebucket.

'We may be sending her over to Addenbrookes for some tests.' Doctor Redmond was watching Sam closely. 'Does she know about her daughter?'

Sam nodded. 'She knows.'

'She's still in a state of shock,' Redmond said, 'Physically as well – the reflexes. These'll likely recover quite spontaneously. Emotionally, well, a lot of that is up to you.' He smiled, and turned to go back into the ward.

Sudden anger shook Sam, with a vision of Dinah's swollen contused face, her stunned uncomprehending expression, her silences.

Dinah was exhausted by Sam's visit, by her anxiety about Simon, and by feelings of guilt caused now by her irritation at Sam's parents moving into the flat in the east wing. She knew how unkind and irrational her feelings were. *Priscilla's wonderful with Si, it's providential her being able to go to Pooks Hall to be with him – I know all that! But it's out of my control, out of my knowledge even, and I'm stuck here – and Georgina*... But she still could neither recall Georgina alive nor accept her death. She drifted into a childish "if only" half dream.

Dinah jerked fully awake. Another visitor stood by her bed.

'Martin!'

His face was aged, ruined by grief. His skin was tight and white, leaving eyes and nose reddened, clashing with the fierce bright orange of his hair – which, Dinah saw with added shock, was threaded with grey. The mask of his face, the glitter in the aquamarine eyes, brought Dinah out in a clammy sweat of fear.

'Why did you have to kill her?'

'She – it was an accident,' Dinah whispered, guilt seeping anew into her soul. Accident? Was it? *Irritation, bad temper, impatience, loss of concentration* ...

'She always tried so hard to get you to love her! You never gave her a chance! I loved her but you took her –' He paused, wiped his mouth. 'You took her, when you'd never ever wanted her! And now – because of you – she is dead!'

For a giddy moment Dinah whirled back in time – so many times – staring into those desperate eyes of his during some crisis of Martin's, trying to hold him together and feeling guilty at wishing that he would just pull *himself* together.

She shook her head. 'It was – a terrible accident. I'm so – so *sorry*.'

*Go away,* her mind screamed at him. *Go away. Leave me alone!*

Uncannily he picked up her thought, but then he had always been like that.

'Alone,' he said. 'You deserve to be alone!'

And he left her, loping away through the ward, one shoulder a little higher than the other in that familiar, nervous stride.

Dinah asked about the estate car.

'Complete write-off.' Sam shook his head.

'The truck driver? It was a truck, wasn't it?'

'Unhurt. A Dutchman. He – he sent a wreath.'

Sam had brought roses from Pooks Hall, velvety dark red almost full-blown roses. 'Smell this one, Di – it's fantastic. Priscilla says it's called Hugh Dixon.'

'You know I can't smell anything.' Dinah stared at the flowers. *A wreath – the truck driver was a Dutchman – sent a wreath.* She turned resentfully away from the flowers, away from Sam. *Easier if I was dead too – stop thinking then.*

'What about those tests you're supposed to go to Cambridge for?'

'Tomorrow – so don't come tomorrow evening, as I'll stay there overnight.' Dinah paused, dragging her thoughts into the present again. 'You'll be able to spend a little more time with Simon, then.'

'Yes.' Sam sighed. He pushed the red roses into a vase of carnations which had a card from Dinah's parents. 'Do you need anything? Clothes? Books?'

'Not books – eyes don't focus well enough for long enough for me to read properly.' Dinah covered them with her right hand. 'Oh, Sam, *why* am I such a mess? And don't say I'm lucky to be alive and in one piece or I'll scream!'

Sam gently took her hands away from her face and kissed her trembling lips. 'You're not in such a mess as you were – your sweet face is much less swollen.' He stared into her eyes until rewarded by a smile. 'Now, anything else I can bring after tomorrow?'

'Yes, fresh nightdresses. But I haven't got any more at home. Will you buy me a couple in Ipswich tomorrow? Not too frilly, and pure cotton, please.'

When Sam took Dinah the new nightdresses she had been to Cambridge, spending the night in the neurological department.

'It was a foul experience,' she told Sam. 'I felt sick there and back in the ambulance – and I'm *never* travel-sick – and I don't think they *proved* anything. They gave me an injection that made my head hot inside. It felt as though my brain was *blushing*! I'm actually glad to be back in this place!'

'I don't think you'll be here very much longer.' Sam smoothed her hair.

'I can't go home like this, though!' Dinah exclaimed. 'My left arm and leg are still asleep the whole time – I'm like a semi-paralytic drunk or something!'

'Doctor Redmond said that the reflexes would probably correct quite spontaneously.'

'When?' Dinah's voice was sharp. 'In fifty years' time? I could be dead by then!'

'Don't!'

*Dead.* Dinah frowned, turning her head away. The questions she had been avoiding asking were rising like vomit, uncontrollably, in her throat. 'Sam, was there an inquest? Was there – a funeral? You said – that Dutchman sent a wreath.'

She stared at Sam's reflection in the window. He nodded.

'An inquest, yes. Straight forward. No one's fault.'

Dinah closed her eyes for a moment then stared at Sam fiercely, stared at his anxious eyes, kind face. '*No one's fault?* Christ almighty, Sam, it was my fault – *mine!* I was angry, should have been able to pull out of trouble.' She nodded sombrely. 'It was my fault.'

Silence. And after a time Dinah whispered, 'And the funeral? Not a cremation?' She shuddered.

'No, Georgina was buried.'

'Where?' Hardly audible.

'In the village – at Monks Hempstall.' Sam paused. 'I know she'd lived most of her life at Snailwell but I thought – I thought we shouldn't – sort of – leave her behind.'

'And Martin?'

'He was there. He sent *you* flowers, too. Those gladioli are from him, just his name on the card.'

She nodded. 'He wouldn't send a message.' She paused, recalling Martin's accusation. Did Sam know that he had been to the hospital? She didn't want to ask him, to talk about it with Sam. 'Who else?'

'Priscilla and Talbot, of course. Simon stayed with the Steggles' – he's our neighbouring farmer – there was a litter of puppies there for him to play with. And your parents sent flowers.' Sam paused. 'Martin said he had been to see them, and that your mother was too upset to travel.'

Dinah nodded. No surprise there.

'David and Jean came,' Sam continued. 'They didn't stay because they had to get back for the children.'

Dinah tried to visualise the scene, but having little experience of funerals all she could conjure was a group of completely unfamiliar people looking like cardboard cutouts, standing round a neat grave surrounded by heaps of earth and wreaths – all in sepia and faded like an antique photograph. One thing, one person, *was* familiar, a little boy who had suddenly appeared close to the open grave – peering in. Dinah jerked herself back to reality.

'I must see Simon,' she said, and clutched at Sam's arm with her right hand. 'Please bring him tomorrow – I can't go on any longer without seeing him!'

Her tone was excited and agitated, and suddenly she realised that her left hand and foot had pins and needles again, alive and tingling after their cotton-wool inertia.

When Sam, knowing what store Dinah set by the visit, told his parents of the arrangement to take Simon to the hospital, Talbot Warner nodded vaguely, continuing to watch the television news. He looked pale and tired, and Sam felt a pang of concern. He had fetched his father from Elveden the same day that Simon came home, and Sam's mother and her dogs and goats travelled to Monks Hempstall in a horsebox.

The goats were housed in the stables and covered yard. They were hornless, gentle, elegant creatures, with golden eyes and long golden coats – except for one pale-eyed white milker and her kid.

There was something almost goatlike about Priscilla, not the least of it her name, for the goat is *capra prisca.* She had a narrow face and golden-hazel eyes, and she moved with a delicate precision.

Sam resembled his father in looks. It was his brother David who had the narrow bones and dark hair of their mother's family.

Simon seemed content to be with his grandparents, and would even smile when he was with the dogs or the goats. On Saturday he cried and fought when Priscilla and Sam fetched him from his haunt in the yard.

He fought all the way to the house where Priscilla changed his clothes, and washed his face and hands. Then the fact that he was going to see Dinah seemed at last to dawn on him and he quite calmly went out to the car and climbed on to Priscilla's lap in the rear seat.

At the hospital Simon at first showed no emotion. He sucked his thumb and held on to Sam's hand, looking back once at Priscilla, who stayed down in the entrance foyer, settled in an armchair with her crossword puzzle.

Dinah sat in a chair by the window, impatient, feeling sick with excitement. Her left arm and leg still tingled with pins and needles, but she could actually wriggle her fingers and toes today.

There were children in the ward. Those who had come last week now stared curiously at the patient who had then been concealed behind curtains.

'Mum – ' and some urgent whispering.

'No,' the woman with the jolly, ginny voice said, 'not like your Auntie Sue. *This* lady was in a motor accident.'

Dinah was sure that the child thought that she was a battered wife, and she found that the first amusing thought since – since the morning of Michaelmas day. *I must tell Sam. It's quite a giggle, considering it was Martin who thumped me . . .*

Now she heard more footsteps, turned towards the entry, as excited as a child.

Sam was there, with Simon, hand in hand.

Dinah saw at once that Simon's lower lip was badly marked still, tiny stitches repairing a cut, smaller cuts on cheeks and chin, bruises yellowish and fading. He stared at her and his hazel eyes were shadowed and sick-looking.

'Hallo, Si,' Dinah said, feeling her mouth and chin shake, trying not to blink or tears might splash out of her eyes. He looked so small.

Simon silently put his hands up before his chest and backed away a few steps. His face twisted into a tragic mask and his mouth opened, wider and wider.

Helplessly Dinah held out her arms.

'Simon – Si – darling, it's your mum. *It's me!*'

Sam picked Simon up and tried to sit him on Dinah's lap, but Simon fought his way to the floor again and began to wail loudly.

'It must be my face.' Dinah tried to rationalise, and to control her emotions. 'I don't – I don't look like *me,* do I?'

She leaned towards Simon again, but he glared at her sidelong, moaning and hiccupping, his hands curled like paws over his chest. Then he jerked one elbow towards Dinah, making an explosive snorting sound.

'Di,' Sam said softly, 'he – I didn't tell you – I thought he'd change when he saw you – but he doesn't *talk*. When he wants to – to object – to warn you off – he makes that noise. The doctor says – '

Dinah almost screamed. With an effort she restrained herself but exclaimed, 'Sod the doctor! I want my son to recognise me!'

People were trying not to stare.

A nurse came with a tube of Smarties and offered some to Simon.

He shook his head, jerking his hands and snorting.

'Oh my god!' Dinah stared at Sam. 'He doesn't talk – what else is wrong with him? You might as well tell me.'

'He, well, he has regressed – it's only natural after an experience like – ' Sam held Dinah's hands, both of them looking at Simon.

'Regressed – how?'
'He's wet at night.'
'Doesn't – ?'
'Oh, yes, Priscilla lifts him a couple of times, of course,' Sam said, shaking his head. Simon's crying had subsided a little. 'Darling, it'll pass. Look, you can use your fingers today. He'll be all right, like your hand and foot.'
'What else? Sam, he can hear all right, can he?'
'Oh yes, nothing wrong there – it's just the speech. He loves the animals, and he potters about with Talbot. *They* seem to communicate.'
'Is he eating?' Dinah asked after a short silence.
Sam's face lightened with a grin. 'Like a gannet! Can't fill him – he'll be all right, like you will.' He paused. 'I want you home, Dinah.'
'I'm doing my best!' she exclaimed. 'my eyes don't squint nearly so often now. Anyway, I'm sure they want my bed. Sam – I'm going to be home before next Saturday.'
'I'll hold you to that.'
'Hold me now, just for a moment.'
Sam bent and hugged her, gently because of the cracked ribs.
Simon came behind him, butting Sam's knees like a little goat and pulling at his trouser legs. He was crying again.
Dinah pushed Sam away. 'You'd better take him away. This isn't doing any of us any good!'
Sam bent and kissed her.
Dinah whispered ''Bye', tears in her eyes.
Sam picked Simon up and left the ward.

In the car Dinah sat rigid with excitement, almost overwhelmed by the bombardment of light and colour and movement. She was also assailed by fear, although she knew Sam for a safe driver. In the town Sam bought – at Dinah's request – a large set of painting sticks for Simon, flowers and wine for Priscilla, and pipe tobacco for Talbot.
Then they headed out on the A45, for home, for Pooks Hall, and Dinah's fear subsided, her mind filling with questions. How would Simon react to her this time? *It must be different today! Will I miss Georgina, when she never*

lived there? Dinah began to sweat. She felt sick.

Sam pulled off the road into a lay-by and they got out and stood in the fresh air, air that was cool and laced with the sharpness of future winter easterlies although the sun still had much of the warmth of summer.

'It was summer still then,' Dinah said, eyes closed and face turned to the sun, the breeze cool on her lips. 'Now it's autumn and everything is different. What shall I do?'

Sam put his arm round her and they walkd a little, past the car to the end of the lay-by, then back. Dinah flinched and shook when a container-truck roared by.

As they walked Dinah bent her head, watching her feet. 'Two left feet – a right left foot and a left left foot,' Martin had laughed, teasing, at Dinah's dancing. 'How did I take up with a girl who has about as much sense of rhythm as she has of a tune – and that's about zero!' Dinah frowned. Why think of Martin? Why now?

'I'll just have to take it sort of moment by moment, I suppose.'

'Best thing.' And Sam thought: *She'll find out – like I did.* 'It's not easy. How are you feeling now?'

'Better. Let's go.' She essayed a little laugh. 'I can't stay in limbo forever!'

After fastening her seat belt Dinah looked at her hands and saw the veins standing out, hard, like worms. *Oh God! "Then worms shall try That long-preserv'd virginity . . ." Poor little virgin – buried – Monks Hempstall. Shall I have to go and see the grave? Flowers – but I'd sooner forget – forget! People are so sorry for me but it's Sam who deserves the sorrow, and Martin.* Dinah inwardly chided herself for weakness as her eyes filled with tears again. She tried to force herself back into some sort of excitement and anticipation.

A barn owl flew ghostly out of the shadowed woods as they approached the gate of Pooks Hall.

Dinah wound the window down, sniffing urgently. She should be able to smell the earth, the autumn smells of dead leaves and damp ditches, the untidy half-wild chrysanthemum and Michaelmas daisy smells, the fragrance of brambles still fruiting . . . Nothing. No smells at all.

Frustrated, she looked at the watching windows of the house

as Sam drew the car up in the forecourt. It was strange to hear a dog bark, and from the farmsteading the bleat of a goat. Birds still sang and twittered.

Suddenly there were voices, the dogs again, and the sound of the main door of the house being opened.

Sam held Dinah tightly by the hand. She felt his warmth a comfort and a strength.

In the bare few instants, not even a second, between anticipation and actuality, Dinah's mind played over the scene.

Simon would free himself from Priscilla's arms and run to Dinah, and he would shout "Mummy" and "Here's my Mum!" and he would talk and babble wonderfully of the excitement of his new home.

Reality hit Dinah like a physical blow, and she was upheld only by Sam's strength, his hand grasping hers, and then his arms – his laughing voice – as he literally swept her off her feet and bore her over the threshold of Pooks Hall, like a bride.

In the hall he set her down. 'My God! Never again – you may *look* delicate, my darling, but you're a weighty armful!'

'Dinah, *dear*.' Priscilla kissed her. 'I'm so very pleased to see you – so happy to see you home!'

But Simon still stood, fists at his chest, elbows out, staring out of his shadowed eyes.

Simultaneously Sam, Priscilla and Dinah all spoke.

'Come and see the house.' Sam.

'Shall I give him his tea and get him ready for bed?' Priscilla.

'Do you mind – if I lie down for a while?' Dinah.

Neither Talbot nor his grandson said anything, Talbot with one hand on Simon's hunched shoulder.

Dinah felt she must retreat from this. She ached to hold Simon, to cuddle him, find him again. But she was defeated. She felt sick again, faint, and her legs were trembling. She nodded at Priscilla, dumbly, and saw the scene dissolve in movement as well as in the haze of her tears.

Sam supported Dinah up the main entrance staircase and into the landing from which the two largest bedrooms opened.

Landing and bedrooms had been made by the original great hall of the house being horizontally sliced into two storeys, then partitioned. The landing had therefore a sloping raftered ceiling, and each of the bedrooms had a tie-beam spanning it and crown post joining the beam to the ridge of the tall roof. Each of these rooms had also a mullioned window which reached upwards from the floor, since the splitting of the great hall into two floors had also divided the tall mullioned windows of the orginal building, mullions which reached right up to the eaves.

It was strange how the great hall was sliced into two floors, Dinah had remarked on first seeing the house – how the upstairs rooms were made with wooden walls, not clay, and all the smaller rooms, too – as though whoever lived here had suddenly decided that they wanted a whole lot of extra rooms.

Now she noticed vaguely how small their furniture seemed, how much floor showed around and between the faded oriental rugs and strips of plain Wilton, and the few rugs of Dinah's own weaving or stitching. She caught sight of herself in the glass as she passed the dressing table on the way to the bed. White – white face – pale, lank hair – and those bruises. *No wonder Si freaked out. Must wash my hair. Head aches. Lovely to lie on my own bed. Beautiful room. Beautiful windows.*

Dinah dozed, warm under the duvet, and soothed by the pills that Sam had given her under Doctor Redmond's orders. Vaguely she heard movement below in the house. Vaguely she heard the barn owl out in the deepening dusk. Vaguely she was aware of lights moving across the high, beamed ceiling as Sam turned the car and drove it to the garage, of the line of yellow light round the door from the hall. There was peace, which for Dinah lasted for an hour and a half.

'Priscilla wanted to do a special meal for us tonight,' Sam said after rather apologetically waking her.

'I feel quite hungry!' Sitting at her dressing table, she sounded surprised. 'I feel strange, though. One part of me seems to be really at home here, and another part feels that I'm sort of in a hotel.' She frowned at her wan reflection. 'I suppose it's because I missed the move.'

Sam was thinking, *Not a word about Georgina. She missed the move, too – missed staying alive – but Dinah mustn't blame herself. It was an accident!* He put his hands on Dinah's shoulders, looking at her reflection in the glass as she regarded him. 'You *are* home – really home!'

They went out of the house and into the autumn dark and Dinah was again frustrated by the loss of any sense of smell. She also anticipated the further frustration of, hungry, being presented with excellent food which she would not be able to taste.

The evening star shone, steady and clear, in a greenish blue afterglow. Owls called – the barn owl, and then two tawny owls in antiphony from either side of the garden.

The front door to the east wing flat stood open. Dinah and Sam crossed the little staircase hall and entered the sitting room. A table had been set for four, the seating comprising three kitchen chairs, and one packing case. Talbot's colour television set was up on another packing case, the vision on but sound off, and one easy chair and a pile of books by the fireplace completed the furnishings.

The dogs, black and white Border collies, barked sharply at the intrusion and then wove around the floor in intricate patterns of nervous movement, becoming reacquainted with the rather uncertain smell of Dinah.

She, glad to be able to do something, mixed the dressing and tossed the salad, telling Priscilla and Talbot how grateful she was for all they done for Simon and for Sam.

Still no one spoke of Georgina.

Priscilla smiled, warm in her flame-coloured dress, badger-grey hair breaking loose from its knot. She was so amazingly different from Dinah's mother, who played bridge fanatically and wore her blue-tinted hair in the style of Margaret Thatcher.

Sam's father beamed at Dinah. He wiped his mouth on his handkerchief and with tremendous energy and effort produced a series of sounds which, with concentration, could be understood as Talbot's articulation of: 'My dear Dinah – it's so good to have you home!'

The final M was clear and firm, a sound made with closed lips and no tongue. This, or much of it, as well as most of his lower jaw had been shot away as the most horrifying effect of multiple war wounds, which had also left him lessened in height and a little lame from a back injury. M, P and B were all the letters he could use to shape his vowels.

Dinah raised her glass to him and to Priscilla. 'May I see Simon before supper?' she asked.

'Of course. My dear, you needn't *ask*!' Priscilla's smile suddenly faded. 'Only – you know he'll probably be asleep.'

The two women went upstairs. Two bedrooms opened off the landing where a narrower stair led to the loft rooms. Both bedroom doors were open and Dinah saw in one the end of a camp bed and an air mattress, and an open suitcase.

In the other room a dim light burned, and she could hear the breathing of the sleeping child. Priscilla left Dinah there and went into the other room. Dinah heard her switch on the light and move about in there, beyond the wall which was made of broad, plain wooden panelling, several hundred years old.

Simon lay on his side, rosy now with sleep, long silky lashes closed on his cheeks and his hair pushed up off his rounded brow. His mouth was slightly open. Gently Dinah bent down and kissed the soft lips.

She jerked upright, recoiling with a harsh gasp, her hand to her mouth.

There was a rank, sour and almost overpowering reek of urine from the child's bed.

'Oh God!' Dinah said in a strangled whisper. She sniffed again, cautiously. Simon had never smelled so bad even when he was less than half his present age and slept in nappies. He had always been so clean, out of daytime nappies as soon as he could walk.

Hurrying out of the room across to the little bathroom which had been built into the space round the chimney, Dinah desperately picked things up and smelled them, sniffing her way round the bathroom – soap, dusting powder, Talbot's shaving soap, cologne – but she could smell none of those things.

Trembling, she sat on the edge of the bath for a while. *But I didn't imagine it – I really smelled him.* She shook her head, avoided looking at her reflection in the glass, and went downstairs.

Dinah forced herself to eat, trying to imagine how the food would taste: roast pheasant with wine sauce, carrots, potatoes and the salad, followed by apple charlotte. She drank her wine and enjoyed the warm and slightly dissociated feeling it induced. *Perhaps I'll take to the bottle. At least it has a more interesting effect than the food, though it's just as tasteless.* But she recalled her mother's sister, who lived in a permanent state of alternate alcoholic haze and wretched hangover, and was even more difficult to communicate with than Talbot with his garbling.

Dinah tried to concentrate. Priscilla and Talbot were having some sort of amicable altercation about the goats. Sam was laughing. Dinah frowned. Sam's parents couldn't continue camping here for much longer, she thought. *I must get myself together – look after Simon – look after Sam and myself – responsibility – get organised – work – yes – yes, work again – and move Simon into his own bedroom.*

Going out with Sam later into the cool blue night for the short walk to their own nearest door, Dinah felt pleasantly fuddled with wine. She heard rustlings of leaves, heard the sound of a motor car some miles away, and longed to be able to smell the night scents. How was it she had been able to smell Simon? The memory of that sickening moment sobered her instantly, and an echo of Georgina's voice teased chilly across her mind: "Si's gone and peed himself and he *stinks*;"

At last they lay in bed, Dinah's body inclined towards Sam and one of his arms across her hips. The loom of the night sky, blue and clear, showed at the tall mullioned window, four vertical strips of sky joining the floor to the ceiling. The small casements further along the wall were both open to the night sounds. Dinah could just make out the pattern of the rafters, the tie beam and crown post. Quiet – so quiet. Sam was asleep. As his breathing deepened he moved his arm and turned a little away from Dinah, her bent knees fitting into the backs of his.

Then the voices began.

Dinah lay for what seemed like hours while they babbled on, too far away to be distinct, no words, and yet too close to ignore. There were sometimes many of them, sometimes only three, two – and occasionally a blessed gap of silence. She tried to rationalise. *I'm overtired, that's all, just in my head.* Then the voices would start again: men, women, children.

For a while Dinah wondered if she might be asleep. *No – if*

*I'm asleep, I wouldn't be wondering. If I'm thinking, I must be awake.* Finally she sat up and reached for the bottle of pills and glass of water. Sitting up in bed, shivering a little, Sam asleep beside her, she felt completely alone, and afraid. She was actually as afraid of whatever drug was contained in the pills as she was of her sensation of utter forsaken solitude – "You deserve to be alone!" Martin's tense voice accused. But taking the pills meant sleep, and sleep meant not hearing anything. She took two pills and lay down again.

She heard a murmur, a faint laugh – a whisper – a sigh – then she slept.

October was nearly gone, but in sunshine. A blue and gold Indian summer flared still with roses and the hard bright shine of ripe apples, the tight-packed purple gloss of blackberries.

Still Simon did not talk.

Still Dinah *could* not – not about Georgina, not about something appearing only in dreams and then not fully recalled. Georgina – a name – *Red hair – I can just remember the hair* – and the voices? Dinah could not bring herself to mention them, tried not to think of them during the day, anyhow. *Am I more afraid of hearing these voices or of thinking I am going mad? I know that there's no-one there!*

Sam drove Dinah to the hospital for her examination after a week or so at Pooks Hall, an exhausting time for the whole family. Sam and his parents assumed that Dinah's moodiness, that her sometime air of preoccupation which would alternate with almost frenetic bursts of activity – of planning and organising – were owing to shock still at Georgina's death, worry about Simon.

Sam tried to reassure her, to urge her not to let Simon's silence and changed behaviour become an obsession, and each time he raised the subject she looked at him as though she despaired of him ever understanding.

No sooner was the medical examination finished than Dinah rounded on Doctor Redmond. Sam heard her as they came to join him in the anteroom.

' – was going to bring my little boy – on second thoughts I decided not to, but to find out a bit more about what actually happened when he was brought in after — after the accident,' she said. 'Do you know that he is not speaking *at all*? He doesn't make a single intelligible sound. Oh, yes, he wails and cries like a baby – when he wakes up in the morning, or in the night. He wets his bed every night, and he can't or won't talk!'

Sam put a hand on her arm. 'Steady on, love.' He felt her shaking.

'Of course, *I* wasn't – ' the doctor began.

'Ok, well, Simon was *someone's* patient – someone was responsible for whatever treatment he did or didn't have, so please will you tell me who I should see?'

'The boy was obviously take into Casualty first.' Doctor Redmond's voice was professionally soothing. 'They'd have records, of course. Perhaps, though, if you went to see the Sister in charge of the Children's Ward.'

'Thanks,' Dinah said, then abruptly she rushed out of the room.

Suddenly she had become appallingly aware of the smell of ether and disinfectant, and – worse – of blood, the unmistakable and metallic smell of blood. She had, even as she fled, directed a frantic glance round the room. *Is someone haemorrhaging? Has someone smashed a transfusion bottle?* But there was nothing, nothing except the smell.

Dinah fought with both nausea and fear as she hurried to the stairs, and by the time she had reached Reception all was as usual. She could not smell anything.

The Sister in charge of the Children's Ward had not been on duty during the days Simon was in hospital, and the pediatrician was not available.

Dinah waited for Sam at the main entrance. 'There must be someone – something – '

'Darling, Redmond says it will pass – it's shock. It's Simon's way of – of sort of *going to ground* so that he can heal in his own time. He doesn't recommend psychiatric help at the moment.'

'We could make private arrangements.'

'Give him some more time – he already *looks* better,' Sam urged.

'Just one word – anything – rather than his awful crying, or that terrible snort!' Dinah mourned. If only Simon would speak and those others – the voices – take on his silence. She agonised over this on the return journey, arriving home with a fierce headache.

'How was it?' Priscilla asked when Sam and Dinah called in to collect Simon, now sleeping in his own room and with the run of the whole house.

Dinah shrugged. 'All right, I suppose, except they can't seem to think of a way to get me back my lost senses. Still – ' she sighed – 'it's easier to live without taste or smell than without hearing or sight – or speech.' She looked at Simon, sharing with his grandfather the one easy chair, watching television. He certainly did look brighter. That sick, dull look had gone from his eyes. Intent on the wild-life programme, he sucked his thumb, the fingers of the other hand clutching his elbow.

Later that evening after she had put silent Simon to bed, Dinah helped Sam prepare apples for wine. 'I really must have a car,' she said, 'even a banger – I don't feel I can wait until the insurance on the Volvo comes through.'

He stared.

'It's all right – I'm not scared of driving again,' Dinah protested. 'You must see it's absurd the way I'm grounded – Priscilla and Talbot as well except when you're home.'

'We can't really afford all that fancy a car, you know.' Sam ate a piece of apple. 'Shall we risk answering an ad in the local paper? Or shall I advertise? Nothing over eight hundred, must be a runner, MOT and so on?'

'Why not?' Dinah said.

Three days later she became the owner of an elderly but sound and active Morris 1000 Traveller, which the three of them went to collect on a pleasant outing to Framlingham.

Dinah could not face walking round on top of the curtain wall of the castle and fretted the minutes away in a bookshop while Sam took Simon round. She bought two paperbacks for herself – she read voraciously now, particularly in the evenings before bedtime – then she bought a *Doctor Seuss* book for Simon.

Dinah drove the Morris home, following Sam with Simon in the Maxi. 'I do like it.' She patted the car as she left it in the garage. 'Such a nice, solid, sensible car,'

'How did you feel about driving?'

'Fine,' Dinah smiled at him. The bruises on her face were fading fast, the swelling almost completely gone. 'I told you I wasn't scared. Somehow I haven't lost my nerve – I suppose it wasn't that sort of accident.'

She read the new book to Simon that evening, sitting on his bed. The book was all a play on words and rhymes, with nonsensical pictures, and tremendous pace and rhythm. Simon listened, and sometimes he laughed – silently. Dinah read the book through a second time, becoming quite excited by Simon's reactions. He was hugging himself, and so nearly letting himself laugh out loud. He twisted the corner of his comforter, a piece of old towelling, against his mouth with one hand while his other hand beat accurate time to the fall of the words.

Dinah came again to the end of the book.

'Do you want me to read it again?' she asked quickly.

Simon, taken by surprise, drew breath, opening his mouth as though to speak.

*Say yes. Say yes.*

He looked at Dinah, full in her eyes, his mouth open. Then he ducked his head and began to suck one corner of his comforter with ferocious concentration.

Dinah's hand moved to strike him.

The movement was so automatic, the urge so strong, that she broke out in a sweat of shock as she snatched her hand back close to her side, sucking in her breath. She trembled, and Simon's eyes moved again to her face, wide open in quick fear. The air seemed to shudder between them, humming as though charged with sudden energy.

'Lie down, now, Si.' Dinah, carefully controlling her movements and her voice, put the book on Simon's bedside table and stood up. 'Time for sleep and sweet dreams.'

Obediently, almost limply, Simon lay down. Dinah moved across the room to draw the curtains over the windows which were open to the clear, damp dusk. Tomorrow the clocks would be put back and by this time in the evening it would be quite dark.

Now it was the night before dark, and warm enough for the bats to be out, darting about the open spaces of dusk with their pin-squeaks and rapid rush of wings.

At midnight Simon awoke, screaming.

The late evening had been peaceful and quiet. Following her shock at how close she had been to hitting Simon, Dinah applied her thoughts to anything rather than herself and the child, and what seemed to her to be a hopelessly deteriorating and totally negative relationship.

She went upstairs to the rooms which had originally been intended for Georgina. Since the east wing flat was being used at present by Sam's parents, he had temporarily stored Dinah's studio and workshop equipment in the third room on this floor. These west wing rooms all had connecting doors, the centre one without a door into the passage, indicating that two original rooms had been later partitioned.

Dinah switched on the light in the first room and looked about. Nothing. No ghost. No atmosphere of regret, nor of waste. Georgina had not actually come up here, Dinah recalled then, with some relief.

The ceilings were beamed and peaked almost to the roof ridge, the windows peering out from beneath their brows of thatch. The partitions between the rooms were of broad wooden planks roughly feathered, and the doors were absurdly small and crooked. There was a tiny square window between this and the centre room, and Dinah forced herself to go and look through it, her face close to the flawed glass. No-one looked back at her.

She collected a half-filled sketchbook and a folder of photographs and returned downstairs, to sit at the kitchen table since the light was better there than in the sitting room where Sam watched a television programme.

When the programme was ended he went to the kitchen and stood looking over Dinah's shoulder. She was drawing together random motifs – plant shapes, animals, birds, human figures – into a border pattern, working with painting sticks in browns, reds and greens. The shapes were drawn from photographs she had taken on an African journey with Martin Crane.

Dinah was surprised how little emotion was attached to these photographs and the memories they conjured.

Martin had been collecting music for his doctoral thesis. Dinah had been collecting graphic designs. Both had been drawn together by their excitement over their work. That had been the good time, before Dinah realised that she was pregnant.

'We need more rugs,' Dinah said after a while. 'Maybe I'll do one in strips, I don't know yet. Really thick, and yet smooth. Too much texture would detract from the simplicity of the shapes.'

Sam smiled, watching her work. He wondered how she had felt, up in those rooms where he had dumped all her equipment, her portfolios and books – two of which rooms should have been furnished with Georgina's things. Georgina should be asleep in bed up there now, foxy hair tangled on the pillow, grubby Pooh bear tucked in the crook of one elbow. Sam had had the bear buried with Georgina though he hadn't told anyone. His throat ached, remembering, and he bent and kissed Dinah's hair.

'Want some beer?'

She shook her head and Sam helped himself.

Dinah went to bed that night more at peace with herself than she had been since Michaelmas, relieved at the return of her old capacity and enthusiasm for work, and with the way the African pictures were lending themselves to her design. She was tired, but agreeably so.

She lay in bed waiting for Sam.

There was a slight sound of wind in the trees, the solitary cry of an owl.

Dinah became aware of a new silence in the house. Where were they? The voices were silent. She lay very still, listening: the blood in her ears, the beat of her heart, her breathing, the crack of old wood settling as the night temperature changed, Sam moving about in the bathroom, the trees outside – and silence. She smiled into the silence of the lofty room, silence from wall to wall, floor to ceiling.

When Sam came to bed and switched off the light, Dinah curved her body into the pattern of his and listened with delight to the strong beat of his heart, her cheek against his chest. No voices. Just her and Sam at last.

They made love slowly, with deep and infinite pleasure.

For the first time since her coming to Pooks Hall both Sam and Dinah forgot Dinah's cracked ribs, forgot all but the increasing and delightful urgency of their passion – two people completely engrossed in themselves, in one another. Sam moaned briefly as he held back. Dinah gave a great gasp as her body escaped the confines of her thoughts and rushed her surging into her climax, then found the added pleasure of feeling him reach his.

Dinah sighed in pure content. She heard Sam laugh softly in the dark. They drifted into sleep, still joined.

Before he slept Sam murmured 'Are you – all right?'

'Of course,' she whispered against the smooth warm skin of Sam's shoulder. 'I want to conceive as soon as possible.' A laugh 'I think I just have.'

When they were awakened by Simon's screaming Dinah struggled to a sitting position, her heart racing. The screams were terrible, and matched some tatters of a dream which fled shrieking out of her head.

Sam rolled over and switched on the light.

'Good god! I feel as though I've been asleep for hours – it's only midnight. I'll go.'

But Dinah had already pulled on her dressing-gown as she ran out of the room, bumping her shoulder painfully on the door post. Sam followed her.

Simon sat up in his tumbled and soaking wet bed, screaming and screaming.

Sam, feeling as though he watched characters in a slightly unsynchronised film, stopped and rubbed his eyes. Dinah had switched the rheostat light fully up as she entered Simon's room, but for a moment Sam thought the bulb must be failing. The light was so dim, flickering, like a candle flame. Then it steadied and brightened to normal.

Simon's screams stopped. He opened his eyes.

He resisted Dinah fiercely as she scooped him up in her arms, then he made himself stiff, but she held him, sitting down in the low chair, crooning, rocking.

At last he relaxed enough to allow her to dress him in clean pyjamas, while Sam made up the bed with fresh sheets. Simon wept a little, but it was a relief to see normal tears, hear normal sobbing after the previous wrenching screams.

In bed again Simon lay sniffing and heaving occasional great shuddering sighs, but he permitted Dinah to stroke his hair and face, even to kiss him.

'Oh my little love – what a dream you must have had!' Dinah murmured. 'Can you tell us what it was? What frightened you?'

Simon made a piteous face and his eyes filled with tears again, then he twitched convulsively and his eyes began to roll upwards. His breathing steadied. A faint beading of sweat showed on his downy skin. He heaved one more sigh, and slept.

'I hope he doesn't make a habit of this.' Sam put his arms round Dinah. Both were shivering; Sam cold in his nakedness, Dinah from shock.

Suddenly they turned to the bed again, listening almost in disbelief.

*Simon's voice. Simon was talking.*

Rolling his head on the pillow he was muttering.

Dinah's mind reeled. *He sounds like one of THEM! His voice . . . words which sound intelligible but are not.*

Then Simon said clearly, loudly, 'No – no – not – no don't!' The muttering resumed, the almost-words, chattering on for a few eerie seconds, then died away.

Simon turned over and curled on his side, one fist, clutching his comforter, against his mouth.

Dinah began to cry.

Back in bed Sam tried to soothe her. Occasional words and phrases jerked through her sobbing. 'Talking – talking – in his sleep – words – why not awake? Why not to us?'

She dozed a little, half dreaming, even while she cried, and Sam felt himself sliding across into sleep more than once. He murmured to Dinah and she eventually quietened like Simon, catching her breath in intermittent shuddering sobs.

The sound of the wind had changed. Rain pattered on the windows and the pattern of night sky seen through the glass seemed a lighter blue. Sam let himself go back to sleep, warm now, Dinah quiet beside him, her head on his shoulder.

Dinah lay still, awake again, her head buzzing with weariness and thick from weeping. She heard the wind, the rain, Sam's breathing and Sam's heart.

Then, true to her expectation when she had seemed dragged

out of sleep, she heard them again. Sometimes it was one voice alone, then others would join in in a sort of chant – no words clear, of course, and several rooms away. Dinah tried not to think of it being in Simon's room – and a child cried briefly and was hushed. Then a man's voice spoke much closer. Dinah's heart thumped and she held her breath. Then there was silence again in the house, and the wind and the rain outside.

Dinah went to the telephone. Sam and Simon were starting their breakfast.

'Is that Mrs Warner? Dinah Warner?' a young woman's voice enquired. 'This is Annabel Brooks.'

Dinah could hear Simon wailing in the kitchen. He still cried every morning on waking, a hopeless irritation to Dinah. Sam, though, remained amazingly patient and apparently unruffled. 'Do you want to speak to Sam?' Dinah asked.

Annabel, laughing, said: 'No I don't – I want to speak to you.'

Dinah sat down. The telephone was in the sitting room. The pale misty daylight filled the spaces between the mullions which reached from knee-high up to the ceiling and beyond into the upper storey. A hint of sunshine edged in at the casement windows in the wall opposite the mullions.

Caught between the two sources of light Dinah felt exposed. She felt brittle, bedevilled still by the memories of last night and her misery when she had heard Simon talking unintelligible gibberish in his sleep, and the urgent: "No don't!" Simon's voice, the voice she longed to hear, even badgering and annoying her! The wailing stopped at last. There were sounds of bowls and spoons in use.

'Oh, yes,' she said hurriedly. 'We've still got your map.'

'Ah, you can bring it with you,' Annabel said. 'Look, I'm feeling social, and not in the mood for exam revision. I'd like to meet you and your little boy. Have you got transport?'

'Yes, I have.'

'Come over this afternoon – we'll throw the children together, and we can talk. Sam can give you directions for finding us or has he already left for Ispwich?'

'No, not yet, but he won't be back until much too late to

come.' Dinah wondered when Sam had been to the Brooks' house.

'Pete's working, too – but to hell with *them*.' Annabel laughed. 'I want to get to know *you*. So you bring young Simon over this afternoon for tea, will you? Please?'

Sam was pleased when she told him she would go, and Dinah asked him directions to Annabel's house.

Sam drew a rough road map in Dinah's sketchbook, saying, 'We had a tutorial there last spring. I think Pete's with Eastern Counties Farmers. You'll like meeting Annabel, and it'll be good for Si to meet other children.' He paused, 'Perhaps he'll even – '

'Talk? With the other children,' Dinah mouthed, and they both looked at Simon, who was picking the raisins out of his muesli rather as though they were dead flies, or live ones.

For a moment Simon's gaze flicked up, taking in both Sam and Dinah.

'Simon,' Sam said, 'you are going to eat all those raisins – every one – or you don't get an egg.'

'Oh, Sam.'

'Di, you mustn't let him get away with things all the time – he'll end up like David's awful, bossy Lulu!'

Dinah began to smile. 'Lulu, I kept on calling her Fifi the last time – do you remember?'

'As if I could forget.' Sam did not smile.

Georgina had been there that time, alive and lively.

Georgina had referred to Lulu tartly as a *boiled rat,* until corrected by Lulu herself saying with unchildlike dignity that she was *not* to be called a spoiled brat!

'Don't forget the map – I've forgotten twice to take it to tutorials to give back to her and I won't see her again before the exam.' He was sorting out his briefcase before leaving. 'Why don't you get her to come over and have a feel of the atmosphere here – you suggested it.' He stopped, and they both remembered Michaelmas. 'Anyhow, darling, have a good time.'

'I don't really think you *mean* me to ask her that!' Dinah said. 'You don't hold with that sort of thing.'

He kissed her. 'Nor I do – but she could come over anyway.'

'Of course,' Dinah said, frowning. Sam's words had reminded her of her previous determination to find out as much as possible about Pooks Hall and its past owners and residents. Now she felt that the present was more important than the past, and the present was being difficult enough to deal with – made more so now by the experiencing of sudden and random memories of Georgina, and of Martin. Waking, these only lasted for the time taken in recognising them, but Dinah knew that in her dreams they not only lasted, but stretched. She was afraid of fully recalling the dreams.

'Have you got Si?' Dinah knocked on the door of the east wing kitchen, and pushed it open.

'Down the garden with Talbot, dear – Talbot's planning what to plant for you, and when, and generally tidying up.' Priscilla was covering jars of bramble jelly with clingfilm, writing labels.

Dinah said, 'I'm taking Simon out to tea with Annabel Brooks and her children – she's an OU student of Sam's. Do you want any shopping while I'm on my way?'

Priscilla smiled ruefully round the kitchen. She shook her head.

'Oh, god! Priscilla – you must feel like *squatters* here! I do feel guilty, honestly. And you were so marvellous when – when I was in hospital – looking after things. Still are!'

'Darling Dinah, we'll stay so long as we can help out in any way. I know that you planned to use the flat – Sam told us.' She finished labelling the last jar. 'And meanwhile you're not to go shifting presses and looms and lord knows what else by yourself! You shout for Talbot – he'll help you gladly. He may be short on one leg but he's as strong as a bear!'

'I shall. It was providential him coming up this morning. I couldn't have done it on my own.'

'Come on, dogs, let's go with Dinah to get Simon.' Priscilla put on a cardigan and she and Dinah stepped out into the sweet November air, slightly damp but mild, birds still singing.

The two collies ran round in wild circles, baring sharp, foxy little teeth and snapping at the air between them when their tracks passed. Then they stopped, and busied away into the hedge bordering the woods.

Talbot was raking leaves in the old walled garden and transporting them in a battered barrow to a compost heap. He was followed by Simon, using a forked stick and a cardboard carton as his own rake and barrow.

'Seems a shame to drag him away,' Dinah sighed. 'He'll probably hate it anyhow.'

'Now, dear, don't make an Eeyore of him – he may not pass any comments, but he takes everything in,' Priscilla said.

'Yes.' Dinah felt suddenly cold. She hugged her arms round herself, trying to remember, to visualise Simon with other children, but she could only recall the irritations of Michaelmas Day and that he and Georgina had been behaving so much out of character.

Priscilla touched her lightly on the hand. 'You take him out with you – it'll do you both good. Come on, Simon, your mum is going to take you out to tea with some new friends.'

Simon scowled, poking about by his feet with the forked stick.

He cried all the way back to the house, cried while Dinah was washing his hands and face and putting him in clean sweater and dungarees. She tried to ignore it but she could feel her tension mounting.

'Will you bloody well *shut up*!' She finally shouted. 'Simon – shut that noise, or I'll *belt* you one!'

The sound rang in the rafters and Simon hiccupped into frightened silence. There was an echo, like laughter, and Dinah was struck by a sudden recollection – only it couldn't be – of Georgina standing beside Simon, here in Simon's bedroom, and laughing while Simon cowered in just his present attitude. *Impossible.* She shook her head.

'And don't you dare start up again,' she warned. 'If you want to make a noise you can damn well *talk* – with *words*!'

Dinah drove to the Brooks' with the child sniffling and fidgeting on the seat behind her. 'Sit *down*, Simon!' She must get a seat and a belt fixed for him tomorrow. The thought of him shaking about loose behind her made her acutely nervous.

She was nervous anyway, though she certainly would not have admitted it to Sam. Dinah had in her imagination built Annabel up as a positive paragon – thought of her as "the fair Annabel" – and so clever, too.

'Here we are,' she said to Simon, slowing down. He snorted explosively. 'And don't you snort like that in the Brooks' house or I'll give you something to snort about!' *Perhaps I shouldn't have brought him – he's not normal, is he? Maybe they'll hate him. I used to hate freaks when I was a kid!* Too late to turn back.

The Brooks' house, two cottages converted, was shabby and the garden untidy. A small blonde girl had just alighted from a school bus by the green and Dinah waited for her to come across the road and precede the car in through the gate to stop by the house.

'Hallo,' Dinah said as she got Simon out of the car. 'Your mother asked us over.'

'Yes,' said the child. 'I know. I'm Amanda. He's Simon, isn't he? Come in.' She opened the front door and led Dinah and Simon from a narrow hall through a staircase hall into a large, cluttered and untidy kitchen. 'Here they are, Mummy. Can I have a biscuit?'

Surprised by the warm, friendly, untidy house, Dinah was further surprised to find Sam's star maths student up to the elbows in flour, making bread.

An enormous black cat sat on the further end of the large table. A smaller, ginger cat sat on the draining board under a window, through which could be seen an angle of still colourful garden backed by heavily laden apple trees and further a rank of elms, pale green and yellow leaves still defiantly clinging to the twigs of the few standing alive amid their skeleton dead companions.

Two small girls were curled up, themselves like cats, in a broken down old wicker armchair beside the Rayburn, playing cat's cradle with scarlet wool.

Annabel Brooks was indeed fair, very fair. She was a true blonde, with pink and white complexion and hyacinth eyes. She wore a fuchsia-coloured smock over gentian-blue blouse and slacks, and Dinah felt monochrome and negative confronted with the colour, brightness and warmth.

'Hallo, Dinah, Simon. Don't mind this, I'll be done soon.' Annabel smiled. 'Yes, Amanda, take the tin with you and you can share them.' She turned to the two on the chair. 'Go on, Charis, Dumpling, get off that chair and take Simon into the playroom. I'll call you when tea's ready. You can play in the garden while it's still light if you want to.'

The child referred to as Dumpling was about Simon's size, and Dinah was pleased when he went with her and her sisters without a backward glance.

'How is he?' Annabel continued, working her bread dough. 'Do sit down. Do you smoke? I try not to, but studying makes me fall from grace from time to time. No?' She indicated a pack and a lighter across the table near Dinah, who shook her head.

Dinah moved a stack of books off a Windsor chair and sat down.

'Simon? Oh, he – ' She paused. How much did Annabel know? Then she had a strange feeling that Annabel knew everything, whether or not it was Sam who had told her. She took a deep breath. 'I don't know if you know but Simon, at present, doesn't speak.'

Annabel looked up quickly, as though she hadn't known.

'Yes, since the accident,' Dinah nodded, keeping her voice very steady at first. 'Either he can't or he won't speak at all. He cries, yes, a lot more than he ever used to. He was such a – real little extrovert, always talking, singing. Now he doesn't say a word. But – oh God! last night he had a dream, woke up screaming, and then when he went back to sleep he was talking, *talking in his sleep,* but it was all gibberish, until he suddenly quite clearly said "No – no don't!" It was so *eerie*, and frustrating, because when he's awake – '

'What do they say at the hospital?'

'They don't want him to see a psychiatrist yet, seem to think it'll just get back to normal naturally.' Dinah was afraid she would become too emotional. She reached into her handbag. 'Here's your map – I actually remembered it.'

Annabel covered the mixing bowl and set it on one of the closed lids of the stove. She washed her hands. 'Come through into the sitting room.'

An open fire smouldered low amid piles of silvery ash in the large fireplace. Dinah became slowly aware with no sudden shock this time, that she could smell the woodsmoke, tangy and aromatic. She was aware of the warm scent of Annabel as the other woman passed her to put fresh logs on the fire. Dinah was aware of the smells of her own skin and hair, of the flowers and leaves in the bowl on the table beside her, of the smells of books and of carpets, of dust. *Oh, let it stay.* she concentrated hard, gathering it up. *Let it stay. Don't take it away again.*

Annabel sat down and watched her, dropping a hand to be butted by the ginger cat. Annabel was smiling at Dinah, a cat smile, eyes narrowing as the cheek muscles lifted.

After a while she said, 'Simon is relaxed while he is asleep. I suppose that's why he was able to talk. It's some tension while he is awake and aware that blocks his speech.'

'I can see that.' Dinah shook her head, and enjoyed the smell of her recently shampooed hair, although she was feeling anger again, and tension. 'I get so irritable with him, poor little Si. Every day I say to myself, "Today he'll be normal". And yet – ' She stopped, the tension lessened.

Annabel was looking at her expectantly.

Dinah began to smile. 'In here, just now, *I* became normal again – so perhaps there *is* hope with Si, I just mustn't let myself despair. You see, one of the effects of the accident on me was that I lost all sense of smell. And just now when I came into this room – I got it back!' She laughed. 'Oh, you've no idea: the *release,* the gain! This room smells so marvellous, an *adventure* in smells!' She felt elated, almost intoxicated. She wished she could tell Sam, now.

'Oh, Dinah, that's wonderful! I'm so glad for you.' Annabel laughed. 'I hope the smells in our house are really worth getting your senses back for!'

After a while she said, 'You've mentioned Simon's trauma, and yours.' Softly she asked: 'Do you want to talk about Georgina, your girl?'

Dinah froze, then sighed out her held breath.

She shook her head. 'You may not believe me but I can't. I dream about her – I know that I do – but I just can't *remember* her.' Her voice faded.

There was a silence punctuated by the rough in and out of the cat's purring as it sat on Annabel's lap. Dinah stood up and went to one of the windows.

The children had left the house and were playing on the slide in the garden in the fading afternoon light, red clouds streaking a purple sky.

Simon stood at the bottom of the ladder, his fists raised in his defensive position. Then he and Dumpling each grasped the rails and put a foot on the bottom rung.

Dinah felt a wild hope that Simon would assert himself, though simultaneously she was anxious that he would behave reasonably well and not thump his hostess.

Amanda was at the top, and Charis on her way down, flat on her back, legs in the air. Then Amanda was on her way down and Charis had landed, like a cast ladybird, arms and legs waving.

Simon and Dumpling assayed the ladder together, struggling against one another, Simon reaching the top first. Launching himself with reckless panache he appeared to be halfway down the slide before his rump came into contact with it. Dumpling followed, slowly and cautiously, and then the whole performance was repeated.

'Dumpling is my despair,' Annabel laughed, joining Dinah at the window. '*Imogen.* I ask you – does she look like an Imogen?'

She went to open the French windows in the other half of the big room and the startling chatter of the children's voices, their laughter, was clear – three voices, three laughs. And Dinah felt a vicious surge of rage at the cruelty of whatever had happened to lock up Simon's speech, and at what she feared might be cruel insensitivity on the part of the laughing little girls. How could they resist teasing him?

Indeed even now she heard: 'What's the matter with him, then?'

'He's shy.'

'He can't be shy – we're his friends!'

'Cat's got his tongue. *Pussy got his tongue, then*?'

'Only little *piggies* snort.'

Annabel put a hand on Dinah's arm and drew her back into the room, closing the window. 'We don't know – that may be just what he needs – let's go and make the tea.'

The bread was ready to knead again.

'Are you happy with Pooks Hall?' Annabel asked. 'Pete and I went round the outside just after it was put on the market. You know, peering in at the windows and hoping to find a door unlocked. It looks a fascinating house.'

'It is, and I really love it –' Dinah broke off, before she could voice the remainder of her thoughts: *Except for the voices. But how can I tell anyone I hear voices almost every night. They'd laugh. Who do you think you are? Joan of Arc?'*

'Sam says his parents are in the "granny flat" at present.' Annabel took bread from a bin, put eggs in a pan to boil.

Dinah said nothing, stroking the big black cat, now on the windowsill.

'I should think that's an excellent idea,' Annabel went on. 'I sometimes wish this house lent itself to resident grans.'

'Do you know a lot about Pooks Hall?' Dinah asked.

'Not really – I'd have liked to have done some research, but I'm still doing a project on *this* village for the community council, and there never seems time, especially with the OU.' She finished setting the table. 'Would you make the tea while I go and fetch the kids?'

Dinah tried to ignore Simon's silence throughout the meal, glad though that the three little girls seemed to have accepted it now. Amanda was all but smothering him with attention, playing the little mother, the big sister. *So like Georgina . . .*

Annabel asked Dinah about her work, the design, the weaving.

Distracted as she was by the children's chatter – and Simon's silence – Dinah was drawn to Annabel, and after a while began talking freely, using her hands to help explain visual points, and seeking colour comparisons round the room.

'We need more rugs!' she exclaimed. 'Pooks Hall looks so sparsely furnished – you must come over and see it, all of you. Why not November the Fifth, Saturday? We could have a bonfire party.' She had not intended inviting them, or indeed anyone, but it seemed that her volition was temporarily hijacked. The invitation was eagerly accepted by all.

Dinah was about to leave when Peter Brooks came in. He greeted Dinah, kissed Annabel. 'Drinks?' He took off his tie and ruffled up his already untidy dark hair.

Dinah accepted a weak gin and tonic, tasting its flavours with a new and greedy interest.

Pete stoked up the fire and said he would certainly bring the family to Pooks Hall on the fifth. 'I'm an absolute kid about bonfires and fireworks – we'll bring some, of course.' He fetched the children from the playroom, Dumpling riding on his shoulders, ducking her head under the beams.

'But you'll have to behave yourselves between now and them,' Pete smilingly warned his daughters.

They made extravagant promises, and Annabel suddenly cried: 'My God – I've forgotten the bread,' and fled to the kitchen.

'I must say, your cats are very well-behaved,' Dinah remarked when Annabel returned. 'I'm sure if I were a cat I'd have had my paw into that marvellous, bulging dough!'

'Ah,' Annabel said, 'both my cats have quite recently been people. They know more about right and wrong than many two-legged people.'

Dinah was slightly taken aback. Then she remembered Sam's remark about Annabel being a witch.

'Oh, wish on a star!' Amanda cried, pointing, as they all went out to Dinah's car.

'Star light, star bright,' Charis and Dumpling chanted, and Amanda joined in. Simon stared first at the star, then at the three girls. He said nothing, of course.

Annabel raised her eyebrows. 'Really, such superstition!'

'I'm looking forward to the party,' Pete Brooks said as he closed the car door for Dinah. 'I've had a secret longing to see inside Pooks Hall ever since I knew of its existence. Can't think why we never managed it – I believe it has quite a history – though all I actually *know* about it is that for a long time it was the hospital for the surrounding parishes. The pest house, you know, lazar house. That's why it's called Pooks Hall – Pox.'

' – and after I'd got my sense of smell back like that,' Dinah was saying, 'and was feeling quite relaxed – Pete goes and blows it with his information that this place was the *pest-house* and is really *Pox Hall*! And *she* must have known, though when I asked her earlier she said she knew nothing about the house's history!'

Sam looked startled, then annoyed. 'Of course!' he exclaimed. 'Damn it – I should have worked that one out myself!'

'Anyway, they're all coming on Saturday afternoon,' Dinah shrugged. 'It's Guy Fawkes Day so we'll have to build a bonfire and get fireworks and so on.'

'Perhaps Annabel didn't want to upset you,' Sam suggested. Then after a while he said, 'And, Simon, did he join in with the other kids – verbally, I mean?'

Dinah shook her head, turning away from him to hide her expression.

She had suddenly connected the voices with what Pete Brooks had told her.

*Oh, my god! How awful! They're getting through to me – the people who were here at Pox Hall, the sick in the lazar-house! I must be sensitive, after all, and I am getting in touch with the house's past, just as I wanted to – but I don't want THAT past*!

'What's the matter?'

'Oh, nothing really. I'm just a bit confused. But it shouldn't really make any difference, should it? I mean – the house is still lovely, and it's ours, and it's the present that counts, isn't it?' *It's ours – not theirs. I won't let them have it back*!

'Oh, Dinah, darling – unless you are literally the first ever occupier of a house you can't go on believing that you can't live in a house anyone has died in – people die all over the place!'

'But so many, such suffering.'

'I think I prefer that to perhaps knowing I lived in a house where *murder* had been done.' Sam went to answer the telephone.

'Perhaps sone of them *were* murdered,' Dinah murmured, 'to put them out of their misery, for money, or to make room for others – there were dreadful epidemics.' She shut her eyes for a moment, her painting stick idly moving on the page of her open sketchbook.

'Hallo, yes, this is Sam. Hallo there – oh fine, really.' Dinah heard him pause as he listened, then he said: 'I'm sure it will be, nothing much happens here – hang on, I'll ask her.' He turned to Dinah. 'Hey, love, it's David. They want to come for the weekend. Sorry it's such short notice and all that but Lulu's been ill and they want to get out of London for a few days with her.'

Dinah looked up sharply. 'Oh? What's the matter with her?'

Sam relayed the question. He turned back to Dinah. 'An infected middle-ear, strictly non-infectious to others.'

Dinah smiled and Sam looked relieved. It was always a relief these days when Dinah smiled.

Indeed, she began to look quite animated. 'Well why not?' she said. 'Tell them they must come – we'd love to see them – and Priscilla and Talbot will be thrilled! When will they come? Oh, and Sam, can they bring sleeping bags for the children?'

Sam nodded, and the telephone conversation was resumed.

Dinah stood up. Before closing the sketchbook she glanced at the open page.

She discovered then what it meant to feel that one's blood ran cold.

On the white paper, previously blank, was a clear and precise drawing – a flower on its stem, with three seed-heads – and beside it was written the words *Never bury deep enow*.

Dinah heard a strange humming sound, and the air shivered and shimmered as though reality were a gauzy coloured curtain blowing in some wind – a wind blowing from where?

She slammed the book shut and dropped it on the seat of her chair. Now her heart was racing as though she had been running up a steep hill. As though from far away came Sam's voice, still talking with his brother. Dinah concentrated hard upon what he said, tying herself to the present.

Later, when she went to see to Simon, Dinah found him restless and very flushed. He lay damp with sweat as well as urine, and in a mess of vomit. Almost unaware of the foul smell – that ancient foul smell she had previously experienced – she cleaned up, remade the bed, washed Simon and changed his clothes. He was heavy with sleep, and gradually became less flushed.

Looking at him as he lay in bed again, drowsy, Dinah thought: *But Si is never bilious*! She fetched the thermometer and checked his temperature. Normal. He slept easily now, no telltale rash on his fair skin, no nightmare babbling. Dinah sighed with relief, and then realised that since entering Simon's room she had been moving quite automatically, performing the physical necessities, whilst her panicking mind tangled with thoughts of pestilence and terror. *Pox Hall – lazar-house – plague* – Shaking, she sat down in the chair by her son's bed.

'You've been a long time, love,' Sam remarked as Dinah joined him in the kitchen. 'I've made up the Aga. I think I'll go to bed. Got to get to College early and cheer my little flock of this year's OU lambs into their first exam.' He paused, frowning. 'Is Si all right? What happened? You look a bit battered.' He put his arm round her.

'He'd been sick,' Dinah said. 'I had to wash and change him, change the bedding. He's OK. No fever or spots or anything.'

'Simon's never sick.' Sam was surprised.

Dinah nodded, and gave a wry smile. 'Let's hope this is simply an exception.'

She meant to tear the page with the flower drawing out of her book and burn it, but Sam had already done the stove.

The page remained in the book, which Dinah put away in a drawer of the bureau brought from her old home to her various other houses, homes with Martin Crane, with Sam Warner. She would take two pills tonight and blot out those voices before they could even begin to torment her.

She lay listening to Sam's breathing, to the night sounds of the house and of the damp breeziness outside, waiting for the sedative to take effect.

Dinah heard a voice – a child's voice, but not Simon's – singing a monotonous little tune. It sounded two or three rooms away. *But it's not Si – if only it could be*! Then a man's voice spoke, unintelligibly, and Dinah, angry, lay concentrating on her thoughts. *Go away. I hate you – however much you've suffered – just go away and leave me in peace*! Hypnagogic images presented themselves to her: grass – tufts of grass and weeds – flowers: purplish, five-petalled flowers with strangely shaped seed-heads.

She jerked fully awake.

Voices, three or more. The child's song was ended. The voices chattered on.

Then a sharply defined memory, a picture in her mind, riveted Dinah's attention.

Georgina. She could see in her memory Georgina standing in the doorway between Dinah's two workrooms upstairs – Georgina in a dark dress, saying something that Dinah could not hear because of the other voices. *But Georgina was never there*!

The sedative began to take effect, reality faded and the visions – the voices last, following her into sleep.

Annabel was on the telephone. 'Meant to ring before – I'm absolutely pissed off with Pete, telling you about Pooks Hall being *Pox Hall*. How could he! And can you forgive him for telling you – and *me* for *not* telling you?'

Dinah sat down, clutching the telephone.

She was alone.

Simon was out for a walk with Talbot and the dogs.

'Forgive? Good Lord.' Remembering her anger when telling Sam: 'Oh – of course – don't worry!' She pulled her thoughts together.

Upstairs this afternoon she had for the first time felt uneasy. She thought she heard voices though it might have been the wind in the trees, something else outside, the plumbing, Priscilla's radio – sounds carried along the purlins and roof beams of the central gable of the house, perhaps the television in the east wing. She would stop whatever she was doing and stand still, listening – not wanting to hear what she thought she might be forced to hear – but she could not be certain.

Then the telephone rang.

'I suppose I'd have found out sooner or later, anyhow,' Dinah continued. 'It's very – interesting. Perhaps that's why all but two of the big upstairs rooms were partitioned off, and why the main hall was divided into two storeys.'

'I wouldn't be surprised' Annabel paused. 'How's Simon?'

'Oh, he's fine.' Dinah frowned. So much to worry about apart from Simon – the house and the voices, Priscilla and Talbot and what to decide about the flat, and then that "automatic writing", the drawing and the words – *Never bury deep enow* – added to the knowledge of the past role of Pooks Hall. *But what has it got to do with ME? Why do I remember seeing Georgina in places where she never was! I must be going bananas*. Dinah made an effort to concentrate. 'Sorry. Yes, he's OK. As OK as he ever seems to be.'

'Dinah,' Annabel said, 'would you like to talk about it? I'm used to peoples' troubles – confidences – part of my New Age group therapies.'

Although consciously she held back – being the person she was – silently Dinah's signals went out: *Oh yes, yes.*

She could not talk about her worries and fears to Sam, not the deep, crazy anxieties. There was no-one – until now.

'I'll see you tomorrow, of course,' Annabel broke the silence. 'But with the children around we won't really be able to *talk*.'

'I know.' Dinah bit her lip, suddenly longing for a cigarette, glad that there weren't any in the house any more. 'I must – I must talk to someone! It's stupid – I'm getting worse – and I never used to be a neurotic person, not neurotic at all.' Her voice went into a husky squeak.

'I could come over sort of *now*' Annabel suggested. 'The children are out for tea and not due to be delivered back until six. Shall I – '

'Hold on!' Dinah cried, hearing a sudden commotion outside, by the back door: Simon screaming, Talbot's voice raised . . .

Dinah shot out of the room and through to the back door, which was opened by Talbot just as she reached it.

Simon projected himself through to fasten himself to Dinah's legs, where he clung, wailing and shrieking.

The two collies were slinking about on the path outside and Talbot in the doorway was white-faced, and more than usually hard to understand.

Dinah finally grasped his explanation of *what* had happened, though, like him, she was completely mystified as to *why*.

Talbot, Simon and the dogs had been approaching the house after their walk when Simon, who had been playing with a stick, had for no apparent reason – and quite uncharacteristically – attacked Nimble with it. Nimble, taken by surprise, had snapped, drawing blood from Simon's leg above his half-wellington.

Talbot talked about having Nimble put down.

Dinah angrily and shakily stripped off boot and rolled up jeans leg and examined Simon's leg, feeling at first in agreement with Talbot. If a dog bites, get rid of it. Then she said: 'No. No, Talbot. On *no account* have her put down . I don't know,' Dinah glanced down at Simon, 'I feel that it was more his fault than Nimble's. I mean it – ' she spoke vehemently. 'She doesn't expect that sort of thing from Si, or from anyone, so her reactions were to defend herself – '

Talbot was grateful. He didn't like what had happened, but

he felt instinctively that the whole horror of Simon's affliction would become worse if the collie had to die.

'I'll take Si over to the health centre for an anti-tetanus boost and whatever they give for dog-bites – ' And Dinah stared in frustration at Simon, thinking, *Maybe the jabs will bring him to his senses*! She felt an immediate twinge of guilt at her senseless vindictiveness. 'Don't fret, Talbot dear, it's not your fault, or the dog's. It's whatever is wrong with Simon.' Then she remembered: 'Oh lord – Annabel's still on the phone! Can you put this hankie round Si's leg while I go.' She ran back to the sitting room. 'Annabel, I'm so sorry – a mishap! Simon – of all things – went and took a stick to one of the collies and she nipped him, of course. It's not much but I'm going to take him to the doctor. I'll see you tomorow, anyhow. Come soon after lunch. Oh, my brother-in-law and his family will be here too – three more children!'

Her hands were shaking as she replaced the telephone. It had happened so quickly. So stupidly. *What on earth was Simon thinking of? What possessed him to do such a thing? WHO possessed – Oh no, I can't. . . .*

At the health centre Simon was given an anti-tetanus shot, and Dinah was given a course of anti-biotic medicine for him. The tooth marks were clean, and the punctures shallow, with no tearing. The young doctor put a plaster on Simon's leg.

'There you are, young man, you won't have much of a scar to boast about, I'm afraid!'

Simon subjected him to a withering stare, and the doctor put out a hand and gently touched the healed scar on the little boy's chin. The senior partner at the centre had taken the stitches out, Sam having undertaken the possibly painful trip with Simon who had been stoically – disinterestedly almost – co-operative.

The doctor smiled at Simon. 'Your leg doesn't hurt now does it?'

The only answer was a snort.

'Simon doesn't talk,' Dinah said. 'Not since the end of September, when he was hurt – that scar on his chin's from a motor accident. I don't know if you know about it, his half-sister was killed.' She carefully controlled her voice, her expression, feeling a knot of tension in her gut. Simon gave no sign of feeling at her words about Georgina. It was difficult sometimes to remember that he was only dumb and not deaf as well.

Doctor Meadows gave both Simon and Dinah a long and considering look. 'How about sleeping – both you and the boy?'

'He sometimes wakes with a bad dream,' Dinah said, 'and I'm afraid I'm turning into a junkie. I still take the sedative I was given at the hospital, though I haven't many left.'

Dinah did not want to say any more about Simon just now, nor about how he happened to get the dog bite. 'He trod on her tail,' she had lied.

Meadows was looking at both their medical records, Simon's first. He sat on the examining couch staring passively at the door of the room. Dinah felt again that awful desire to shake him, strike him – to get *some* reaction. She clenched her fists in her lap. She wanted to get home. Sam would be worried.

'Appetite?' Meadows looked up.

Dinah nodded. 'Quite normal. At times he's really greedy – he always liked his food.'

'And he still wets his bed.'

'*Still*? He was *dry* before he was two. Oh, I see what you mean.' The angry flush faded from her face. 'Since the accident, yes, every night and all night! I don't know where it all *comes* from! He doesn't drink any more than any other child I know.'

'Would you like another opinion?'

Instead of leaping at this suggestion – a thing she and Sam had been wanting to ask and yet afraid of doing – Dinah again felt angry. 'Would it do any good? Have you a practising *magician* in your partnership? Or a witch?'

Surprisingly the doctor grinned. 'It's as bad as that, is it?'

'Christ almighty, Doctor Meadows! Simon was a bright, forward child – noisy and full of fun. Now he's – well, he seems to have lost the will and the ability to *communicate*!' She paused. 'Sometimes I get so angry I want to hit him – no, I don't care if he hears me say it!' She tightened her lips and blinked, looking away from the doctor, away from Simon.

Meadows stood up and walked round his desk again to stand

looking at Simon, who still sat on the edge of the couch, legs dangling. His large, expressive hazel eyes moved. He stopped staring at the door and looked up at the doctor, a questioning look, now, and a little apprehensive.

'I sometimes wonder if taking him to a *vet* might be more rewarding!' Dinah spoke bitterly. 'At least they're used to dealing with patients who don't speak our language!'

'Hypnosis?' Doctor Meadows suggested.

Dinah's expression answered him.

She was afraid.

'Well I can only repeat, Mrs Warner, that from the results of all the tests, apart from a recent dog-bite, nothing is clinically wrong with Simon.'

Dinah sighed, eased Simon off the couch and took his hand.

'And you?' The doctor opened the door for them but stood blocking it. 'This afternoon must have shaken you.'

'Oh, when things like that happen with children you just go on to automatic pilot.' She smiled a little. 'It's afterwards you get the shakes.' She shrugged, feeling Simon tug at her hand. She looked down. 'But I sometimes wonder if he'll ever talk again!'

'I think that he will,' Doctor Meadows said. 'As so frequently happens in cases of amnesia, something will happen to shift him quite spontaneously out of his non-verbal phase.'

'Don't use jargon to me!' Dinah snapped, then her tone softened as she said, 'One night he did speak, but it was in his sleep – and it was quite horrible!'

'Oh?' Doctor Meadows pounced. 'Do you know if he cried out, or actually said anything – exclaimed – when the dog nipped him?'

Simon was now pulling hard at Dinah's hand.

'I don't know – I didn't ask – I wasn't there myself. My father-in-law was with Simon, and I never thought of asking him.'

'Ask him, and bring Simon in again in a week's time.' Meadows' smile was warm, caring, and Dinah thought that he must be very popular with the old ladies of the practice. The thought actually made her smile – it was nice to have a thought like that, although Simon seemed angry with her as they got into the car.

Most children, when taxed with supplying a reason for some misdeed will either claim no knowledge, no motive – 'I don't know why I did it' – will break down and weep, hoping for quick forgiveness, will lie, or will retreat into stubborn silence.

Simon Warner, although maintaining silence, did none of these things. Placidly and with obvious enjoyment he ate his tea. He actually seemed pleased about something, no longer angry with Dinah, even pleased with himself. And from time to time he would scan the room as though looking for someone to whom to tell his cheerful secret.

'But, Simon, don't you – ' Priscilla began again.

Talbot remarked sadly that it was no use.

Sam then asked the question that the doctor had earlier asked Dinah.

'Dad, did he *say* anything – cry out at all – when Nimble bit him?'

Simon suddenly fixed his father with a narrow stare.

The atmosphere in the large, beamed kitchen was heavy with negative expectation, but Simon simply looked down again at his plate, picked up his empty eggshell and peered into it. He then put it carefully back in the eggcup, upside down. Smiling a little at his joke egg, he drank his milk whilst now staring towards the dark sky at the windows.

Talbot was shaking his head. He didn't *think* that Simon had spoken – there was the bitch's surprised yelp as she snapped, and then Simon's first scream. Talbot couldn't be sure. The whole scene was confused and over in a second.

For Talbot, it was a long and difficult speech.

'Well, I don't suppose Si will do that again in a hurry.' Dinah turned away, went to the dresser for four glasses, and to the Suffolk cupboard built into one corner of the room, taking out bottles of sherry and whisky. 'Pour out, Sam, darling, will you?' Trying to sound as though the whole dog-bite incident was not only closed but already forgotten.

She went to stand by Simon, watching him. Was it natural to have such an extremely healthy appetite after antibiotics and shock? 'Hurry up, Simon, love – it's only half an hour to your bed time.' She wanted to get him to bed early – yes, out of the way – before David and Jean arrived with their children. Tonight she could not face exposing Simon's silence.

The telephone rang. Sam took a sip of his whisky and went to answer it.

'Must've been a wrong number,' he said on returning. 'So irritating that – when you've taken the trouble to answer politely and the idiot just cuts the connection.'

Later, at Simon's bed time, Dinah took him through to the sitting room. 'Come on, Si, say good night to Daddy, and to Gran and Talbot.' *One day it'll work – he'll just say it without thinking.*

But Simon began to cry, silently.

Dinah picked him up in her arms and went out of the room, Simon's silver-blond head bobbing at her shoulder as his sobs shook him.

In the bathroom he obediently took the second dose of medicine and the prescribed sedative pill. Dinah watched him as he washed the pill down with the bare mouthful of water she had given him.

She had a vision of that mouthful of water swelling and generating in Simon's body, until the waters must burst forth in some great tidal wave. Shuddering, she carried him to bed.

Simon slept. Priscilla was milking her goats. Talbot was with Sam in the study of the main staircase hall, and Dinah was in the kitchen.

She had become aware of the *timing* of the afternoon's accident – if indeed it was one. She had been arranging that Annabel come over for a talk – and at that moment Simon had elected to get himself bitten by the affectionate and happy-natured Nimble, thus making certain that Dinah and Annabel did not meet. *Christ, that's absurd, crazy, that a child of four could be so devious. And why? And, anyway, how would he know*?

Other things pricked at her memory, but she could not see them clearly, and what she did see didn't make sense to her.

There was the sound of a car drawing up, doors, voices, barking. Dinah had forgotten the dog, Lulu's dog.

Outside, the yard light flooding the scene, the other Warner family emerged from the large and elegant estate car which displayed the most recent possible registration letter on its licence plates.

Dinah and Sam went out to greet the visitors.

'Great to see you!' David thumped Sam on the shoulder, kissed Dinah's cheek. 'I wish we'd arrived in daylight but that's life – work!'

Jean Warner was not of the kissing kind, but her smile was warm and affectionate.

Sam had once remarked to Dinah that he found it impossible to imagine David and Jean in bed together. Dinah knew what he meant. It surprised her that elegant Jean allowed her elder daughter Louisa to be called Lulu, and that she permitted her to possess a shaggy mongrel dog.

Lulu, palely recovering from her ear infection, was ten and a half years old, Victoria six, and Matthew four. Lulu informed Dinah that she would 'eat with the grown-ups'. Victoria and Matthew, groggy with travel and weariness, drank milk and allowed Jean and Dinah to put them to bed. Lulu would join them later.

Meanwhile Lulu took her dog out to meet the collies. Rowlf at first grovelled in submission, then went into circular ecstasies with the collies round the lawn outside the east wing – stage-lit by light from the house windows.

'What a fantastic, beautiful house,' Jean remarked as she and Dinah left the children's room.

'All right if you're immune to the plague' Dinah almost said.

She showed Jean into the big room which matched hers and Sam's. 'I'm afraid it's not very well furnished yet – the cottage was the biggest place Sam and I have lived in until now! We have got to adjust to space.'

'I like it as it is.' Jean paused, then awkwardly she put her arms round Dinah's shoulders for a moment.

'Thank you, Jean.' Dinah gave her a quick, grateful hug. Nothing more needed to be said between them about Georgina not being there.

Downstairs Sam and his brother were having a drink, talking. Lulu was in the east wing with her grandparents.

'How are things?' David had asked. 'Not this place – my God! I'm almost envious – but Dinah, and Simon?'

'It's really Simon.' Sam poked the fire. 'It's difficult to tell with Di. About Georgina, I mean, she doesn't say much. But Simon – you'll see tomorrow – he doesn't say anything at all.'

'About his sister?'

'No, about *anything*. He hasn't spoken since the accident.'

David looked shocked.

Sam continued 'You remember him, noisy little sod – on and on all day like a dripping tap? Now, silence. And another thing – a sort of character change – for instance there was a bit of a crisis today because he hit one of Priscilla's collies with a stick and got himself nipped. Now, Si adores those dogs – Dinah has this sad little fantasy that he *talks* to the dogs and the goats.'

'And Georgina – I mean obviously Simon doesn't talk about her – but does Dinah?'

'No, we don't talk about Georgie.' Sam's distress showed in his face. 'I want to but she doesn't.'

Both turned as Dinah and Jean entered the rom.

'Where's Lulu? She can't be out with that dog still – her ear!'

'She went next door, darling,' David reassured his wife, 'Mum and Dad won't let her get chilled.'

'Oh, the "granny flat" of course,' Jean laughed.

'Yes, but it's not a new invention, you know,' Sam said. 'This granny flat was probably an original, seventeenth-century or earlier.' He handed out drinks. 'Quite often when the elder son married – and they married much later than we're usually led to believe – old Dad was dead already and the widowed mother was left running the farm. Well, the elder son would then build on an extra wing to the house or cut off an existing wing, and install his mother in her own quarters – giving the management of the main household to his wife.'

'All very diplomatic and sensible.' Jean remarked. 'Is it true?'

Sam nodded. 'Annabel, a friend of ours, has done a local history project on her village. Ah, here they are.'

When Priscilla and Talbot, with Lulu and the dog, came in, Sam, his brother and sister-in-law all looked at Dinah.

Lulu came dancing into the room ahead of her grandparents.

But Dinah was not seeing Lulu.

*Dinah saw Georgina.*

The light gleamed on her fiery hair, lighting her smile, her aquamarine eyes, fair freckled skin. Then suddenly it was not Georgina at all, but dark-haired, hazel-eyed Lulu.

Dinah's glass shattered on the floor and she knelt swiftly to retrieve the peices.

She was aware of Lulu squatting beside her to help clear up the mess, her dark plaits swinging, the only child in the room.

Dinah's skin felt taut and prickly. She was tense, and sweating slightly. Blood pounded in her ears. She told herself to relax. *It's imagination, you're getting paranoid – and that's just what THEY* want.

Dinah could only assume that she behaved quite normally at supper and afterwards, for she could remember nothing of it. Much later, in bed, her mind began to allow her to recall her feelings about the events of the day, if not the events themselves. She lay tensely waiting for Sam, waiting for some scream from Simon, waiting for the voices to begin their teasing. Shock waves from the day's events threw up odd and apparently unconnected pictures. The connection, she knew, was there – if only she could see it.

At last Dinah heard Sam come upstairs. She heard his voice, David's, Jean's – footsteps and the movement in the bedroom next door. A child murmured – Victoria. There was a slow quietening of activity and noise. Sam slid into bed, kissed Dinah gently and switched off the bedside light.

He was asleep in a few minutes, finding himself exhausted suddenly by his emotions, by his feelings at having Lulu in the house but not Georgina.

Dinah gradually relaxed. It took a long time. She lay listening, and tentatively began to recall more about the evening, edging memory back to that moment when the glass had slid through her fingers to shatter on the floor.

She recalled the child dancing through the doorway, but she remembered Lulu – only Lulu.

Dinah relaxed towards sleep. The house was silent about her, with only the occasional crack of settling wood, and a slight stirring of wind at the windows.

No voices.

In the dark Dinah felt herself smiling. *That's it – too many Warners in the house. With all these Warners THEY don't stand a chance.*

Dinah slept well.

At first light she and Sam both awakened, and made love. Then they slept, close in one another's arms, until newly awakened by the alarm clock, whose ringing was closely followed by a further alarm of the sound of voices, and of running feet.

For a moment of sheer horror Dinah stiffened, cold. Then she awoke fully. These were real voices, real footsteps, real children.

She listened for the sound of Simon's voice. Always it seemed that she listened for his voice – and she never heard it, except for the crying.

In Simon's room she sniffed the air, then turned to the windows.

So far Dinah had not been aware of the day itself.

Now she noticed the gusty wind which shrieked and whooped across the roofs and boomed, amplified, in the tall chimneys. The misty sunshine appeared oddly serene at the windows – as though, Dinah thought, the sound-track of an event had been superimposed on another quite opposite happening.

One of the casements suddenly banged shut, then slammed open again.

*But I put it on the catch last night, I always do.* She closed the window and turned to Simon, who was awake, watching her, sucking the corner of his comforter. Dinah washed and dressed him and they went down to the kitchen.

Lulu was already downstairs, about to open the door of the back hall to let out Rowlf, who had slept in the lobby.

She greeted Dinah and Simon and they watched the woolly black dog bounce out into the wind, tossing like a blown feather. 'He's very good, Auntie, and he doesn't even smell, does he?' Lulu tidied Rowlf's bean-bag into a corner.

Dinah smiled, sniffing. 'No, he doesn't smell at all.' She turned to Simon. 'Do you remember Lulu, Si? And her dog is called Rowlf after the Muppet dog you love watching on television.'

Lulu giggled. 'Only *my* Rowlf can't play the piano!'

Simon, who had been watching the dog, looked at Lulu and scowled, then went to the door, the wind catching him and standing his pale hair up in a crest.

'What funny weather you have here.' Lulu observed, as though the weather were peculiar to Dinah's garden, or switched on especially for the weekend.

It was indeed a strange sort of day.

The mist was laced and suffused with sunshine – in perfect stillness at one moment, while at the next the vapours were churning and shredding, the trees tossing in wild gusts of wind. Leaves and twigs flew like birds, and birds tossed and tumbled on the restless air like so many blown leaves.

'Can I do anything to help?' Lulu shut the door when the dog returned. She smoothed her hair. Her plaits were very neat. Dinah wondered if they had kept in so neatly all night, or had Lulu herself redone them this morning.

'Well, yes, there's the table to set.'

Dinah noticed how Simon at first watched, and then began to follow Lulu, looking faintly puzzled. Once he ventured to touch her hair, and he looked even more nonplussed when Victoria and Matthew appeared.

'Come along, children.' Lulu swept the three young ones into action. 'We're all going to help get the breakfast. Come on Matthew – and you, Simon. We need spoons and things – where are they kept?' Simon opened the cutlery drawer, and Lulu directed the counting of knives and spoons and the placing of them on the big table in the annexe made from the old dairy, the plaster work removed from between the stout studs.

Dinah, cooking porridge, was overwhelmed with guilt at the injustice she had done to just such a child as Lulu. *OK, so I didn't want a child then – so I never even liked Georgina – I might've tried harder! And here's Lulu behaving exactly as Georgie used to, and I'm smiling at HER*. Dinah would, she knew, have been irritated by Georgina in such a situation.

Sam and his brother arrived, hungry, Jean following, then they were all sitting at the table in the old dairy. Priscilla came in with a can of fresh milk.

'Coffee, Mum?' Sam poured her a cup.

Dinah stood up and went to fetch a jug for the milk.

A feeling of pent-up energy was increasing within her. She was becoming more and more restless, so much so that she could feel her skin tingling and her muscles tense and twitching to be active again whenever she tried to slow down. It was a strange feeling, a really painful sense of excitement and anticipation that set her looking expectantly at doors and even windows as though looking for a visitation.

Visitation? *Of course, visitors, and Annabel and her family are coming.*

'You all look very bright,' Priscilla remarked. 'Are you going shopping at all, you girls?' She looked at her two daughters-in-law.

'Yes, fresh buns for a bun race.' Dinah was setting up the coffee maker for a new brew. 'Give me a list if you want anything.'

'A *bun* race?' Victoria made a face. 'How can *buns* race?'

'You bite them off string and eat them,' Lulu began.

'You'll find it tough going, Vicky, with your gappy teeth!' David laughed and ruffled Victoria's brown curls.

'Daddy, that's mean!' Lulu frowned at him. 'It's just her age. Are we doing apple bobbing, too? But it's Guy Fawkes, not Halloween.'

'So we'll have a bonfire, and fireworks, and anything else to entertain us – like bun races and apple bobbing,' Sam said.

'Fireworks?' Matthew looked up eagerly, spluttering the word through a mouthful of milk.

'A bonfire!' Victoria breathed happily.

'Yes, a *huge* one,' Sam told the children. 'But we're not going to put a guy on top to burn because we don't like pretending to burn people.'

Matthew groaned to show his disappointment. Simon scowled.

Dinah felt a finger of cold touch her. She put a hand quickly to the back of her neck. Nothing. Her skin was warm. But the cold remained. It became a little icy core at the centre of her excitement.

'Matthew, you can't even *remember* the last time you saw a guy on a bonfire!' Jean leaned across and topped up his mug with milk. 'And you seem to have spilled more milk than you've drunk – '

'There's always plenty of milk.' Dinah began clearing the table.

Priscilla then became the centre of attention for the visiting children.

'Can we see the goats?'

'Could I learn to milk?'

'Let's take all the dogs for a walk, too.'

'Can we take the goats out?'

'What are their names?'

Children's eager voices – but not Simon's.

Dinah stopped at the Steggles' farm at Outwood Green not far from the Pooks Hall gates. Stowing two trays of eggs in the back of the Traveller, she then drove to Stowmarket.

Jean adjusted her seat belt. 'This car,' she said, as Dinah left the slip road for the A45, she shrugged. 'It's so different!'

Dinah didn't want to think about the Volvo. 'I know,' she forced a laugh. 'Sam calls it a half-timbered jelly-mould – but I love driving it. It's so basic and solid.'

'You're looking better this morning,' Jean observed. 'You must have been exhausted last night, what with that accident of Simon's and us arriving.' She paused. 'David told me what Sam said about Simon not speaking since the crash, but Dinah, the *children* told me that it wasn't Nimble who bit him but another dog – a *white* dog!'

The Morris jinked, held the road. Both women gasped, and Dinah's knuckles were white as she grasped the wheel.

'Why do kids have to make up such awful – hurtful – lies!' Dinah exclaimed. 'I hate.... Oh, I suppose they must have simply made it up, but why – why?' She felt sick and shaky, her heart thumping heavily.

There was a long silence.

'Dinah, perhaps Simon *did* speak. Children do trust other children at times when they won't confide in an adult,' Jean said. 'On the other hand – if Lulu and the others made it up – well, I'm sorry. They're a law unto themselves, I'm afraid. This *au pair* business and going back to work again is a mixed blessing, but one is so much pressurised not to be domestic.'

Dinah nodded. 'Except by men – and the Prime Minister!'

*Men like Martin.* And suddenly all the old pain, fear and frustration surfaced again. Martin had shown her off at first – his clever, creative, original girl friend – then when they married he changed towards her. He still openly admired *other* clever, creative, original women – but with Dinah became increasingly possessive, exacting, even tyranical. Dinah must replace Martin's mother as prime source of nurture and confidence. But Dinah had no wish to replace Rosemary Crane, no desire at all to play the mother to spoiled-brat Martin. When she wanted a child she would bear her own. But in the event, she bore Georgina, at the wrong time, in the wrong place, *the wrong child*. Rosemary Crane was bitter. Dinah was a bad wife and a worse mother – couldn't even bear Martin a son! Martin was besotted. This alien little child became his delight, and he would be a father to put Dinah's faulty mothering to shame – whenever his work gave him time. *Men like Martin*. Exciting, charming, attractive – and yet so destructive.

Dinah bit her lip as the car was rocked in the slipstream of a convoy of container trucks. She relaxed a little when they left the main road at the turning to the town.

Jean sighed. 'That awful vulnerability little boys have! Oh, my god! If the same thing had happened to me – Lulu, or the little ones. You must miss Georgina so much! I know that's putting it too absurdly mildly – I can never fully understand your loss – '

'It's Sam who misses her the most. He's – he was – a wonderful step-father to her.' Dinah said quickly. She could not accept the sympathy she did not deserve.

Sam and his brother had prepared lunch. The washing had been hung out, now alternately flapping, snapping and straining on the lines, now hanging limp and lifeless. All Dinah had to do was call in the children to wash.

She wanted to ask Lulu about Simon, whether he had really spoken, where the idea about the other dog had come from, but she couldn't bring herself to draw the little girl aside and ask her.

She felt even more tense and excited, almost like stage-fright, almost like dread, and almost like the wild and breathless anticipation of a child on the eve of a birthday.

At lunch she was too strung up and excited to eat much, and her throat kept on contracting, making it hard to swallow.

She looked down at her hands, the left hand displaying a slight tremor, veins prominent, pins and needles prickling like nettle stings. 'By the pricking of my thumbs, Something wicked this way comes. Open locks, Whoever knocks.'

A flying twig struck the window near her and Dinah gave a half-stifled shriek, dropping her fork with a clatter.

Simon knocked over his glass and water spread across the table, dripped off the edge.

'Bloody damn!' Dinah's voice was a shocked whisper as she fought to hold down the rising head of hysteria. 'I'll get a cloth – how is it that four ounces of water changes into four *gallons* when it's spilt!'

'Is that magic?' Victoria asked.

'Magic I can well do without.' Dinah sat down again, picking up her fork.

'More – more please.' Matthew picked up his empty plate.

'What's the mater, Di?' Sam asked. 'Not our cooking, I hope.'

She shook her head. 'It's lovely, I'm just not very hungry.'

*Perhaps I am pregnant again.*

Excitement like a knot was twisting inside her, tighter and tighter.

'Darling,' Jean was saying to David, 'why is it you never cook anything at home?'

Laughter, and David said, 'My image, darling – think of my image!'

'Mary-cloud does the cooking,' Victoria remarked. 'I don't like all the pepper.'

'*Marie-Claude*,' Jean corrected , articulating carefully.

Victoria shrugged. 'I still don't like her cooking.'

Later, when washing up was mentioned, Lulu firmly said, 'Me – me and Grandpa. Aren't we, love?' And she went and put her arms round his neck.

Talbot grinned. Simon scowled.

'She's so like Georgina,' Priscilla said. 'Pure chance, of course, but – ' She shrugged.

'She'll grow out of it,' David said quickly, glancing at Dinah. 'She'll soon catch a dose of radical feminism from somewhere. Mum, I do believe that you were always a closet women's libber. Why else would you have taught Sam and me to cook and sew?'

'In case you never got married, of course.' Priscilla smiled.

'Who's Georgina?' Victoria asked, frowning, half remembering. 'Why isn't she here? Is she a girl or a lady?'

No-one answered her, and she followed the two little boys out of the room. 'Wait for me – wait for me – '

The weather had remained bright and dry, though the strange wind still crashed and shouted, hurtling through the trees, suddenly and completely dropping from time to time, before picking up and raging away again.

Dinah stood in the depression that was part of the old moat, grassy and overgrown with brambles. She was on the woodland side of the walled garden where today the goats were browsing. She could hear murmurings from them as they kept in touch with one another, but these bleatings seemed as remote as sounds from another planet.

A game of hide and seek – adults as well as the children – had been in progress. Now it seemed that Dinah had found, as well as been found.

There was suddenly a complete absence of wind, though the space between them shimmered and hummed as Dinah and the man looked at one another. He was leaning on a spade, looking at her from beneath the brim of his hat. *But he isn't in the game! Who is he*? Beside him, not quite solid, almost ectoplasmic, the impression of a squat white dog with dark ears.

As she mentally grappled with what her eyes reported, the man moved closer, the dog-shape became more solid.

Dinah found herself sitting on the damp ground, hands clutching at the rough grass as though to steady herself on the spinning earth, prevent her from flying off.

After a breathless moment of shock she found that she could move, scramble to her feet, run – through the brambles and up out of the moat, fleeing into the garden, towards the house, panic riding on the back of her neck.

She collided with Annabel round the trunk of the old thorn tree.

'Hey, where were *you*?' Annabel grabbed her wrist, feeling the galloping pulse like some little wild creature trying to break through the fine, pale skin. Softly she asked, 'What scared you so?'

'I – I – don't know – ' Dinah stammered, shaking her head. *I can't – she'll think I'm hallucinating – but I did see – who?* 'I was down in the dry moat and it spooked me – how silly!' She forced a shaky laugh and knew that Annabel didn't believe her.

As she spoke the wind rose again to a greater force, whirling dead leaves up around the two women, raining them down from above.

Dinah tried to rationalise as she watched the game of rounders which followed the hide-and-seek.

*Imagination? But why? Real? Who was he and where did he come from? Where did he go? Maybe he went back into the wood when I passed out – no business to be in the wood anyway, it's ours – and the dog?* Dinah liked that even less than she liked the idea of the man, a white dog which the children said had bitten Simon, not Nimble at all. She recalled the strange cold, the humming sound and the trembling air, and felt a little faint.

Dinah went into the house, where Annabel had been on a solitary tour.

'Do you mind if I stand on my head for a while, Dinah? It's a sort of yoga exercise that helps if I'm boiling up for a migraine attack.' Annabel found Dinah in the kitchen, leaning against the warmth of the Aga.

Annabel had felt hostility and rejection in every room she had entered. She began herself to feel the pressure of Dinah's unusual, unnatural excitement. She also felt the first warnings of an attack of migraine. She must fight it off. She needed all her strength against the forces centring on Pooks Hall.

Dinah stared. 'Of course not. Have a cushion. Do you want anything else?'

Jean came into the kitchen and stood briefly aghast at the sight of Annabel Brooks standing on her head in a corner of the old dairy, and at Dinah's apparent unconcern. Jean retreated hastily, muttering something about Priscilla and butter, and a little later Annabel righted herself gracefully, cheeks scarlet, eyes bright.

'If only we'd felt free to laugh that would have been so funny!' Annabel said. 'Jean doesn't like me. No – really, she doesn't. But it doesn't matter.' She paused. 'Dinah, listen –

*we can't talk, not here, not now*!'

Dinah stared at Annabel. 'Why not? It's my house. Who's to stop us talking? I want to.'

Disappointment rocked her like a physical blow, and Annabel put an arm round her shoulders and leaned close. 'Dinah, *it's here*, in the house! There's such anger.' She paused, a spasm of pain above her eyes. 'So *much* anger, frustration and resentment. Oh, my God, we must be careful! Watch – but I'm not sure *who*. I don't think – ' She broke off, listening.

Only the wind. The house shook and the windows rattled.

Annabel said, 'On my map, did you see the lines? All those lines meeting here? It's a place for the gathering of forces, of power, so we must be careful. If you open up the gates you must be careful who you let in.'

Dinah shook her head and glanced behind her. She grimaced, rubbing her arms and hunching her shoulders. Then she ran a hand over her wind-blown hair and was surprised not to feel it standing up on end like charged wires. Her scalp prickled and her skin crawled and twitched and she was filled with a sudden irrational fear, *a fear of Martin Crane*. She feared his coming to Pooks Hall, though why he should come here she could not think, since Georgina – the link – was gone. But Martin had accused her of killing Georgina. He had accused her that day in the hospital of never loving Georgina, of killing her. Guilt and fear flowed through her. *I killed my first marriage and my first child. What am I doing to Sam and to Simon*? Her love for Martin had died with Georgina's birth, only a certain physical attraction remaining. All her capacity for loving seemed to have gone and she was left simply trying to recapture her feelings for Martin, and to discover a love for the changeling child – the child who had replaced her in Martin's emotional world. And when she stopped loving Martin, fear filled the vacuum.

'I was afraid – always afraid of Martin, really,' she whispered, shaking. 'Sam is so safe. Mad Martin and Safe Sam.' A sad little giggle. 'I said to Sam, thinking about feeling so safe with him, you know, that my feminist friends would say I was absolutely *sick*, to turn to him – another man! And Sam said "Really? How very sexist!" '

'You know, I think he had a point.' Annabel smiled. 'But *mad* Martin? How mad?'

'Over-indulged by his mother, spoiled all his life.' Dinah shrugged. 'Sam said it was "terminal insecurity." Like a spoiled child he'd fall apart or get violently aggressive if things didn't go his way, even trivial things. He's brilliant in his field of work, and selects friends and situations to his own advantage so he usually stays on top, but it was tight-rope stuff all the time. Exciting at first, but it couldn't last.'

'And Georgina? Why did you insist on taking her when you and Martin parted?'

Annabel knew about Georgina. No point in lying, or trying to justify herself. Dinah sighed. 'I thought it was natural for all mothers to love their babies, want them.' She shook her head. 'But she didn't – not like Simon did – Georgina didn't seem like *my* child. I can't explain any better.'

'Would she have been better off left with Martin and his mother?'

'She'd still be *alive*!'

'Who knows?'

Dinah remembered how Martin's mother had sold her flat and moved into his and Dinah's home, and gradually all traces and reminders of the marriage were erased – except for Georgina's room always ready for her to visit.

Now Georgina was dead, and Dinah was afraid again.

Children's voices occasionally reached them, carried on the wind. The afternoon darkened rapidly. Dinah glanced apprehensively at the windows. She tried vainly to ignore the tension. Her skin felt too tight. She imagined it splitting into a myriad thread-thin bleeding cracks.

Why she had resented Georgina so much? Her thoughts edged round the worst facets of herself, recalling her daughter's gestation and birth, comparing it with Simon's.

With Georgina Dinah had dragged herself from nauseous mornings to weary nights, the embryo's presence consistently irksome, changing Dinah's familiar and comfortable young body into something not wholly her own. The months in Africa were the best time, before Georgina was even conceived. The birth took place in a large teaching hospital in the Midlands, and afterwards Dinah, physically ill with influenza and emotionally drained, had allowed herself to become a cypher, a numbered bed in a ward. And the child, when it was born – ugly and orange-haired, skin curiously citrus at first – was simply labelled 'Baby Crane'. The baby had indeed a pitifully birdlike look after the first few days, all pink skin, orange fluff, gaping mouth and perpetual hunger.

Dinah could not love her. She could not feed her, either, and Dinah gave up the last of her instinctive struggle to prove herself a complete mother. The nursing staff was relieved. Martin was reproachful. Georgina sucked from the bottle with greedy self-absorption, and became the object of great friction between Martin and Dinah. Martin, unlike Sam later, knew how Dinah felt about her daughter.

Simon's conception had led to a different style of pregnancy and birth. Supported by Sam's acceptance of her as she was, Dinah sailed healthily through the nine months, immune to any germs and full of energy. Simon's birth occured, somewhat unexpectedly since dates were not in agreement, at home in the cottage at Snailwell, Sam and the District Nurse in attendance, Georgina wandering in and out.

Georgina never *appeared* to be deprived, resentful or jealous. *She adored Simon*, Dinah recalled, *she worshipped him. For her he could do no wrong, and for me, while SHE could do no right! And I loved Simon. She must have known the difference and she tried so hard to please me*. Dinah's sense of shame and guilt almost overrode the tension and excitement.

Georgina had tried so hard to be the perfect little daughter, the perfect elder sister – until that last day. *The first time we brought them here*, Dinah thought. *What did Annabel say? Anger, resentment, frustration – all emotions Georgina had never displayed until Michaelmas, here, at Pooks Hall.*

The wind still blew from the same quarter, a gusting gale, and the sparks from the blazing bonfire flew harmlessly away from the house, streaming across the orchards and the woods.

Perhaps this would be a cleansing fire and she would feel better, Dinah had hoped, but felt worse. She could not remain still. She found herself searching constantly for something or someone that she surely must soon see, and she listened for the voices which she felt she could almost hear.

Annabel also looked tense and expectant. Her beautiful hyacinth eyes were clouded with pain, and sweat glistened on her skin. *Migraine, or the heat from the bonfire*? Dinah wondered. *Or what she felt in the house today*? She moved towards Annabel, and received a warm smile, a straw to the drowning.

Dumpling kept on asking when they could have the potatoes set to roast in the bonfire, and Pete picked her up and swung her round. 'After that tea you ate?' He laughed. 'What a gutsy little pod you are!'

'We should call her Beanpole, and then perhaps she'd get to be thin like one,' Amanda suggested.

'That's a perceptive remark for a girl of her age.' Sam looked in surprise at Amanda Brooks.

'She's quite wise from time to time.' Annabel smiled at Sam.

'She's a witch's daughter,' Pete had put Dumpling down and had his arms now round Annabel's waist.

'Has she got a proper name?' Lulu asked. 'My real name is Louisa – I don't always feel like one, though.'

'Imogen, I'm Imogen,' Dumpling chanted. 'And I don't feel like a dumpling now – I feel like a *potato*!'

Matthew and Victoria joined her, with Charis, all jumping up and down shouting 'potato.' Simon, a little apart from them, jumped up and down silently, firelight glittering in his eyes.

The children's faces were beautiful in their delight at the bonfire and the light of the flames, and lit up further in wonderment as Sam, David and Pete began to light the fireworks.

The firelight touched Amanda's and Charis's hair to red-gold and for a moment it was as though Dinah saw Georgina too – hair the colour of fire. She felt as though she would explode like a firework herself, sizzling with sparks.

The fireworks banged and sizzled and whirled, bright wheels and brilliant fountains, and showers of gold, silver and coloured stars and flares and flashes feasted the eyes. Whizzing comets of colour and light draped the dark sky, green and blue, red, gold, silver – and floating up through them and away on the wind, the red and orange sparks from the bonfire.

Priscilla and Talbot had brought sparklers for the children. Now the five of them danced around the blaze, starry sparklers held in either hand, tracing patterns with the sparks.

After the fireworks were ended Sam said that they would have to wait until the fire died down before raking out the potatoes.

'Come on back to the house and we'll have a drink, and the kids can have a round of indoor hide and seek.' He turned to look back at the fire, and suddenly shouted: 'Simon!'

At the same moment Dinah screamed.

It seemed that Simon was being projected towards the fire, feet scarcely touching the ground, hands up in protest.

'*You bloody little idiot*!' Sam dragged him back, amid the pungent smell of scorching hair and singeing woollen sweater, flinching at the surge of heat as the chancy wind bent the flames towards him and the child.

Dinah was beside them, snatching Simon from his father and staring in horror at his shocked eyes and scorched nose and cheeks. She felt hysteria very close.

'I'm sorry, I didn't mean to shout. Simon, it's *all right* – I'm not angry now,' Sam coaxed, and the other children drew near, staring. 'It's just that – well – we don't really fancy *roast boy* this evening, just roast potatoes.'

The other children thought that was hilarious.

But Simon snorted, then began to cry as though all Dinah's hysteria were coming out in him.

Dinah began to walk towards the house, as fast as she was able, with Simon now a dead weight in her arms. She elbowed Sam aside when he wanted to carry the child.

When Dinah later joined the party in the sitting room she was strongly aware of the smells of bonfire smoke and of dead fireworks, of sherry, whisky, and of mingled fragrances of scents and soaps brought out in the warmth.

She moved towards Annabel, and as she did so a gust of wind blew a great puff of smoke down the chimney and a tongue-like spurt of flame licked out of the fireplace into the room.

The casements rattled. Dinah's teeth chattered.

She clenched her jaws, and then saw that Simon was standing staring at the fire with a look of horrifying, helpless terror.

*It's here. It's in the house. It's in this room*!

Dinah put out a hand to Annabel, nodding her head towards Simon. She saw Jean looking at her curiously, and thrust her hands into the pockets of her slacks. Then she, with everyone else, flinched and gasped as Sam exclaimed, '*Christ*!'

Two loud and heavy explosions had shaken the house, and made two of the girls squeal and Matthew clutch at Jean's legs.

'What on earth was that?' Jean had a hand to her mouth.

'Farmer – shooting – ' was what Talbot articulated.

'Steggles shooting in the *dark*? And it sounded a bit too bloody loud and close, Dad,' Sam said doubtfully. 'He wouldn't be lamping after bunnies round here anyhow, too overgrown.'

Pete Brooks had opened one of the casements and hung out, the wild wind rushing in past him to stir the air in the big room.

'Can't see any lights – too noisy to listen for anything.' He withdrew and closed the window.

'Hey, have you been letting off bangers in here?' David came into the room looking startled.

Dinah's heart was hammering. 'It's outside,' she whispered, licking her lips, knowing that she lied.

'Outside, shooting the poor, poor peasants,' Victoria intoned. Then, 'What's lamping bunnies? Is it shooting them, too?'

She and Charis Brooks clung together, round-eyed, excited by drama.

'*Pheasants*, Vicky,' Lulu corrected. 'Pheasants – you know – with an EFF.'

No-one actually believed Sam or Talbot, but what else was there to think, or to suggest? If it was not someone shooting in the woods – though it had sounded more like artillery than like a couple of shots from a twelve-bore and if not fireworks, what could it be?

'None of us have any connections with any terrorists, have we?' David asked, grinning at his brother, then at Pete Brooks. 'Or the CIA?'

The mention of terrorists paradoxically seemed to ease the

tension a little, and Jean suggested that maybe some bangers had been forgotten, and left too close to the dying bonfire.

'It's not over,' Annabel muttered, and Dinah stared at her, ripples of apprehension up and down her spine, a tight, congested feeling in her chest.

And, simultaneously with another loud explosion, which was followed by a volley of sharp bangs apparently coming from above the house, a wave of smell rolled into the room – nauseating, sweet and sour all at once, thick, contaminating, bad.

'My god, what a *smell*!' Priscilla was white. 'Sam, what *is* it?'

'Who – '

'What – '

' – bangs from above – the smell is down *here* – '

'Oh, *poo* – '

'Yuk – '

*This is what Georgina meant*! Dinah held a tissue over her nose and mouth, tried to catch Sam's attention. He too had heard Georgina complain of a sickening smell in the house.

'Mummy, I think I'm a little bit frightened.' Victoria crept over to Jean, who sat down and took the little girl on her lap.

David turned to Sam. 'What could have happened? Those bangs . . . my god, could the central heating have exploded?'

'Smells more like drains.' Sam felt as though things were beyond his control, and he was scared – recalling, as Dinah had, that Georgina had been obsessed by some disgusting smell she claimed was in the house.

'It's sick. It's a *charnel* smell,' Dinah whispered, shaking, and it seemed that she could hear voices – *the* voices – troubled, gabbling and moaning.

The smell was gone as suddenly as it had come – and unlike smells usually do, it went completely – no vestiges remaining, no aftertaste in the nose or mouth.

There was sudden movement.

Sam and David headed upstairs. Talbot, with Pete Brooks, went through to the kitchen and the rear of the house.

The house, physically, was totally normal.

In the sitting room Priscilla began a game of 'I-spy' with the children, all but Simon taking part, all of them aware of the sounds of searching, aware of the thumping of footsteps through the house, the switching on and off of lights, opening and closing of doors.

Talbot returned last. He had been round the outside of the house, and down the drive in the wild night, flashing a torch beam, seeing only what he knew should be there. He also checked the east wing, where the three dogs were restless and whimpering. He left lights burning in the flat for the nervous animals, and returned to the family carrying a treasured bottle of Glenfiddich.

'Nobody saw anything? Or heard anything?' Priscilla asked. 'Did we – did we all smell it?'

No-one asked 'smell what'?

'Stink bomb?' David suggested.

'But who?' Priscilla's voice almost mocked.

'The lads from the village – Guy Fawkes night, you know – stink bombs and thunder flashes!' Sam wondered if he should call the police.

'What else could it have been, really?' Jean looked from him to David, who looked as unconvinced as any of them.

'Yes,' Pete Brooks said, uneasy about Annabel's silence, the look on her face. 'Someone from the village saw your fireworks and the glow from the bonfire and came along to play silly-buggers.'

'Daddy, silly *what*?' Amanda, excited and puzzled by the atmosphere and the questions, played for attention by teasing.

The tension should have been relieved, particularly as Talbot had not reported anything out of the ordinary when he was checking round outside. There was a conscious effort at relaxation, though the wind seemed to be vibrating through the very fabric of the house, now a monstrous, whirring noise, and a hammering of giant fists at doors and windows.

A crackle like thunder ripped across the roof and Dinah saw Simon jerk, rocking on his feet.

'I don't really *like* thunder,' Lulu said rather apologetically, and squeezed herself on the sofa between Priscilla and Talbot.

Now Annabel and Simon stood facing Dinah, before the fireplace as though on a stage, set apart from the others by their own tension.

Annabel's eyes darkened. The migraine was taking hold –

or if not the migraine, something else. Shimmering lights flashed behind her eyes, and in front of them everyone and everything in the room had a rainbow aura. To her as well as to Dinah, the new humming in the air and the sound of strange voices was growing in persistence and volume.

Simon also seemed to be listening to the voices – louder now, and more insistent than the occasional voice of a living person within the room. Louder, clearer, yet the words still unintelligible.

Time stretched.

Time contracted.

Then the night erupted in a heavy banging, apparently approaching, but from which direction impossible to guess. Like a stick of bombs – *bang, bang, three, four, five, bang* – the sequence culminating in a series of random explosions at doors and windows, above, below, as if to shatter them, the walls, the house, the people and all.

Dinah thought that she screamed, but it was Jean who made the sound.

Talbot Warner slid to his knees on the floor, recalling the barrage at Mersah Matruh. He felt Priscilla's thin, hard little hand on his shoulder and retained his sanity.

The glasses on the table trembled and chimed.

Dinah's spirit erupted in a silent screaming. She felt as though all the events since Michaelmas – events in time, in space, in the countryside – indeed that the house itself and all its past existence were streaming through her like a great coloured wind. Lights and colours pumped and flowed like breath and blood. Her skin tingled and burned and felt icy at the same time. She was awed and breathless with it, her heart racing, and felt that she must run, fly, out and away from the fire, from the room and the people – run out into the wind and the night.

She looked at Simon.

He stood with his shoulders hunched, hands raised as though praying, beseeching. He jerked like a puppet with each crash – but seemed eagerly to await the next.

As if to break the spell Dinah made herself look at the other children and she saw the three little Brooks girls huddled now on the sofa like the three wise monkeys: hands over eyes,

Dumpling; hands over ears, Charis; hands over mouth, Amanda.

Lulu and Victoria were clutching at David and Jean, and Matthew was curled as tightly as possible on Priscilla's lap, like Simon twitching with each explosion.

The last of the series of crashes reverberated into silence.

Seconds felt like minutes, like hours.

In the silence – only the crackling of the fire, and the roar of the wind – Dinah stared at Simon.

In his extreme excitement he looked incandescent.

Dinah's heart seemed to stop. Surely no child could stand that pressure? She would see him snap like a flower on its stem and die before her eyes!

'The gates opened.' Annabel's whisper reached through Dinah's preoccupation.

An explosion crashed into the room through the door from the hall.

Miraculously it seemed, the room, the house, the world, remained intact and untouched. No plaster poured from the cracked walls. No glass splintered deadly glittering shards across the room. There was no wreckage – yet the blast did crash the door open.

In a concerted intake of breath, all turned – even Simon – to see, dreading what was there . . .

*Nothing. No-one.*

There was a wild hollow rattling like a roll of drums, and the final explosion cracked tamely, like a shot from an air pistol, somewhere high above.

A tempestuous gust of wind shook the house like a terrier shaking a rat and drew a burst of flame up the chimney.

Dinah, rigid with concentration, was so intent upon him that she felt for a dizzy moment that she actually *was* Simon, and swayed towards him a little.

He opened his eyes, tightly closed since the banging open of the door. Now he shuddered a little, shook himself like a dog coming out of water, and looked about – face shining with eagerness.

Turning to Dinah, he broke the stunned silence.

'Why've all the fireworks stopped, Mum? I want my potatoes out of the fire.'

## *Part Three*

# William

'I felt as though I'd just *given birth*!'

Dinah's eyes were bright, healthy colour in her cheeks. Even her hair looked glossier. 'All we could find outside on Sunday were remains of fireworks, rocket sticks and paper wrappers.'

Tuesday morning, and Dinah, still a little dizzy from the events of Saturday, was still trying to explain to herself, as much as to anyone else, the events of Bonfire Night – and the attitudes of those involved.

As mystifying as the phemomena of the battery of explosions and the appalling smell, was the fact that after Simon had spoken it seemed as though no-one thought that anything untoward had occurred – or else that there was a spontaneous and thorough conspiracy of silence.

It seemed that only Dinah was still shaken from the effects of the culmination of inexplicable occurrences. 'I know,' she said to Annabel, 'you were totally crippled by your migraine. But do you – can *you* remember it at all?'

Annabel, glancing at Simon and Dumpling who were painting pictures of bonfires and fireworks at the kitchen table, smiled and nodded. 'Let's go and light the sitting room fire – I'll bring more coffee.'

Dinah, nursing her coffee cup in her hands, the fragrant steam teasing her senses, apologised for neither telephoning or visiting Annabel sooner. 'Sunday was chaos as you can imagine – the children were hung-over with excitement still. Then yesterday I went to visit the school in Monks Hempstall, they'll take Simon in the mornings for the rest of this term and full time after the New Year, although he won't be five until February.'

'I confess that I spent Sunday in bed blacked out, with no-one allowed near me.' Annabel added sticks to the infant blaze. 'I'm so glad about the school. He's a bright little boy – I only wish our local would take Dumps before her birthday, but they're really rigid.'

'So it seems that it's just you and me who recall it all, 'Dinah said after finishing her coffee.

'Simon?' Annabel looked up from the fire. 'He *did* remember that there were potatoes in the fire.'

Dinah sighed. 'I don't want to question him.'

'No, neither would I, actually – although I'm burning with curiosity.'

After a while Dinah burst out with 'No-one said *anything* about it! It was as though we'd all come in from the bonfire and sat about drinking and talking, and the kids playing "I-spy" and *lost* all that time while the – the *happenings* were going on!' She paused. The fire had caught and was crackling well, the scent of apple-wood stealing out into the room. 'And then Simon said he wanted his potatoes out of the fire – so we all put on our outdoor things again, even Talbot and Priscilla, and trooped out to the bonfire to rake out the spuds. Jean even remembered to bring the butter and knives.'

'All except me,' Annabel said. 'I watched you go, and you couldn't let Simon out of your sight – I saw your face when he came and cuddled you and let you cuddle him – then the damned migraine hit me again, worse than ever before.'

'And another thing,' Dinah said after a while, 'yesterday I came to a decision. I told Priscilla and Talbot that they must put the small-holding on the market and make their permanent home at Pooks Hall.'

'Oh, what a good idea! And you still have plenty of space, don't you!' Annabel turned as the two children came into the room, displaying their finished paintings. 'Oh, darlings, they're *beautiful*. What did you like most about the party on Saturday?'

Dumpling pondered, staring at her painting. 'I liked – I liked the fire and the firewords – I liked the sparklers best because I don't really like bangs – and they did bang awfully much.' She held out her picture again. 'Look there's me and Charis and Simon with the sparklers writing our names in the air.'

'How about those potatoes?' Annabel gave the little girl a squeeze.

'I wish I'd eaten more: four – five – six!'

'I ate three and a half,' Simon said. 'Then Auntie Jean said I'd burst and she ate my other half.'

'Aren't grown-ups mean!' Dinah laughed, delighting anew in her happy, *normal* son.

When the children went off out to the slide, Dinah said, 'What do *you* think is the explanation? And *is* there one at all?'

'Oh yes, and I believe that no-one – after Simon spoke – asked any questions or made any more conjectures, because *everyone* – even the children in their own instinctive way – knew that whatever explanation any of us could offer would be either inadequate or simply unbelievable.'

Dinah frowned. 'What do you think *is* the explanation?'

Annabel was silent for a while. 'There was a tremendous amount of anger in the house that day. Whose anger we may never find out. You remember what I said about opening the gates? And I felt also that there was danger – for you and Simon. There was such power there, such *force*, I was afraid that it would break Simon and perhaps you, too – even me.' Her eyes darkened. 'I wonder – did it – did it get what it came for?'

Dinah's lightness of spirit, her new buoyancy, flagged. Since Sunday, after a good night's sleep and no voices to worry her, there had been an almost honeymoon flavour to her life. Now she wanted nothing to spoil it again for her and Sam and Simon.

'What do you mean?' she whispered. 'Didn't it *give* – you know, Simon's speech?'

'We can talk here, possibly even in your house now,' Annabel said.

Dinah nodded.

'How about some of the things you can't talk to Sam about?'

Then at last Dinah began to cry.

Weeping with relief and abandon, she found that she was on the floor, on her knees, her head wrapped in her arms and resting on Annabel's knees. 'I'm wetting your clothes – my tears – bloody great pool – like Alice we'll be swimming – '

She tried to move away but Annabel held her, stroking her hair, her neck, her shoulders.

She was aware that the door had opened, heard Annabel say, 'Hush.'

Then, 'Oh, poor lady.' Dumpling's voice. 'Come back, Simon, we've got to find the cats.'

Dinah raised her head and sniffed, glad of the handful of tissues Annabel gave to her. 'I feel – it's not only that I'm guilty about Georgina – it's poor little Simon, and Sam, who I *love*. What sort of person am I? And it's Martin, too, what I did to him – because I was afraid of him.'

'Who's been telling you that everything is your fault?' Annabel eased Dinah up into the low easy chair she had just vacated. 'More coffee, right? Strong and black. Look, you can't take *all* the guilt! Leave some for someone else! Anyhow – how can you be guilty over something that is not in your control?'

*What had she said? 'You can't take all the guilt.' Well – that accuses me of being selfish, doesn't it? No, she'd never accuse or judge, it's just bloody true and it does make me selfish – which makes me all the more guilty*!

Dinah's head throbbed, her nose was blocked, her eyes were swollen and her throat hurt. And every time she tried to think of what she was going to tell Annabel, her treacherous eyes filled with tears again.

Annabel returned with the coffee, which was black and strong, as promised, and also laced with brandy.

'The children are eating cheese sarneys and yogurt in the kitchen.' She sat on the floor by the fire. 'They're teaching Black Tom to read – though little do they know that Black Tom can already read fluently in seven languages! I can't think how they are doing it as Dumpling's such a lazy little devil she can only read her own name, and things like FISH AND CHIPS and ICE CREAM!'

Dinah spluttered what was almost a laugh, and then tears welled up in her eyes again.

'I haven't bothered to teach Simon *anything*! I've just loved and enjoyed him, I suppose – and tried to get him to behave nicely, you know.' She took a deep and shaky breath. 'Martin and I – we taught Georgina to read before she was three.

There was just time before we split up. I'd met Sam by then.'

'Drink up,' Annabel held the cup out to Dinah. 'While it's hot. Then tell me.'

'My god!' Dinah breathed, staring into the fire, eyes wide and dry now. '*I can remember Georgina again* – picture her – I'd forgotten! After the crash I forgot what she looked like – only remembered that she had red hair. But that day, Michaelmas, was full of anger and petty irritation and Georgina was – oh – quite unlike herself! She is – was – a gentle, happy child who adored Simon, but that day she was pert and tiresome, at times really rotten to Simon. They were scrapping like – well, quite unlike *themselves* – and then at other times she seemed half asleep.' Dinah's mind followed the rolling of the memories like a not quite fully remembered film. Then she exclaimed, 'The smell! Of course, *the smell*! Georgina never told lies – but she kept on talking about a terrible smell in the house, and saying that she couldn't go into the house or she'd puke.'

'Had she been to the house before?'

Dinah shook her head. 'She'd been really excited before we got there, you know – longing to see her rooms. But when we did get there she never went upstairs at all! She'd tied up the name of the house with Kipling's *Puck of Pook's Hill* and was full of lovely fantasies – just as well she didn't know it's really Pox Hall!'

They looked at one another, and Annabel murmured: 'I wonder – did she?'

'Sam said he had heard her that day talking some extraordinary nonsense in a broad Suffolk accent.'

'Did he tell you what she'd actually said?'

'No, and afterwards – well – we couldn't talk about it.' Then, after a moment or two's hesitation, Dinah told Annabel about the voices.

They could hear the children playing again. Annabel said, 'You haven't heard them since Saturday evening? Then, when it was all winding up to the climax, I think I heard them too.'

'That's right,' Dinah agreed. Her head and eyes felt less heavy and swollen, and she could breathe clearly through her nose again. She was also conscious of the fact that for some time now, Annabel's hands had been on her feet and ankles, gently and firmly massaging – when had she removed the shoes? It felt good, like standing in shallow, warm, running water. She gave a little gasp as a vivid picture flashed into her mind – Georgina, standing ankle-deep in shallow, warm, running water. Georgina laughing, holding her dress bunched up at her hips, bare white legs, foxy hair blowing in the sharp sunlight. The water was aquamarine blue, Georgina's eyes also. The sound of laughter and Sam's voice: 'Why don't we ever have the camera at the right moment!' But the unconscious camera in Dinah had clicked its shutter and taken a copy of the memory.

'Anything else?' Annabel prompted.

'Just a memory – from before.' Then Dinah said, 'When I think of Saturday I can still feel a sort of backlash of excitement – I felt so tense then that it seemed unbearable and yet it went on winding up tighter and higher, and still I hadn't flown into pieces!'

Annabel nodded. 'At first I could feel it coming from you, and then it got into me, too. With the damned migraine attack as well, *something* had it in for us.' She paused, deep in thought. 'And yet, in the event, Simon was released from whatever had held him speechless.'

'There's another thing,' Dinah said, 'you remember when I rushed out of the old moat – when we were playing hide and seek? Well, down there, in the dry moat, I saw a man – a stranger – looking at me. He was leaning on a spade – *and there was a small white dog*. The air became very still – and then it sort of hummed and shivered and I began to feel – well, that *one* of us was unreal. Then I must have fainted, which is weird in itself, because I don't faint. I remember sitting on the ground, and then running like hell!'

'Good God!' Annabel exclaimed. 'That tale the children told, that it was a white dog which bit Simon!'

Dinah frowned, then nodded. 'It would explain – I mean, if he was scared of a dog he might hit out at it. He'd *never* have attacked Nimble or Quick.'

'Children are much more psychically receptive than adults, yet you've been receiving an amazing amount.' Annabel paused. 'Do you feel up to doing some research on the house, now that Simon is OK and we think whatever it was is over? We can find out about the people who lived at Pooks Hall from the Parish Registers. They're still in Monks Hempstall church, I know.'

'Will she – will Georgina be in the register? A burial?' They both stared silently into the fire, then Dinah nodded, answering herself. 'Maybe,' she said, 'Maybe. But I don't think I'm ready yet.'

They went to join the children in the kitchen. Simon and Dumpling were doing a jigsaw. The cats were asleep together on the wicker chair. Annabel made fresh sandwiches, and sliced up some tomatoes and celery.

Dinah felt confident now that her emotions were under control, she was even quite hungry, yet she was nagged by a thought that there was still something that she hadn't told Annabel.

'And did the cats learn to write as well as to read?' Annabel asked.

Simon was scornful. '*They* can't write!'

'Paws,' Dumping giggled, spreading out her plump and paint-stained hands.

'Can't hold pencils,' Simon explained, and added, 'Anyhow, I think Black old Tom knows it all.'

Dinah gasped, but Annabel simply laughed, holding up her own hands. 'No thumbs, of course, cats and dogs both.' Her own hands were shapely and supple. 'And we, we *people*, have hands with good strong thumbs – which is why we can do and make things and how we got to be what's called *civilised*!'

Dinah suddenly remembered what she had left out: the sketchbook.

'I suppose it must have been me,' she said, when the children had gone to the playroom. 'I must have drawn those things, written those words without realising what I was doing.'

'And you can't identify the flowers?'

'I haven't tried – I didn't even want to look at the page again! And the writing – I mean the actual writing – the *hand*, was totally unfamiliar. And I never spell enough E-N-O-W!'

Annabel put a hand over Dinah's, which were clenched together on the table. 'Will you show it to me?'

'I suppose.' Dinah sounded more cheerful, even hopeful, 'I

suppose that maybe if I find the book and open it, the page might be blank again, mightn't it? I mean it might never have happened, like the others on Saturday – behaving afterwards as though nothing had happened.' She paused, then tightened her lips with a quick frown. 'What I'm saying is that I *hope* that I imagined that drawing and the words but I think I know I'm wrong. The page won't be blank. You see why I can't talk to Sam? Sometimes I feel I'm really going insane'

Doctor Meadows rang the buzzer for his next patient and picked up the top-most folder on the remaining pile. Two cards in the folder: Simon Talbot Warner and Dinah Margaret Weston Warner. He looked up as the door was opened.

They came in smiling, both of them.

Much of the look of strain was gone from the woman's face, and the boy had shed his previous cringeing stance and lowering gaze. He looked like any bright, blond, four-year-old. Yet a childhood memory teased Meadows, a fragment of his own concern and worry over how the king and queen could be absolutely certain when the changeling was replaced by the real prince that it was a real boy and not just the changeling again – or another one! Simon Warner looked like a real boy, however, and even more so when his gaze was drawn by the scale model of the vintage Rolls-Royce car on the doctor's desk-top.

Dinah sat down, watching.

'Would you like to play with it?' Doctor Meadows asked. On his previous visit the child hadn't even seemed to notice the model.

Simon turned agate-coloured eyes to his mother, and then to the doctor. 'I like these sort of cars – and tractors too,' he said.

'Right – a bargain, Simon. You pick up that car and have a look at it while I look at your leg.'

Simon grinned and carefully, lovingly, picked up the model and then clambered up on to the couch.

'Your mother told me she didn't want to wait the whole week because you've started scratching at the dressing, so let's see what's underneath.' Tiny, clean scabs came away with the dressing. 'Well, look at *that*! Clean as a whistle. You don't even need another plaster. You heal very well, Simon, I can't really see any marks. How's the dog?'

For a moment Simon looked doubtful, uncertain, and he threw Dinah a questioning glance as the doctor pulled the sock up again over the apparently unscarred leg. 'Which – oh, we had a dog called Rowlf staying with us for the bonfire. Dogs don't like fireworks though. They were shut inside.'

Dinah was glad that the signs of scorching had gone from Simon's cheeks, nose and chin.

'Right, clean bill of health,' Doctor Meadows resumed his desk and marked Simon's card. 'In more ways than one. When did it happen, Mrs Warner? Saturday evening – I see. And completely spontaneous? Caused by anything in particular, or just the excitement of bonfires and fireworks?'

Simon was crouched on the floor now, moving the model car about and keeping up a running commentary on what the driver – called for some reason William – was doing.

'Fireworks, I think.' Dinah said.

'Ah.' Meadows wrote on Simon's card. 'Some form of amnesia as we thought, probably in connection with the sound at the time of the accident: explosions, fireworks . . . '

Dinah watched as Meadows made his notes, and thought wryly: *If you only could have heard the fireworks I'm thinking about*!

'Does he remember everything now? Does he talk about things that happened before Saturday?'

'I haven't asked him, and I asked his father not to. I feel – it's up to Simon. I don't want to probe.' Dinah glanced down at him. 'One thing,' she said, 'on Saturday, when he started speaking again, he asked for his potatoes out of the fire. So he remembered that we put potatoes in the bottom of the fire to roast.'

'Ah.'

'Doctor Meadows, please, don't you probe, either. We don't want him upset by any searching into those weeks of blocked off memories. We want to leave it and just count ourselves marvellously lucky that not only is he alive and well, but that he has started to communicate again. There – a little bit of jargon for you!'

Simon looked up at her. 'Can I have one, just like this?' he asked.

'You can have that one, Simon, if you like.' Doctor Meadows, after a brief look of frustrated disappointment had crossed his face, stood up, smiling. 'Then I won't have to feel guilty when the other little boys have to give it back to me.'

'You can have it back, if you like,' Simon held the car out.

'What I'd like is for *you* to have it as a present, a late Guy Fawkes Day present!' The doctor turned to Dinah. 'You look well.'

'Oh, I am – now. And I intend to throw away the last two sedative pills.'

If the morning was fine Dinah would sometimes cycle with Simon to school, although he was becoming almost too heavy on the cycle seat. More often, however, she used the car to save time. She was at work again, and every possible moment had to be spent up in the rooms at the top of the house.

Priscilla would often go and fetch Simon from the road junction at Outwood Green where the minibus with the mornings-only children let him off. She and Simon together found bright berries and late leaves, feathers, fungi, snailshells, and nutshells neatly robbed of their kernels by mice or squirrels. Frequently they arrived home late for lunch.

Once they heard the sound of the hunting horn plaintive in the distance, some brief hound music, far away shouting, and then a rush of hoofbeats on the road past the drive gate, and the riders trotting by surrounded by a cloud of steam in the frosty air.

Simon was about to ask why the horses and riders were on fire when Nimble and Quick began to whine.

'Look, Si – there,' Priscilla whispered.

Across the drive, going in the opposite direction to that taken by the riders, a fox trotted delicately. Unhurried, he paused and turned his keen gaze on the woman and child, and the two collies. He stood, one front paw raised. Then he flicked his brush and trotted airily away into the woods.

Wildlife and plants drew Simon, especially very small things, and he would poke about for hours under piles of wood, or by the old walls, searching for snails, mice, woodlice, spiders. He collected burrs and seeds and nuts with a squirrel-like perservance and was adept at finding mushrooms.

Simon never went beyond the orchards into Mongwodes, though, never looked for nuts in the hazel thicket there. And when Dinah suggested a walk in Mongwodes one afternoon, he shocked her by suddenly snorting, and momentarily taking on that cowed and yet aggressive mien he had worn during the weeks of his silence.

It was to the old walled garden that the three hives were brought, the last of Talbot's possessions to be transferred from Elveden to Pooks Hall.

The colonies of bees were asleep, well-fed on winter rations, and the hives insulated against possible deadly cold. They were set up against the south-facing wall of the old garden, between an ancient, gnarled and barren fig-tree and a green gage whose roots cracked the base of the wall, and whose fruit Priscilla had preserved last month.

Dinah, Sam and Simon watched Talbot and his friend fussing about with the hives. 'Bees,' Simon said. 'What's bees *really* like? How do they make honey? Honey's in bottles.'

He imagined lines of bees all flying past rows of glass jars and pouring in the honey – but from what? He enjoyed the taste of honey too much to allow of his imaginary bees spitting or anything into the jars. Of course, they held *bubbles* of honey in their claws, and dropped the bubbles into the jars. He had never seen a honey comb. Now he ventured to step towards the nearest hive.

'Have you ever seen a glass hive?' Sam was smiling down at Simon, although he addressed Dinah.

'Yes, last summer in the wine and honey tent at the Suffolk Show.' She paused. 'And there was a museum somewhere – I remember, Haslemere – it used to have a hive built into the wall so that the bees could work normally, but inside it was glass and you could watch them. Hypnotic.'

She remembered the three-year-old Georgina, standing enraptured watching the bees, Martin squatting beside her, telling her what they were doing. Georgina had pressed her tiny, pale hands on to the glass and felt the warmth of the hive. 'Bees are *hot*!' There was a song she had learned in the little kindergarten run by the local doctor's wife – Dinah could not remember the tune.

'Came a roaring Bumble-Bee' she said, 'Pockets full of money, Said "Good morning, Clover sweet – What's the price of honey?" She stopped. 'I've forgotten the rest – and the tune.'

'Go on, Mum,' Simon urged.

'I can't sing – you know that! Anyhow, I think that Clover said the Bumble Bee could have it for nothing.'

Sam laughed. 'Where did you get that? I like the idea of the bee roaring!'

Martin had set the damned jingle for voice, piano and bassoon – had it performed at a concert in Guildford. Dinah closed her eyes for a moment, but opened them again quickly as an unbidden vision of Martin at the piano had imprinted much too clearly on her mind and memory.

'Oh, it floated up from my childhood, I think.' She picked up Simon and swung him round. 'OK, Roaring Bumble Bee?'

He roared, but very gently.

On the ground again, he asked: 'Do they sting? I think they do.'

'Only if you frighten them,' Talbot said.

'Like dogs biting?' Simon was round-eyed.

Talbot nodded. 'Just like that.'

A few days later Simon had to go to the hospital for a final check up. They had to wait a long time at the hospital, and he was edgy and fractious, missing his walk with the dogs, his ferreting about in the wild damp garden. He was also unnerved by the hospital, and was sullen and awkward with the doctor. But he was pronounced wholly fit.

Dinah drove into Monks Hempstall instead of turning off at Outwood Green. She passed the green, and at the top of Upstreet parked on the little green opposite the lychgate of the Church of All Saints. She undid her seat belt and got out of the car. Simon slept, sagging in his seat-harness.

It was dark in the church porch, loud with the sound of the wind, filled with strange lesser sounds, like those made by the scuttering of blown leaves scurried along by the wind to silt up huddling in the corners. Twigs creaked and cracked, and branches squeaked in the ancient yews bordering the path. Dinah tried the church door – locked, of course.

She went out and looked up at the square tower, the racing

clouds beyond in the evening sky. The wind was making wild and beautiful music in the trees.

Dinah walked slowly across the graveyard. She knew what she sought, she would recognise it, she had seen it in her imagination and in dreams.

The wind hissed in the hedge and Dinah could hear the sounds of the young cattle grazing in the glebe beyond, blowing and chewing, stamping. A blackbird flew out of the hedge, scolding in a series of staccato notes, as though plucked with a plectrum.

Dinah stopped. She held her breath, then released it in a long sigh, lost on the wind.

Here Sam – and Martin – had stood on a bright autumn day and seen the small coffin lowered into the earth.

Dinah tried to visualise the scene now, but thoughts and images streamed unconnected through her mind, jagged and painful, nothing holding.

The grave was marked by a rectangle of grey-white stone, flat and smooth. A few leaves blew across it, hesitated, then went on before the wind.

Dinah's face felt naked, cold and blank, her whole person behind the face stripped and open. She was aware of a void within herself, no love, no hate, only a whisper of guilt. *Georgina? Georgina*? Nothing.

She bent down and touched the stone. It meant nothing to her, it was as void as her emotions. Here was no marble angel, poised in the frozen act of strewing roses; no weeping cherubs or Grecian urn; not even a death's-head. Just a flat blank stone.

*I never saw her dead, never saw the funeral.* Dinah wondered was this perhaps why she seemed to see Georgina, and did hear the voices? She sighed and stared round her in the grey dusk, looked up at the cloudy damp sky, impatiently brushing a leaf from her sleeve. She stared at the stone. It would have been too dark now to read the lettering – even if there had been any lettering to read.

She shuddered and went back to the car. Simon still slept, slumped in his harness, his hands limply dangling.

In unreasoning terror that he was dead, Dinah leaned in and shook him. He stirred and whimpered.

As she drove in the closing evening light past Outwood

Green, noticing in the beam of the headlights a hedgehog trundling hastily away off the road, Dinah suddenly recalled a tomb she had seen – where? A tomb in a tall place, with echoes. It was a raised tomb, like a table, and on it the statue of a reclining girl-child. *I know, Romsey Abbey with Martin.* Written round the edge of the table-top they had read: 'Is it well with the child?' Dinah couldn't now remember if the question had been answered.

She nearly clipped the gatepost, braked, then accelerated. Gravel spurted beneath the tyres. Simon woke up fully and began to wail, the sound taking Dinah back to the bad days between Michaelmas and November the fifth. She started to yell at him to shut up, but bit the words back, scared at the rush of emotions through her. The moment passed and Simon sniffled into silence.

Later, putting him to bed, Dinah bent to kiss him, and noticed how the scar on his chin was growing daily less noticable. She thought then of the lack of any scar from the dog-bite on his leg.

'Si,' she said, 'you know that bite on your leg that we can't see any more – well, which dog *was* it that snapped at you?'

Simon in bed, lying down, the glint of a bright eye over the sheet. He moved so that his whole face was visible, both eyes wide and guileless.

'That little white dog – the one with the black ears,' he said.

It took Dinah two days to warp the floor loom for the woven rug which was to incorporate the African designs. During the hours spent on this most tedious part of weaving, she listened to the radio, or to tapes.

Sam had found an old-fashioned oil stove in the barn and had cleaned it and fitted a new wick. Dinah liked its homely look and the occasional gentle plop of blue flame. Up here, in the attic rooms with their rough-hewn timbers and peaked ceilings, she generally felt quite relaxed. Here she could be completely herself, driven only by herself. This was a place where no-one came unless invited.

The moment when the actual weaving was begun was one of acute excitement. Dinah adjusted the 'daylight' lamps to supplement the wan winter sunshine in the room, and as she approached the loom again she felt suddenly prickly and sensitive – *sensitised* – as she had felt on November the fifth. For a moment she was scared, then she found the rhythm of the shuttles as the mechanics of the loom gently thumped. She worked the first band of the end border, then stood back.

Her neck and back felt stiff and she moved about the room, stretching. Eleven o'clock. Priscilla would have coffee on in the flat, and would be calling Simon in from the garden. It was Saturday, there was no school. Dinah switched off the lamps and turned down the wick of the stove. The quiet was extreme.

Then a board creaked in the next room and Dinah felt her skin crawling nervously. She opened the door. Nothing. The window was open, however, and Dinah went to close it, surprised and puzzled. She looked out over the garden, the orchards and woods, the blue-hazed winter horizon.

Suddenly she heard Simon's voice, astonishingly loud and clear, as he came round the corner of the house, gesticulating with his hands and talking to an imaginary companion. Dinah closed the window very softly, shot through with a sudden sadness. *He used to have Georgina to share his thoughts and games with.*

Halfway down the stairs she stopped and looked back, as though expecting to be followed – and she recalled Georgina looking at her through the little window between two of the rooms. *Is she coming down*?'

Then she gripped the stair rail, head spinning, palms sweating. Georgina had never been in those rooms, never looked through that tiny window.

Dinah didn't remember how she reached the door of the east wing, only her precipitate entry to find Sam with Priscilla and Talbot drinking coffee at the kitchen table, Simon with them, eating an orange.

Explaining her haste and excitement, she said, 'I've done it – I'm weaving. I've finished the first part of the end border!'

'Oh, Dinah, you shame me.' Priscilla poured coffee for her. 'I shall have to get my spinning wheel set up again.'

'Oh, do!' Dinah exclaimed. 'I love your wool – you know I really do like your spinning much better than my own!'

Priscilla's wheel and spindle had spun the thread which had drawn Dinah and Sam together.

Dinah had been showing some pieces, two wall hangings and a rug, in an exhibition at Kettle's Yard in Cambridge. In the same exhibition was a curious, three-dimensional woven 'sculpture', made of wools the many textures of which had fascinated Dinah, who constantly sought new ways of texturing her work. It was not difficult to find out who had spun the wools, and that was how she had met Priscilla Warner, and Sam.

As they walked with Simon round the house to their own kitchen door, Dinah said, 'Annabel and the kids are back from their post-exam trip to Cornwall. She asked us to take Si along for tea this afternoon. OK?'

'You two go,' Sam said. 'I want to finish putting up the book-shelves in the study.'

'Did you ever find that drawing you told me about?' Annabel asked, while the children watched television after tea.

The warmth faded momentarily from the room. *Why am I such a coward*? Dinah thought, and turned to Annabel. 'I forgot. I – I've been using a different sketchbook.'

Annabel smiled. 'Naturally,' she said. 'No, don't worry. I'd like to see it, though. And have you seen the Parish Registers yet?'

Dinah sighed. 'No, I've been putting it off.' She paused, then spoke faster. 'And of course I've been working every available moment. I'm trying to get this rug finished for the sitting room by Christmas – and I've got ideas for a wall-hanging I want to get on with.'

She thought again of her sketches for the proposed wall-hanging, blocking out the memory of the drawing of the strange flower and the seed-heads, the words written in that cramped, almost tortured hand.

That evening Dinah was full of ideas, and she sat in the bathroom with a sketchbook and crayons while Simon played in the bath. The wall hanging would be organic in its shifting foci of design, slubbed and textured and tufted with patterns of silky whorls like 'Allah's thumbprint' on the neck of an Arabian horse, like the rosettes on Abyssinian cavies, or the whorl of hair on Simon's crown.

Dinah gradually became aware of what he was saying as he

lay in the soapy water ' – I told you – you never listen! We had sausages for tea – and treacle and crumpets.' He sounded impatient, scowled briefly. Then he said. '*And* we had orange squash,' glancing up at Dinah. 'We're not allowed coke. And after tea – ' He stopped suddenly and sat up, grabbing at his floating toy frog and clutching it possessively.

'Who's your friend, Si? Didn't he go out to tea as well?' Dinah asked, wiping the page where Simon's sudden action had splashed her.

He shot her a strangely mature, considering look.

'No,' he shook his head. 'She can't go out – not even to school. She stays here all the time. Silly! Doesn't know crumpets *or* orange squash or coke.'

'*She*?' Dinah stood up and scooped Simon out of the bath to towel him dry. 'What's her name, then?'

Then she stiffened, holding Simon very tight and still. *Oh god, what made me ask? It can't be –*

Simon wriggled, turning his head up to look at her, and Dinah was careful to wipe her fear from her expression.

'Alice,' Simon said. 'She's called Alice.' He made a funny face. 'Sometimes – sometimes I like her.' And he nodded.

'That's a nice name.' Almost faint with relief, Dinah laughed, bent to kiss the soft nape of Simon's neck, then laughed again, and was a little aroused, too, by his miniature erection as she continued to dry him.

Sam laughed when Dinah told him about Simon's imaginary playmate, but he grew serious when she told him of her panic when she asked the playmate's name.

'But, darling Di, it would have been the most natural thing in the world if he *had* called her Georgina – after all, she was part of the scenery, and his playmate, for most of his life.' He kissed Dinah's worried face. 'Maybe this'll help him, and he'll be able to talk about Georgina, too. Hey, I wonder if other little boys invent girl friends and do little girls invent males? Did you?'

Dinah pulled away and shook her head.

'Neither did I,' Sam said. 'Why Alice, I wonder?'

'Do you think – I don't know, Sam – do you think that Simon *knows* that Georgina is dead? Surely he must. He never asks where she is.'

'*Dead* is just a word to children – I think that they fit it to some concept which is familiar to them, then understand it when they are mature enough.' He shook his head. 'I wonder, should we have told him that she, for instance, went to heaven?'

Dinah shook her head. 'Oh, no. But if he *had* said Georgina – ?'

'Dinah, you don't believe in ghosts do you?'

'I honestly don't know.'

Sam lay reading in bed. Dinah, beside him, stared at the raftered ceiling, letting her gaze wander over the beams, the tie-beam and crown-post sending their massive shadows slanting across the high spaces of the lofty room.

Sam finished his chapter and put the book on the table. He left the light on. 'Did Annabel say anything about the exam?' he asked.

'No, only that it was nice to have a break from studying.'

Sam fidgeted, rubbing one foot against the other. 'Have you – do you talk to her about Georgina?'

'You know I can't. I couldn't even *remember* Georgina from the crash, until Simon began to speak again.'

'Has Annabel asked you to join that group of hers: "New Age" or whatever they call it?'

Dinah shook her head and settled back on the pillow, sighing. 'No. I'm not into groups, I don't think.'

Boards settled in the hall outside the bedroom. Far away in the still night the sound of a motorcycle made a small crescendo and faded.

'Or covens, I hope?'

'Sam! And it's said that it's *women* who gossip!'

'What is it, then?'

'Discussion, history, myths, rituals and so on, and they have meditation meetings. They help people with thought and prayer.'

'Sort of psychic Samaritans.'

'I suppose.' Dinah smiled.

'I think I might feel excluded if you did join them, Di. It hurts enough that you talk to Annabel and not to me.'

'Why should I lay my stupid neurotic worries on you?'

'Because if these things are enough to worry you, then they are neither stupid nor neurotic. I don't like standing in the wings feeling ignorant and useless, your worries are my worries!'

The door of the room rattled and the open casement responded. The moonlit fog swirled into the room in a rising wind.

'That wind reminds me,' Sam said. 'What did – I mean, did Annabel say anything about what happened on November the fifth?'

Dinah lay down again. 'She didn't offer any explanation – ' She paused. 'What do you mean – *what happened*?'

'Simon, of course, though I suppose it was the noise of the thunder?'

'Yes,' Dinah agreed.

When she finally fell asleep Dinah had painful confused dreams in which she searched for a girl called Alice. She half woke at one stage and struggled not to go back to the dream, trying to escape from a hall full of mixed farm animals which suddenly all shed their skins and flesh to become instant skeletons. Back in the dream again Dinah screamed and ran, legs clogged with the usual nightmare inertia. Pursued by skeleton pigs and goats she escaped by falling out of a window. She landed in what seemed to be a pit of soft, cold clay, lay staring up at a grey sky streaked with rain. People came and looked down at her, pointing and whispering, and sometimes she heard their words: *A liar and a cheat. No business having children. Pity the poor child, the one she didn't manage to kill.* And Dinah cried out 'No – no!' but her voice would not leave her mouth. 'Pity *me*, please. Help me – I'm so sorry for what I did!' She choked on the words. The sticky, damp pit tipped like a tilted cup and Dinah rolled out, landing on all fours on the floor of a room filled with spinning wheels. 'Alice,' a man's voice said, 'You know you have no call to be here!' She began to cry.

Dinah awoke with tears on her face.

The foggy moonlight had given place to a windy blue dawn.

Dinah felt heavy with the dream. Her head ached and she felt clammy and sticky as though from the clay of the pit. She shuddered, afraid. *Oh, please, no*!

She slid out of bed, pulled on her dressing gown and went to the bathroom. Her period had started. Because it had been several weeks late she had been sure again that she was pregnant.

Dinah crept miserably back to bed, and had almost fallen asleep when she was suddenly awake and alert again, tense.

Voices.

Someone laughed – and there was the murmuring again, just too far away to distinguish words.

'I have these memories,' Dinah said, 'Impossible memories. I remember her, Georgina, in places where I never saw her, because she was never there!'

'Memories?' Annabel looked startled. 'Surely not. Dreams, possibly. Wishes or fantasies – regrets, maybe? Your guilt feelings apparently embodied.' She shook her head, her long blonde hair was loose, hanging half-way down her back.

'Jargon!' Dinah muttered.

They walked along the lane leading to the back of the Brooks' house. The three children – Amanda not yet home from her school – gambolled and scuffed about in the deep drifts of dead leaves, and the air smelled of wet earth, toadstools, and a little of woodsmoke.

'No,' Dinah continued firmly, 'dreams and fantasies are different – you can control fantasies. But how can you remember something that you've never seen!'

They walked on.

'You don't ever hear those voices now, do you?'

'No,' Dinah lied, not knowing why. She switched her mind away from *those* memories and thought instead of work – which was going well – and of the commission she had received for a tapestry hanging for a new Civic Centre in a Midlands town.

Also Sam and she had been lucky at a local auction and bought some good old pieces of furniture, though neither of them wanted to over-furnish Pooks Hall.

'It's incredible what people used to keep in their houses,' Annabel said when Dinah told her about the auction – a sudden change of subject. 'Extraordinary mixtures of objects. For instance I saw in one sixteenth-century inventory that in "the room over the parlour" there were two beds, a truckle-bed, three mattresses, two coffers, four stools, a trestle, five fleeces – yes, really – a sack of grain, *and* – wait for it – two fine cheeses and a length of cloth! There seemed to be beds everywhere.' She paused. 'And there's a house at Walsham-le-Willows that used to be the poor-house, and in the seven-teenth-century they inventoried no fewer than seventeen spinning wheels!'

Dinah gasped, recalling vividly her dream of the night the voices had returned – a room full of spinning wheels – and the voice 'Alice, you know you have no call to be here.' Why Alice? she wondered. And why did Simon choose that name?

'Do the girls have imaginary friends?' Dinah said after a while.

'Amanda has had one for years! You'd never guess what she calls her!' Annabel laughed.

Dinah grinned. 'Tracy? Samantha?' She laughed. 'Coriander?'

'No – she calls her Megalith.'

'Megalith!' Dinah exclaimed in a laughing whisper.

'When I asked her she said it was a very pretty name.' Annabel shrugged. 'I suppose it is! I was at school with a girl called Retina. My mother said she wondered if the parents had meant to call her Renata but couldn't spell – or if her mum had had an affair with an eye specialist.' They laughed, and Annabel said, 'What are you and Sam planning for Christmas?'

Dinah looked as blank as she suddenly felt. 'I don't know – I suppose we're both avoiding thinking about it, really.'

'Yes, of course.' Annabel put an arm out and gave Dinah's shoulders a squeeze. Their feet scuffed in the damp drift of leaves. 'Do you want to have another child, Dinah?'

'Oh yes, I was pregnant at the time of the accident, you know.'

'I didn't know.' Annabel sighed. 'I hope you and Sam have another child – or as many as you wish. Why did you ask about imaginary playmates?' She asked.

'Simon has one now, he talks to her. Yes, it's a girl – and I was afraid – but Sam thinks it's a sort of compensation for Georgina not being there any more.' She paused. 'But Simon doesn't call her Georgina – he calls her Alice.'

'I suppose it's natural for him to choose a female, having only had a sister.'

'He's a funny little soul. He was most emphatic that this invention of his couldn't, for instance, come out to tea. He says she has to stay at Pooks Hall. Oh god, with these crazy sort of memories of mine, if he'd said her name *was* Georgina I'd have freaked! I told Sam, but he said it would have been quite natural for Si to call a fantasy friend that.'

'Were you afraid that Simon had somehow got in touch with her?' Annabel said softly. 'But you said that the one day she went to Pooks Hall she was only in the house for a few moments.'

Dinah nodded. 'Simon also said – when he told me about 'Alice', – that he *sometimes* likes her! Doesn't that strike you as odd? I mean, why create a fantasy that you only sometimes like?'

'Children have ideas – make connections – that often seem bizarre to adults.' Annabel frowned, then pulled her hair into three strands and plaited it, fastening the end with an elastic band she took from her coat pocket. 'You're thinking about ghosts, aren't you?'

'But I don't think I believe – ' Dinah's voice faltered to silence. 'Is it possible? Simon? And me?'

'It's not impossible, but what I'm thinking of now is not a ghost in the usual sense. I'm thinking about the embodiment of a thought – you see, sometimes in moments of extreme emotion the person experiencing the emotion is laid wide open to forces and influences from outside.'

'November the fifth,' Dinah said softly. 'Could *that* have been Georgina? But you said that you felt anger, frustration and resentment then, and I had this terrible feeling of excitement and anticipation.' She gave a sad little laugh. 'Sam believes it was a thunderstorm.'

'I should like to come over to Pooks Hall while Sam is out at work.' Annabel stopped at the garden gate before they followed the children in. 'I can't come tomorrow, but would Thursday morning be all right? I want to come into your house again, and listen, and open myself up to – well, anything. You're becoming too pale and thin – and you looked blooming just after Simon started to speak again! You mustn't become completely transparent or we'll take *you* for a ghost!'

Thursday was a cold, wet day, with a thin, raw wind keening in the now almost bare branches of the trees, sibilant in the hedges.

Simon was off school owing to the full-time pupils being taken to Norwich for the day. He was in an uncertain mood, and followed Dinah about in a way that made her as unsettled and edgy as he was.

'Where's your friend Alice today?' She asked.

'Don't know, don't care,' Simon muttered, scowling.

*Quarrelling? With a fantasy*? This mood of his made Dinah irritable and depressed. She wanted to be upstairs, working, but she knew that Simon would never become engrossed enough in any occupation for her to leave him alone in his own room. *Damn it*, she thought, *why can't bloody ALICE be of more use*! Then she thought of Georgina – 'I'll take care of him, Mummy, it's all right' – and she felt a cold shiver up her spine, a prickling at the back of her neck.

When Annabel arrived Dinah was glad to see Dumpling also. 'Priscilla's asked us to go and have coffee with them, and then with luck Si and Dumpling will feel like staying with her,' she said.

'I'm all for that!' Annabel laughed.

'Where's Talbot?' Dinah asked with surprise as Priscilla settled them in the little sitting room, with coffee and oatcakes, and goats' milk for the children.

'He's having a day in bed, dear. His leg plays up in this sort of weather, and he's much better off in bed with an electric blanket and a good read!'

The children decided to stay with Priscilla, who was dyeing a batch of wool with an aromatic vegetable dye. She gave them scraps of fleece and wool to play with, and showed them how to turn the little spindles she used in demonstrations and classes.

'I suppose a few hundred years ago the village children would be working for their living like that.' Annabel watched as Simon and Dumpling struggled with wool and spindle. 'Adept and earning at four years old, and most likely half-blind and crippled at thirty.'

'Oh Annabel!' Dinah grimaced.

'My dear, it's true – only the children of the rich were treated as anything other than adults!' Annabel laughed. 'I've sometimes said to my lot, "A couple of hundred years ago you'd have spent all day straw-plaiting or stone-picking for pennies – not *playing* or going on outings!" ' She shrugged. 'They simply don't believe me! Anyhow, Dinah, let's see your weaving. Where is it?'

'Attic.'

'Up we go, then.'

'Oh dear, it's pretty arctic up here – I should have lit the stove earlier.' Dinah shivered.

'Don't light it for me.' Annabel still wore her fleece-lined overcoat. She looked at the weaving on the big floor loom. She bent close, then stood back. 'Where did you get those wonderful primitive patterns? And I like the way you're winding it inwards, border after border.'

Dinah nodded. 'I got the basic designs from African weaving and pottery, and some rock paintings.' She fetched her photographs and drawings.

'When was this?'

'While I was in Africa with Martin, before I was pregnant the first time.' Somehow Dinah didn't want to mention Georgina by name, not up in this room. She felt very cold.

'Oh yes, I remember you talking about the trip, and you haven't used any of these designs until now?'

Dinah shook her head.

"Well,' Annabel made a sudden movement, shrugging herself deeper into her warm coat. 'What else do you do up here?'

Dinah showed her the spinning wheel in the next room, and the other spinning tools, the stack of fleeces, the table loom, and the silk-screen printing equipment and jars of dyes.

They went through the house then, into every room – except that part of the east wing that was closed off into the flat – finally coming into the sitting room, which seemed to be under attack from wind and rain from both sides.

In each room Annabel stood very still, a faceted crystal pendulum dangling on a fine cord from finger and thumb.

In each room the crystal remained still, totally motionless.

Dinah was puzzled, a little relieved, but a little disappointed.

Annabel had a strong and uncomfortable feeling that she was being laughed at.

She looked up at the ceiling. Between the heavy beams the wide boards of the upper floor were unplastered. 'Yes,' Annabel murmured, 'I reckon that the floors were divided when the house was made the hospital, to make more rooms.'

Then for a while she stood with her eyes closed, breathing slowly. She made herself open wide to any sound, thought, or force. She became strongly conscious of Dinah's tumbled, anxious thoughts, though she could not read them. She was also strongly aware that although the crystal had not responded there was a force in the house, a force coiled in the dark somewhere.

She opened her eyes.

'Is this simply the force generated by the junction of the ley-lines?' she whispered, as much to herself as to Dinah. Then she shook her head. 'No there's more. But why doesn't the crystal – ?'

Dinah noticed that Annabel's face had paled, looking drawn as though with the onset of another migraine.

She tried the pendulum once more, holding it out away from her body.

The crystal hung so still it was as though something was holding it rigid from beneath. Dinah stared. Did she imagine it or was Annabel's hand being slowly dragged down?

Then Annabel made a small shocked sound and jerked the pendulum up. It hung motionless for a moment then began to swing in rapid circles.

Her hands were shaking as she put the crystal into its soft leather pouch again and replaced it in her handbag. 'I'm sorry, Dinah. I can't explain why it doesn't work normally. Now, how about finding me that drawing?'

Reluctantly Dinah went to the drawer in which she had concealed the sketchbook. Slowly she brought it back to Annabel, leafed through it to find the place. *God, I hope it's not there after all. Let it be a blank page*!

The page was not blank.

'I see what you mean,' Annabel breathed, amazed. 'That *writing*!' She carried the book over to the tall, mullioned windows. ' "Never bury deep enow" Bury what, I wonder, or who? And what's the significance of the drawing?' She turned to Dinah. 'You were on your own in here while Sam was on the phone, just doodling?'

'I wasn't really aware that I *was* doodling – I wasn't looking at the page at all.' Dinah stared out at the wet garden, its colours washed out and flattened by winter and the cold, wet wind. Annabel still looked at the drawing.

'What *is* this flower? I know it perfectly well, so familiar, with those funny seed-heads like little heads with beaks . . . Beaks, that's it!' Annabel exclaimed. 'It's cranesbill!'

Dinah turned abruptly, staring wide eyed. '*Cranesbill*?'

'Yes, cranesbill, I'm certain.' Annabel looked at the drawing again. 'If you've got a Keble Martin or any other wild flower book we could check.'

'I've got a Keble Martin, somewhere.' Dinah spoke slowly, looking again at the page of her sketchbook. She had previously had no idea of what cranesbill looked like.

The missing piece of the puzzle, the name of the flower, was the revelation she needed to complete the connection, to round off the terror.

'There's no need to look it up,' she told Annabel. 'I know you're right – it has to be that.' She paused. 'Cranesbill.' Her whisper seemed to flutter about the ceiling in a feathery echo. '*Georgina's name was Crane.*'

On Friday afternoon, having made an appointment, Dinah alone drove to the church, arriving at the same time as the Rector who greeted her at the lych gate.

'I have met your husband, of course,' he said after greeting Dinah, then stopped, looking surprised and embarrassed. Dinah could almost see the thought, *both your husbands,* crossing his mind. He continued, 'You were in hospital. It was a terrible loss to you. Please accept now my deep sympathy. I did call at the house but you were all out.'

Dinah smiled, gently withdrawing her hand from his, and walked beside the Rector towards the church, both of them stopping to look up at the tower before entering the porch.

'Ten thousand pounds more needed,' he said. 'Ten thousand needed for the tower now, on top of the three thousand spent on the north wall.' He waved a hand. 'Save our churches – save our heritage! But it's so terribly, terribly expensive! And who uses the churches? The faithful few – the few faithful, and now this one needs even more money!' He glared around him and Dinah saw a fanatical gleam in his eyes. 'You know, Mrs Warner, this structural decay is happening all over England, especially here in East Anglia where there are so many churches of the same period. This was a wool church, of course.' The Rector unlocked the door and opened it for Dinah. 'There used to be a guild-hall over there across the green.' He pointed. 'It was burned down in the eighteenth century, along with a row of six cottages. But you see, Mrs Warner, all these churches, these splendid mediaeval buildings – all roughly the same age – are *all* reaching their limit, all falling down, decaying, suffering from this exorbitant senility!'

'Exorbitant senility,' Dinah repeated softly, 'what a nice way to describe it. But because it's so – well – out of reach in many cases, shouldn't they be allowed just to slip away in their own time into graceful ruin?'

'Like pulling the plug on the life-support machinery.' The Rector gave a short barking laugh and preceded Dinah through the echoing building to the vestry, a small party of sparrows flying past them to flutter twittering in the tower among the looped bell ropes.

The vestry smelled damp, and was cold.

Dinah sat at a table and the Parish Registers were placed in front of her. She pulled a notebook and pencils from her shoulder bag and the Rector switched on an electric heater. The smell of scorching dust from the heater elements was now added to the damp and mousey smell in the room and Dinah sneezed.

'Have you a particular interest in the Registers?' the Rector asked.

Dinah suddenly felt nervous, also furtive, and almost guilty. 'Our house,' she said. 'You know – the people who lived there.'

'I don't know a lot about it, I'm afraid. No-one seems to have lived there for quite a time before you came.' He spread his hands, looking round the small room which succeeded in being both stuffy and close, and cold. 'How long do you think you will want to be here?'

'I don't really know. When will you want to lock up?'

'I have a meeting, and I'll make a few calls after that. Don't worry, Mrs Warner. If you finish and I'm not about, just turn off the heater and put the Registers back in the safe. It locks automatically. I hope you find what you're looking for.'

'Thank you,' Dinah said, and almost added, *I hope I really don't find anything!*

She opened the oldest of the three volumes, and was surprised to see that the first record – that of a marriage – was as early as 1594. The writing was faded and difficult to decipher. The book felt icy cold, the cold of subterranean stone, neither clammy nor yet quite dry. She kept on wanting to wipe her hands on the thighs of her cord slacks.

As she turned the first page a spider ran out of the binding and Dinah fumbled, dropping the book on the floor. She picked it up, guiltily looking towards the doorway into the church. Some papers had fallen out and she picked them up and looked at them, at first simply anxious that they might be actual pages misplaced from the Register, then with interest.

Someone had already done some work on the Monks Hempstall Parish Register.

There was a note – a list – on a page torn out of an exercise book. '*See archivist. Tues. 25? June, '64 – about missing entries! Who has them? Don't forget poultry spice. Light bulbs. Present and card for Penelope. Petrol.*'

In the same handwriting there were some notes apparently copied from a book, since there was a page reference. Then there was a list of figures and a graph of baptisms, marriages and burial figures from 1558 to 1699 – apparently complete – and written on heavy quality paper with a Twickenham address embossed but crossed out at the top. Dinah wondered who the researcher was – must have a garden at Twickenham, or why the poultry spice? And why did the list stop at 1699?

The graph showed that the worst years for deaths in the Parish were 1558 with 27 burials, 1559 with 18, and 1656 and 1662 with 12. There was 1679 with 17 burials, 1680 with 15 and 1684 with 14. Dinah noticed that in most years the baptisms exceeded the burials, though she knew that many of those baptised would not have survived the first year. She sighed. In 1558, however there had only been 7 baptisms against the 27 burials, and in 1680 15 people were buried and only 5 infants baptised.

The high figures for some years' burials seemed drastic in a village whose population, according to a footnote to the graph, was numbered on an average as 'about 60 householders and their dependants'.

Dinah tried to recall which were the plague years. The year of the Great Plague, 1665, seemed not to have been a bad year for Monks Hempstall which must have had a lucky escape. On the graph five other years were much worse than 1665. Dinah thought that those were probably years of very cold winters and hot, wet summers.

She turned to the quotation in the notes, and read that in 1690 there had been 'great distress in the neighbourhood of Monks Hempstall. Sickness was very prevalent, and so numerous the deaths that an order was obtained from the Session and afterwards confirmed by the Court of the King's Bench to raise £200 in the Hundreds of Bosmere, Claydon, Hartismere and Stow for the relief of the poor in such parishes as Monks Hempstall who were extremely visited with smallpox.' There was a list of contributions from parishes, from Buxhall with £5.12s.8d. to Creeting St Peter with £2.10s.2d – ten parishes in all, and surprisingly large sums for those times.

*All those deaths, small pox, plague, and other things like colds and bronchitis, measles and accidents.* Dinah, filled with sadness, heard in her memory the voices.

She folded the loose papers back into the cover of the first volume, and opened the Register again.

She read through, page by page, at first with great difficulty. Then a new incumbent came to the parish and the handwriting changed and was clearer. That was in 1675.

In 1676 there were three marriages celebrated in Monks Hempstall.

One of these, on September 17th, was between William Templar Crane of Wood Hall, Outwood Green, and Elizabeth Sarah Stearn of Haughley.

Dinah's hands shook.

Here it was before her, the name Crane – William Crane, – of Wood Hall, Outwood Green.

Dinah pushed back the chair and stood up. She felt sick, suffocated. She must get out in the air and move about. She longed for a cigarette, but had none.

She hurried, almost running, out of the vestry and the church, out to the warmer, living and moving air of the winter day. The smell of damp, of old books and of mice, seemed to cling to her hair and clothing.

Dinah walked about, quartering the graveyard for a stone, some old stone, bearing the name Crane. She found none, and thought wildly: *Perhaps I imagined it. It's not Crane. I misread it, and it's really Dane or something like that!* She had to go back and find out.

Shivering in the vestry again, Dinah read through the next twenty-three years of entries in the Register.

Another incumbent had come to Monks Hempstall, his predecessor being buried in 1684, and the new parson had written after an entry for Wood Hall, Outwood Green, 'likewise known as the Pox House'.

And Dinah had not misread the name Crane.

Forcing herself to write slowly and accurately, although her hand shook, she made a copy of certain entries.

| | |
|---|---|
| William Templar Crane of Wood Hall | |
| Elizabeth Sarah Stearn of Haughley | married Sept. 17 1676 |
| William John Crane | baptised Nov. 12 1676 |
| Mary Crane | baptised Dec. 4 1677 |
| Thomas Crane | baptised Oct. 10 1678 |
| William John Crane | buried Sept. 2 1680 |
| Alice Elizabeth Crane | baptised Nov. 9 1680 |
| William Crane | baptised May 24 1682 |
| Sarah Crane | baptised June 15 1684 |
| Sarah Crane | buried Aug. 20 1684 |

Dinah unclenched cold, cramped fingers from the pencil and shook her head, pushing her hair back off her face. She thought, *Alice – Alice Crane – Simon's Alice who can't leave Pooks Hall – Wood Hall – Pox House.* She looked again at the pathetic history. *Now Thomas is the eldest – and only him, and the second baby William and Alice alive!* She read on, feeling a sense of dread chilling her excitement.

She found another reference to Wood Hall, referred to in brackets as 'the Pesthouse'.

| | |
|---|---|
| Susan Crane | baptised Sept. 29 1690 |
| Elizabeth Crane and Susan Crane | buried Oct. 1 1690 |
| William Crane | buried Oct. 1 1690 |
| Thomas Crane | buried Oct. 1 1690 |

*Now they're all dead, except the father, and Alice.*

Dinah looked up at the greyish plaster wall in front of her and saw in her mind's eye the man with the spade. *If he had not been real, was he William Templar Crane?*

She thought of Simon: Simon and the white dog with black ears; Simon with Alice, whom he only sometimes liked. *This is too much for me, I don't believe it, I can't! But I heard the voices, didn't I? I saw the old man, and the little dog – and Simon talks to Alice, who has to stay at Pox Hall!*

In a cold sweat of fear at her own thoughts and memories, Dinah looked again at the Register – she must finish what she had begun. And she found that William Templar Crane was buried in January 1698 – which Dinah knew by modern reckoning to be 1699, since when William Crane died, the new year would not have begun until Lady Day, March 25th.

She stared at the book and the lines wriggled like worms across and up the page. How old would William have been? Dinah wondered. Possibly in his early fifties, though looking older.

'But where's Alice?' Dinah whispered. 'What happened to Alice? She was born in 1680 and we're now nineteen years later! Perhaps she survived after all – then it's coincidence Simon calling his fantasy Alice!'

Excited now with a new hope Dinah turned the page.

She found that William's burial, the last entry on the previous page, was also the last entry both for the hapless Crane family and for the house at Outwood Green known as Wood Hall, the Pox House, or Pesthouse.

At the top of the new page, before the new entries were listed, a note had been written in a hand so small and fine it might have been scribbled with a pin, the ink very faint.

Dinah worked at it. She had excellent sight.

She finally made out that William Templar Crane had been 'constrained within his house non of the village seeing him excepte in his death. Alice his daughter died in 1691. God reste her soule. Probably in Oct or Nov. That record once kept in Wood Hall is given to the Parish Chest. Amen.'

Dinah felt stunned, her brief hope shattered. *Alice Crane was the same age as Georgina when she died.*

Unlike Georgina, however, Alice was not buried in Monks Hempstall – where then? Dinah tried to think, to be reasonable. Perhaps Alice had been sent to relatives to live, or maybe she had gone into service, dying away from home. But the memory of the writing flicked across her mind: Never bury deep enow.

Dinah stood up and walked into the church, pacing up and down the aisle, besieged by thoughts of burials, and of things that would not remain buried. She wished desperately that by some miracle Annabel would appear.

After five minutes curiosity urged her back into the vestry. She wondered what was wrong with William that he should be 'constrained' so? By whose order was he constrained? Her eyes were aching from reading the fine handwriting, but she sat down again and read through the remainder of the Register, page by page, until the end of last September – when she and Sam and the children had spent Michaelmas at Pooks Hall – and Georgina at times had really seemed a changeling.

She found two other Crane entries.

John Brabrooke Crane from Coddenham had married a Monks Hempstall girl, Mary Ann Curry, in 1805, their address being given as Place Farm – which, Dinah knew, was between Monks Hempstall and Battisford. Their son George was baptised in 1807. Dinah found no further mention of them, but an entry of 1824 showed that a Joseph John Wright of Place Farm had a daughter baptised. Place Farm was still in the Wright family in 1914.

Dinah found it very strange that there was no further record of anyone being baptised, wed or buried who lived at Wood Hall, Outwood Green or whatever other names were given to the house.

She sighed. *That's weird. Someone must have lived there or it would have become derelict!*

Dinah found herself thinking of Martin. Could he be descended from that John Brabrooke Crane from Coddenham? And was *he* descended from a relative of William Templar Crane? Coddenham and Monks Hempstall were not too many miles apart. Perhaps William had been born at Coddenham – more Parish Registers to check. She locked the Monks Hempstall Registers in the safe and switched off the electric heater, leaving the vestry to the mice and the church to the sparrows.

Driving home Dinah concentrated very hard on the road to try to curb the wild conjectures and fears flying about in her mind. Saddened and scared by what she had learned, she found it harder than ever to explain the happenings at Pooks Hall, now peopled with real characters yet still as puzzling. *Unless I simply accept it as a haunting. But I can't, it scares me too much, the thought of Simon playing with a ghost!* And how could she explain it to Sam and his parents? Priscilla and Talbot would be desperately sad and embarrassed, and Sam would feel constrained – that word again – to insist that Dinah see a psychiatrist!

As she entered the Pooks Hall drive, Dinah had a vivid mental picture, like a memory, of a girl of Georgina's size or a little smaller, dressed darkly and simply, fox-red hair only partially hidden by a plain white cap. Dinah gasped, her foot suddenly coming up off the throttle, making the Traveller's engine cough and almost stall.

*She was baptised on November the ninth so she must have been born about November the fifth, and died – eleven years old – possibly on the same date.* Dinah slowed down as she neared the house, recalling that she had felt, as she had told Annabel, as though she had 'just given birth' after the events preceding Simon's recovery of speech.

Dinah sat in the car, in the garage, the afternoon light fading to dusk. She heard the owls begin their nightly patrol, and heard Priscilla on her way to milk the goats. Everything was normal in a beautiful place. Everything was normal except that Dinah would hear again tonight the voices from the past of her house, and except that Simon played with an invisible girl called Alice whom he had never mentioned until *after* November the fifth.

*Opening the gates.* She stopped in the act of getting out of the car. Had those forces gathering, like the alignments crossing, at Pooks Hall opened the gates for Alice Crane to pass from the past to the present? *I must see Annabel. Tell her.*

At the same time that Dinah pored over the Parish registers Sam went to the Records Office in Ipswich. In the search room he asked for information on Monks Hempstall.

The clerk gave him a quizzical look, asked Sam to sign the book and fill in a form, then said 'Wait a moment, please,' and disappeared round the corner of a large bank of filing cabinets.

Sam heard a murmur of subdued voices.

The clerk returned. 'It seems to be a popular place – I'm afraid a lady has all available documents on Monks Hempstall'.

Sam pushed past the clerk. A lady researching Monks Hempstall? *Dinah?* In an adjoining room were the viewers for microfilm, one of them in use.

Sam sighed. It was not Dinah. The immediate impression of amethyst-coloured sweater and blonde hair in an absurd pony-tail confirmed this. Annabel turned and saw him.

'Hi,' she smiled.

'Are you looking for something about Pooks Hall?' Sam asked.

She nodded. 'Without much success at first. There isn't a lot anyway, and most of it I've seen before.'

Sam noticed an air of barely suppressed excitement about her now. 'But?' he said.

'There's something here that wasn't in the file before – look!'

She unfolded a stiff and antique sheet of paper which had obviously been part of a stitched folio. She straightened the paper carefully on the table-top and Sam noticed her hands – plump, with dimpled knuckles and curiously tapered fingers – most unlike Dinah's hands, which were blunt-fingered, lean and sinewy.

'This looks like the end of some sort of register,' Annabel said, and Sam read:

*Tobias Hunt*
Elizabeth his Wife Decd. October 23 1691
Taken for Buryal that same Day

*Alice Crane* Decd. November 5 1691
May God forgive me –
Enow. There will bee no more

'My god!' Sam exclaimed in a low voice. 'So there *was* one, an Alice *Crane!'* He paused, then said almost angrily, 'It must be a coincidence – Georgina was reading *Alice in Wonderland* earlier this year. She must have put the idea of the name into Simon's head – we'll ask him. She was always reading him stories.'

'Crane,' Annabel said. 'Did Dinah's first husband come from Suffolk?'

'So far as I know he was a Londoner – but – ' he pushed his hands through his hair, frowning, reminding Annabel of Simon. 'Do you know if Di has been here? I hope to God she doesn't go making these connections – I don't want her getting neurotic about hauntings and other rubbish.'

Annabel said nothing, turning the paper over so that Sam could see what was written there, the first in an unfamiliar hand, the second entry in the writing from over the page – and, Annabel knew, the hand that had written in Dinah's sketchbook. Sam took the paper and held it to the light. He read:

*Vol. II.*
*Henry Streetsend* 1669 until decd. 1670
*William Templar Crane* 1670 –

*With the Charge of Wood Hall at Outwode Green in the Parish of Monks Hempstalle. To house and care for the Sicke.*

The room was close and hot, and both Sam and Annabel felt the need for fresh air.

At that moment Dinah was walking feverishly about the graveyard at Monks Hempstall, looking for vanished headstones, even looking for one she knew would never even have been there.

'Is this paper part of the records of the old hospital, the pest house, then?' Sam asked.

'Must be,' Annabel said. 'It's no local myth or invention that your house used to be Wood Hall – look at this.' She turned to the microfilm projector again, and leaned to one side so that Sam could read what was on the screen. 'This is part of the first census for Monks Hempstall, in 1801. Look, we've got Outwood Green here as a street – see? Three dwellings. There's Green Farm, occupied then by the King family with two labourers, then here's New Cottage, occupied by the Widow Last with one labourer – one house, whereas now its split into two cottages. And here's Wood Hall. Look, Sam – "otherwise known as Pox Hall or Pooky Hall – owner absent." That's it, and someone called William Crane had charge of the sick there, and Alice Crane died there.'

After a silence during which Sam uncomfortably recalled hearing Georgina talking strangely and in broad Suffolk the only time she had been to Pooks Hall, he said, 'How was it that you didn't see this paper before?' He still held the sheet from the folio.

'Apparently it was folded into an account book, from the Parish Chest. I hadn't looked at that because it covers too late a period, but another researcher found it, quite recently, and replaced it. There's a reference in an article written in 1911 – a sort of potted history of the parish – referring to an account. It's later than our Crane references, though, 1721.'

Sam read through the account, which was rendered to 'the Governor at Pock Hall, Outwode Green', and listed such staples as flour, salt, peas, candles, and barley – and a barrel of oysters.

'Oysters!' Sam laughed, glad of light relief. 'The sick lived well, or was that for the Governer and the peas for the paupers!'

'Very likely,' Annabel smiled, 'though oysters were a much more common food then than they are now, of course. And here's the last reference, a fragment of an inventory.'

*'Pooks Hall, Outwood Green',* was pencilled very lightly

over barely legible writing, but the fragment had been transcribed.

> The Hall: 2 tables, 4 joyned stooles, a long table, 3 spinning wheeles.
>
> The further chamber: 1 half-headed bedstead, a flocke bed, 3 flocke bollsters, a warming panne, one feather bed, 2 spinning wheels.
>
> In the thorofare: 2 smallstooles, a hearthiron, 3 spinning

'No date,' Sam remarked.

'By the writing it's around 1670, I reckon – that would make it at the time that William Crane took over after Streetsend died.' Annabel paused. 'I've never been certain what a half-headed bed is – and by the number of spinning wheels I imagine the house served as the poorhouse as well as hospital.'

'Keep the poor well occupied,' Sam nodded.

After packing up the microfilm and tidying the small pile of relevant papers, Annabel, who like Sam had been deep in thought, said: 'Did Martin Crane ever go to the house – at the time of the funeral, I mean, or ever?'

'No, he didn't,' Sam said. 'He went away directly after the burial. Why?'

'I was just wondering, if he *had* gone into the house – if anything out of the ordinary might have happened.'

'No, he drove right away from the church.'

'Sam, do you think it's all a matter of coincidence?'

'That's certainly what I *want* to think.' Sam frowned as he recalled again, this time with a touch of primitive fear, Georgina in the overgrown garden at Pooks Hall: the way she had walked, and her voice – 'Another one gone' – and then – 'More room' – as though referring to a death freeing a bed in a hospital. His skin felt clammy.

They moved into the main search room, and Sam said, 'Annabel, may I ask a favour of you?'

'Surely.'

'Please don't talk about this to Dinah. I'm afraid – I don't want her becoming obsessional about anything like this particularly now that Simon is completely recovered.'

Annabel said, 'I can't promise. Dinah may talk to me, and I don't want to have to lie to her.'

Sam jingled the loose change in his trousers pocket. 'Well, all right. I can only hope that she'll be too busy between now and Christmas to go delving into the sad past.'

They left together, and as Sam turned to walk back to the college Annabel hurried after him.

'Sam,' she called, and he turned, surprised. 'Sam – I forgot to ask you – I didn't want to ask Dinah but can you describe Martin Crane to me?'

The cold wind pushed dustily at them, smelling of traffic fumes. Sam stared. *Martin? Why?* He said, 'Well, Georgina was really very like him, although she was so pretty.' He paused. 'But of course, you never saw her.'

Annabel waited, her hair plumed by the wind.

Sam shrugged. He didn't particularly want to think about Martin Crane, last seen at the funeral, face blue-white and haggard, the freckles splashed across the taut skin, aquamarine eyes blurred and bloodshot. 'He's about my height, I suppose, maybe taller as he's round-shouldered, thin, sort of gangling and nervous – looks younger than his age or did before – ' He took a deep breath. 'He's pale, freckled, with carroty hair and sort of light blue eyes.' He grinned bleakly. 'Women seem to find him attractive.'

'Yes,' Annabel nodded. 'He came to one of our New Age groups, calling himself Michael Carter. I was certain then that he wasn't what he seemed or claimed to be, but he said he was a friend of one of the members – who just happens to be away out of the country for six months.'

Sam felt a curious chill that had nothing to do with the wind. 'If it was him, I wonder why?'

'He only came that once.'

'What were you doing or discussing at that particular meeting?'

'We were discussing dowsing techniques.' Annabel clearly recalled the evening. 'How queer — dowsing.'

'When was this meeting?'

'Three weeks ago,' Annabel said. 'He didn't give any indication that he would come again.'

'So how can we be sure? Hell, why do we *want* to be sure it was Martin Crane and not simply someone called Michael Carter!' Sam stared at Annabel.

'I knew then that he was not who he claimed to be – I knew it at the time – but I didn't. . . .' Angrily she shook her head, putting up a hand to control her blowing hair. 'Something stopped me from taking him up on it. But I am sure, Sam. It was Georgina's father.'

'Why would he be interested in dowsing? He's a musicologist!' Sam exclaimed. 'And he lives in London, so why should he go to your group to find out about it? How'd he get to hear about – oh, this other person, I suppose.'

Annabel put a hand on his arm. 'I'm going back to the search room to see if he – or Michael Carter – was looking at any of the Monks Hempstall documents.'

Sam went with her.

They found nothing in the register of either Martin Crane, or Michael Carter. They did, however, find an M.J. Carne, who was doing 'family research' some months ago, about the time Sam and Dinah first knew about Pooks Hall.

'I'm worried, and I also feel at fault,' Annabel said as they returned to the street. 'I should have tackled this Carter person then. Why didn't I? I don't think he left an address or phone number with the Group. I'll check up. And I'll ring round the others who were there that evening in case he has been in touch.'

Dinah had no opportunity that evening to telephone Annabel, although she was anxious to. She needed to talk – but not to Sam, not yet. She was very conscious that she was listening for Simon to talk to Alice – which he did not do at all that evening, or not in Dinah's hearing, anyhow.

Work at her loom was the only thing that took Dinah's mind away from everything else, but this evening she had time for but a bare hour's weaving. Her head ached, and she had little heart for anything, being so concerned with what she had seen in the Parish Register, with her own endeavours to rationalise, and with frustration at finding neither time nor opportunity to call Annabel, that she did not notice Sam's unusually preoccupied air.

Simon noticed something. He looked darkly from one to the other of his parents as they said goodnight to him. He glanced often round the room, a little warily, as though expecting to see someone else – an unwelcome someone. He drew back a little when Dinah bent to kiss him, and he cried out when she switched off the light.

'No – no – I want the light on, Mum!'

'You don't need it turned right up,' Dinah said – part of her wanting to leave it, as he wished, to comfort him; another part wanting to deny that there might be anything to worry him.

'Oh, Dinah,' Sam said.

'And you're usually the one who accuses me of spoiling him!' she said quickly. *I mustn't show them that I'm scared too!* 'All right, Si, I'll turn it up a little – a nice little glow, see.' She turned the rheostat up a little. 'And the landing light will be on until we come to bed.'

'Life is a series of compromises,' Sam tried to laugh as they went downstairs.

His mood suddenly became apparent to Dinah, and she put her arms round him. 'Sam, darling, is anything the matter?'

He bent a little and laid his cheek against hers, smelling the scent of her cool skin and hair. His thoughts swirled. Over and over he would tell himself that he did not believe in ghosts, did not believe in influences from beyond the grave. *I can't believe it. There's no proof, no proof.*

'Oh, Sam,' Dinah murmured, and put up a hand to lay its palm against the side of his face.

For a moment Sam thought of telling her, but she must not know that he had discovered that there had been a girl called Alice – Alice Crane – who had lived and died at Pooks Hall.

On Saturday they went to Cambridge. The weather was crisp and brilliant. There had been a frost in the night and it still rimed the ground and the road where the sun had not yet reached. The winter colours of the countryside were intensified by the pure, sharp light, no longer mellow and autumnal.

Talbot sat in the front with Sam, and Simon sat between Dinah and Priscilla in the back of Sam's car.

'Poor old dogs, they couldn't come,' Simon said, noticing a black and white collie sitting in a gateway.

'They wouldn't like it,' Sam said, catching Simon's glance in the rear-view mirror, then Dinah's. 'And how about your friend Alice, Simon? Couldn't she come either?' He paused. 'Simon, do you remember that story – about Alice and her adventures in Wonderland?'

'Oh, Dad.' Simon's voice was touched with scorn. 'Alice isn't in Womble-land – she's at *home!* Dumpling's got the Womble songs.' And he began to hum, until he dozed off, lying across Dinah's lap.

Cambridge was crowded: students still up, residents, winter tourists, shoppers from the surrounding countryside. Christmas music sounded from singing groups, from a brass band, and from a woodwind ensemble in the covered shopping precinct. Simon was awed by a huge cut-out cardboard whale on which supporters of the Friends of the Earth were signing their names, dropping coins into a box. Simon, round-eyed and serious, wrote S- I- M, only the S was back to front. They saw a small anti-abortion faction parading – ALWAYS ROOM AT THE INN! – and a pro-abortion demonstration – MORE ROOM AT THE INN – and a group of Hare Krishna followers gyrated gently in pale robes, muffled over with sweaters and duffel coats, bells tinkling faintly.

'Mum, why don't they have hair?'

After lunch the Warners split up. Priscilla took Simon with her, and Sam took Talbot to the Fitzwilliam Museum where he left him happily engaged while he set off himself for gift buying.

Dinah, on her own, felt young, free, and quite childishly excited, divorced from her fears and worries for a whole carefree afternoon – hours in which to wander, stare, to spend money and to be herself *for* herself. She filled the time.

The sky became a beautiful slate colour, tinged overhead with pink, pale green low down in the west. Mist hung over the trees by the river. Stars were appearing, cold and remote, and the bright lights of festive Cambridge seemed garish and yet insubstantial, unimportant between the earth and the sky.

Dinah stood at the West Door of King's College Chapel. From within she could hear the choir rehearsing – soaring disembodied voices, and a delicate counterpoint of long looping lines of melody. Outside, she stood in a cold shell of evening stillness, with the sounds of the busy city removed a space, almost unreal. She listened, smiling, spellbound by the music. She wished that she were not alone now, that Sam could be with her, sharing this pause and the almost painful beauty of the voices.

The door was opened from inside, and the voices swelled out into the evening, but Dinah was distracted by the sounds of footsteps as three people came out, whispering, and behind them a fourth.

For a shocking and breathless few seconds Dinah found herself staring at Martin Crane, the lights from within the chapel flaring orange through his hair. Then he stepped back, and the door closed; he inside, Dinah outside.

Her heart pounding and her mouth dry, Dinah picked up her shopping basket and additional laden carrier bags, and started off at a panicked run back to King's Parade to mingle with the moving crowds.

She had not been mistaken. It was Martin. Both had recognised one another.

Glancing behind her, Dinah plodded on, avoiding other peoples' shopping bags, almost tripping over baby-buggies. The evening had grown colder, and Dinah bent her head to the rising wind, on which floated an aromatic mingle of smells – tobacco smoke, hot dogs and onions, the scent of patchouli on someone's Afghan coat, coffee, and then petrol fumes as she left the pedestrians-only area. Dinah felt panicky still, but she was certain that Martin had not followed her. Even so, she still glanced round from time to time, even as she reached the car-park on Gonville Place. Happy tears stung her eyes as she saw Sam. She dumped her burdens, flexing her numbed fingers.

'Why didn't I bring a rucksack?' she exclaimed. 'I'm absolutely bushed.'

'Making it obvious that you've been spending a lot of money,' Sam laughed.

'Mum – Mum – look what I've got! Look, Mum!' Simon danced up and down, excitedly waving his hand, above which floated a gas filled balloon of gleaming silver plastic, bobbing gently on its tether.

'Oh, Si, how *lovely!* Did you have a good time?'

'Marvellous,' Priscilla laughed. 'He wore me out! And we

managed to avoid *la grotte de Père Noel!'*

Dinah gave an uninhibited hoot of laughter and felt a warm surge of happiness at being with this family again.

'Come on, Dinah, get in the car and rest your feet! I'll get the soup out.' Priscilla began to organise everyone.

Hot soup, cheese rolls, fruit-cake and coffee were a satisfying meal after the day's activities, and both Talbot and his grandson slept on the way home. Priscilla and Dinah talked a little, then sat within their own thoughts. Sam, driving steadily, even in the swathes of fog which muffled the countryside every few miles, felt happier and less tense than he had been at the start of the day.

Pooks Hall loomed against the frosty, starry sky.

There was a welcoming barking of dogs and bleating of goats, and a tawny owl flew on its silent, muffled wings over the roofs of the house, calling out that he was abroad.

Dinah murmured, 'The owl is abroad, the bat and the mole, and so is the catamountain – '

'What's that?' Sam asked.

*A song that Martin used to sing.* 'Oh, an old poem – can't remember who it's by. In the next bit "The frog peeps out of the fountain." Rather nice!' She spoke too quickly.

Sam went into the main part of the house, switching on the hall and yard lights. 'Good to be home,' he observed, stretching his spine and arms, smiling at the others when he found them still sitting in the car. He glanced back at the house, thinking that it was not haunted, it couldn't be.

Dinah carried Simon into the house and he whimpered and woke, wriggling down out of Dinah's arms, looking round him with dramatic anxiety, clutching the air with his hands.

Talbot appeared, the silver balloon bobbing at his shoulder, and a great smile spread across Simon's face.

Dinah began to laugh, weak with sudden relief. She had thought he might be looking for Alice but it was only his balloon he wanted.

He went to bed that night with the balloon tethered to his bedhead.

'What do we do when the gas runs out of that thing?' Dinah wondered later, as she and Sam showed one another various purchases they had made for Christmas – and hid certain others.

'I know it's a bit extravagant,' Sam confessed, 'but I've ordered one of those marvellous child-sized tractors – you know, on the old pedal-car principle, but much larger and more realistic. Picture it – a genuine Simon-sized John Deere!'

'Oh, Sam, he'll be thrilled.'

Dinah did not tell Sam that Simon, in the bath, had been talking.

'In the car – you know, the *car,* my Dad's car – I ate lots and lots of chips for dinner and I got my silver balloon. Oh, you're *silly.* Everyone knows what – ' and Dinah had crept away, not wanting to listen and yet wanting to, terrified that somehow another voice would answer.

In bed later, Sam asleep beside her, Dinah lifted her head, listening. She remembered that when she had returned to the bathroom, Simon was looking rebellious, and his hair was wet, water running down his face, also, and dripping from his long eyelashes – *as though he had been ducked!*

A little wind rose up stealthily and began blowing about the house, whispering at the windows, sighing in the trees, a desolate sound. The wind had dropped earlier in the evening. Now it was pushing at the house, rattling the windows. Dinah pulled the covers close. She found herself thinking of Martin again. Last year he had visited them at Snailwell on Christmas Eve on his way to a concert in Cambridge. He had brought gifts for both the children, and Georgina had cried when he left. Poor Georgina, loved by her two fathers, but stuck with a mother who didn't love her. *A mother who killed her.* . . .

From being sleepy Dinah was now wide awake, and besieged by unwanted thoughts and memories. She quietly went to the bathroom and took the last two sedative pills in the bottle. She replaced the key to the bathroom cabinet in its hiding place and returned, shivering, to bed.

Drowsiness at last settled over her, through which with a dreadful sense of inevitability, Dinah heard a man's voice, talking urgently – too far away from her to hear clearly, and then joined by another.

'Oh, go away, please,' she whispered futilely.

That night she dreamed of Martin.

About to dial Annabel's number, Dinah was startled when the telephone rang. She snatched her hand back from it as though it might electrocute her, then laughed at herself and picked it up, giving their number.

Nothing. 'Hello?' Dinah said.

There was a small sound at the other end as though the caller had shifted position, then something like a sigh.

'What number do you want? Who do you want to speak to?' Dinah began to feeling uncomfortable, a little angry.

Not even any heavy breathing. Simply – nothing.

Dinah slammed the instrument down and it gave a petulant ping. *Funny phone calls – that's all I need!*

Dinah grimaced, then dialled Annabel's number. 'Annabel, I'm glad it's you who answered. Did one of the girls dial this number just now?'

'No, I've been right here writing letters this half hour and we don't have an extension – not guilty. Why?'

'Then it seems that I've just had one of *those* calls.'

'No talking?'

'No, not really any breathing either. Silly, but unnerving!' Dinah glanced round, feeling vulnerable. She thought of Friday in the mousey chill of the vestry; thought of Alice. 'Annabel – ' she lowered her voice, though she thought that Sam was out in the garden with Simon – 'I've found out that there *was* a Crane family, and they lived here in the late sixteen hundreds – *actually here* – only it was called Wood Hall officially then. I must see you and talk.'

'You've seen the Parish Registers? Did you make copies?'

'Yes. And there was a daughter called Alice.' Dinah's voice was flat.

'Are you all right?'

Dinah sighed. 'It was so weird, seeing it written down – names and dates. I couldn't find any of their headstones. I suppose they were moved, to make space.' She shivered. The light coming in from the tall mullions and the windows on the opposite wall was flat, grey and chill. 'But there's no record of Alice being buried.'

'Damn it, I'm tied up today,' Annabel said. 'How about

tomorrow? Bring Simon over in the afternoon, any time.'

Dinah felt tears of childish disappointment in her eyes as the conversation ended a few minutes later. She didn't want to have to wait until tomorrow – she wanted to talk to Annabel now, today – wanted Annabel to come to Pooks Hall again to reassure her that the house was empty but for the living. *And Alice?*

She scurried upstairs, and once she had taken the dust sheet off the loom and was at work again the ghosts left her alone, for the time being.

She worked on, in her ears the rhythmic thud of the loom, the creaking of the floorboards as she shifted her weight from one foot to the other. She could hear the gentle plopping of the stove, and an occasional scrabbling and argument of sparrows and starlings under the overhanging thatch. A peacock butterfly awoke from its winter roost clinging to a beam. It fluttered slowly about, to land on a skein of wool. It flirted its wings, then snapped them shut over its back so that it looked like a dark leaf caught in the fibres of the wool.

Sam called up the stairs to tell her that he and Simon had prepared lunch.

Priscilla and Talbot were sharing the Sunday lunch, and Dinah found their presence a relief, since she felt a strong urge to blurt out to Sam all her mounting fears and worries, to tell him about the voices, about the old man in the dry moat, about Sam's playmate Alice – who might not be what at first she had seemed. As it happened, the comfortably commonplace conversation was a relief and Dinah was actually happy to talk about her work.

Asked about her progress, she said: 'My rug'll be ready in time for Christmas, if I don't waste any time.' She had tied Simon's balloon so that it floated above his chair and in it she could see the distorted reflection of the table and the people around it. Simon saw her looking at it and tilted his head up to stare at his own eyes, large and strange in the reflection.

'We look funny,' he announced. 'Everything looks funny.' He paused. 'Alice doesn't like it – she's silly to be scared of a silver balloon. Dad, can I have lots? I'm *very* hungry.'

Dinah bit her lip, but no-one commented on the fact that an imaginary child could be scared of a balloon.

'Lucky to get any at all unless I sharpen this knife.' Sam laughed, and fetched the steel to whet the knife.

He had just finished carving the roast when the telephone bell shrilled.

Dinah hurried through the back hall to the sitting room. She returned looking flustered and angry. 'That's the *second* time today! Sunday recreation for some creep, I suppose!'

'What's that, dear?' Priscilla looked up from cutting Simon's meat for him.

'Funny phone calls.' Dinah sat down. Sam looked up sharply. 'No speaking — doesn't even breathe heavily – but there is someone there.' She took a drink of her beer, brewed by Sam. 'That's better. It's not fair though that *I* should be the one left with a nasty taste in my mouth.'

'With the old-fashioned candlestick telephone you could blast them almost deaf by putting the earpiece to the mouthpiece,' Sam said. Then: 'Was it from a call box, Di?'

She was surprised. 'No, that's odd! You always imagine that these characters sneak into call boxes – you know – with the collars of their greasy raincoats turned up.'

'I'll take it next time it rings,' Sam said. 'I'll be indoors for the rest of the day – I've a lot of paper work.'

There were no more telephone calls that day.

It was six-fifteen on Monday morning when Sam hauled himself out of bed to answer the persistent ringing, muttering about an extension in the bedroom.

'Same again – bloody joker.' Sam returned to bed. 'Half an hour before the alarm goes off.' He ran his hands over Dinah's breasts, her ribs, turning towards her.

'Sam! Your knees are *icy!*' Dinah exclaimed.

'Soon get warm again.'

Later, as he left for college, Dinah said, 'Simon and I are going to the Brooks' this afternoon.'

'May I take my silver balloon?' Simon asked, the balloon floating above his head.

'I don't see why not,' Dinah said, 'but I don't think you'd better take it to school – I'll tie it up in the kitchen.'

Simon nodded. 'It doesn't fly, Mum.' They went to put the balloon in the kitchen, then to get Simon ready for school.

'No, it bothers.'

'Bothers?' Dinah smiled. 'Oh, yes – *hovers!*'

'Yes,' Simon agreed. 'Talbot says it's a you-foe. It is, isn't it?'

Dinah hurried Simon to school in the car, hurried back to her therapy – her work. She was at the loom all morning, seeing the near approach of the final angles and last lines of the last border at the end of the rug. She wanted to see it finished, was impatient to make a start on the wall-hanging at the same time as she made sketches for the commissioned work. When on form, Dinah always liked to be working on several projects simultaneously.

That afternoon over tea in Annabel's kitchen, Dinah at first talked about the visit to Cambridge, saying nothing, though, about seeing Martin.

'I love Cambridge, too,' Annabel said. 'It's a place I wouldn't mind living in if I had to live in a city.'

'Have we been to Cambridge?' Amanda asked.

'Of course you have — don't you remember the river and the bridges, and going in a punt?' Annabel laughed. 'It shook Pete rigid when I was better with the punt pole than he was!'

'Oh, yes.' Amanda smiled.

'There was ponies in a field in the town,' Charis recalled Midsummer Common.

'That's right – and we got a parking ticket, just to round off that particular day!' Annabel grimaced. 'Have you all finished your tea?'

The children went to the playroom, where Amanda and Charis were setting up their toy theatre.

Annabel looked at Dinah and a buzz of excitement vibrated between them.

'Do you know something too?' Dinah whispered.

'Did Sam tell you?'

'*Sam?* Did Sam tell me what?'

'Oh,' Annabel poured the last of the tea into her cup. 'It was just that I went to the Records Office in Ipswich on Friday afternoon. Pete had some time off and he took the girls over to Southwold to see his parents. They don't like me so I had time to myself. So — I went to Ipswich, and Sam was there.'

'*Sam?* In the Records Office?' Dinah's face was flushed.

'He never said.' She twisted her hands together. 'But he's always been against researching into anything – you know – that might make us think Pooks Hall *is* haunted. It's so difficult to explain.' She shook her head. 'I suppose he is really trying to protect me and Simon.'

'Well, he did go to look at the documents,' Annabel told her.

There was a silence like a spiral staircase, thoughts curling up and then spiralling down.

After a while Dinah said, 'Did you find out anything?'

'What did *you* find?'

'People called Crane lived at Pooks Hall – a family. He was the sort of warden of the hospital, and there *was* a girl called Alice.' Dinah stopped, recalling Simon in the bath, face flushed, water running out of his hair.

Laughter and delighted shouts came from the playroom, and the sound of 'The Ash Grove' played on a descant recorder.

'Show me your copy.' Annabel quickly cleared their end of the table, moving her chair closer, and Dinah took out her notebook and laid it on the table between them.

Then Black Tom materialised and leapt light as a shadow onto the table, couching himself neatly, front paws folded in, staring at Annabel as his sides expanded and contracted purringly.

The cat was so intent upon the notebook that it seemed as though he actually read Dinah's script upside down. And Dinah's script, Annabel noted, was a rounded and pretty variation of school-room italic – and did not in any way resemble the cursive hand of William Templar Crane in the page torn from the vanished folio or in Dinah's sketchbook.

'Cranesbill, the flower and the seed-heads,' Annabel said, and Dinah looked up, startled. 'You remember your drawing? Don't you see? It fits. Crane – William himself, and the little Williams – *bills!* At that time, if one child died another would carry its name, especially boys.' Annabel sighed as Dinah nodded tensely. Annabel felt a need and a longing for her companions of her New Age group. She felt that she might be unable to handle this on her own. Yet she knew she could never ask the group to Pooks Hall. That simply would not be fair on Sam Warner. She bent her head and read and re-read the information given in the Parish Register.

'You see,' Dinah said, 'there's no record of Alice being buried. Yet this note says she died in 1691, when she was the same age – as Georgina.'

Annabel, suddenly reluctant to pursue the subject of Alice, flipped the page and saw the later Crane entry.

'Perhaps I should look at the Coddenham registers,' Dinah suggested. 'I thought that perhaps William might have come from there. If he did there might be a possible connection. I mean, if Martin's father was descended from this George Crane – and in a round-about way from William's family too – '

Annabel took a pencil and drew a rough pedigree. She shook her head. 'We don't know – the two families *may* have been connected.'

'So it could be the link between Georgina and Pooks Hall.' Then Dinah's expression changed. *Georgina, yes, she was a Crane – but why me? Why Simon?*

'What's the matter?'

'The idea works for Georgina.' Dinah was surprised that each time she mentioned her daughter it seemed easier to do. 'But it doesn't for Simon or me. And it was Sam who bought Pooks Hall, not Martin.' Frowning, she went on: 'But even if this place is strong enough to draw people to it, Georgina was just a child and *we* chose to live there. The decision wasn't hers!'

'How did you find it?'

A cold finger of fear tracked down Dinah's spine.

'The estate agents who had it on their books claimed they never sent us the information – but someone did, as though we were meant to want to choose Pooks Hall.'

Annabel pushed her fingers up into her hair and the slithery knot loosened and uncoiled, sliding like golden syrup in the light. Hairpins in mouth, Annabel twisted it up again.

Dinah watched her, silently questioning.

Annabel sighed. 'But you saw the house, and moved in. And now Sam and you and I know some things that might fit together. I found some more information, missing when I looked previously – I admit very briefly – before.' She stood up and went to the cluttered dresser, returning with a folder and showing Dinah a photocopy of the page torn from the folio kept by William Crane at Wood Hall, and before him by Henry Streetsend – and the familiar handwriting.

Dinah was shocked.

After a while she whispered, 'Am I the connection, then? That writing – *my* hand holding the – it's the same!' She stared at her right hand, as though seeing it for the first time.

'A force will find its outlet where it can.' Annabel hesitated 'And of course, you carried Georgina in your body.'

There was a long pause, during which they were conscious of the children's voices from the playroom, and during which Dinah was thinking: *I don't believe – I can't handle this. What would happen if I went away, if we all did, sold the house?* She shuddered, the children's voices sounded so like the others – no words, just the tones and inflections and periods. She shook herself and forced herself to speak. 'What should I do now?'

'Is it quiet at the moment?'

*Only those damned awful voices – and Simon talking to Alice!* Dinah nodded.

'It seems that in many instances when the dead can't seem to, so to speak, *resolve* cases of haunting – ' Annabel looked seriously into Dinah's eyes ' – the death was unexpected, cut off from friendship or love, maybe unmourned, frequently violent. Even miscarried or aborted children can cause disturbances. They have not been properly released, sent off – the result being hauntings like I said, or maybe psychoses in relatives or descendants – waiting for resolution.'

Dinah shuddered, flinching back, and Annabel leaned forward and touched her hand. 'Of course, what I believe need not necessarily be the truth. I admit that.'

Dinah moistened her lips. 'I see. William, and maybe Alice, too, didn't have an easy end, and probably no great funeral send-off.' She thought of herself, and of Georgina, but she said: 'We still don't know where Alice was buried.'

'No, and I am not going to do any table-turning or ouija-board in your house – you could say that the walls are just too thin.' Annabel stroked the cat.

'But whose was all that anger you said was in the house! Why was William constrained?' Dinah thumped one fist down on the folder of notes. 'What actually happened to Alice? And why the "God forgive mee?" Is Alice actually buried *there,* in my house?'

'Dinah, we're not living in a Stephen King novel!' Annabel exclaimed. 'She could have died in another parish.'

That evening Sam and Dinah were in the kitchen racking wine.

When the telephone rang Dinah went to answer it, determined to force the silent caller to talk – if the call was a silent one. It was not.

'Hello, is that Dinah?'

A voice, female, familiar, somehow both overbearing and whining. *Oh, no!*

'Yes?' Dinah said, tense.

'Dinah, this is Rosemary Crane, Martin's mother.'

'I know – how are you?' What else was there to say?

'I'm worried, Dinah, worried out of my mind! It's Martin – have you been seeing him?'

'Good God, no!' Dinah exclaimed, a flash of memory showing her Martin Crane staring at her in the doorway of King's College Chapel. But that didn't count, surely?

'Dinah, I wouldn't phone *you* – you know that. At least we can be honest with each other. But I just have to know. You see, he keeps going up to Suffolk – he won't say exactly where, or who he's seeing. He's so strange these last months, and getting worse, as though he's in a dream – or a nightmare! I'm desperately worried. He's not working, you know. Last week he missed giving an important lecture-recital! I didn't even know where he was!'

Dinah stared helplessly into space, clutching the telephone.

She had no wish to continue the conversation, but she was unable to cut the connection. Not only her mother's early training prevented her from abruptly ending the call, but perversely, she felt a certain sympathy for Martin's mother – widowed and emotionally dependent on her son. Also, what did Rosemary Crane mean about Martin coming to Suffolk?

Dinah sat down. She heard some sighing and fidgeting, not the almost complete silence of the other calls. 'When did all this start?' she asked. 'Is it – is it since Georgina – ?'

'He was a bit – ah – *distrait* during the summer, but when

he came home after poor little Georgina's funeral he was really a changed man.' Mrs Crane paused. 'I should have gone with him but I didn't really feel well enough, strong enough, and anyway, he insisted on going alone – used quite violent words.' Again she paused. 'It hasn't been bad all the time. You know he was always, well, moody. He's still my Martin the rest of the time.'

Dinah carefully uncurled her tense toes, straightened her spine. 'Yes?' she prompted.

'Then he went to Suffolk again – for the first time in October. He said he was visiting friends but he stayed in an hotel – I found the receipt in his pocket – a hotel in Needham Market. I had to send the coat to the cleaners.'

'I never saw him,' Dinah said.

'And then on the thirteenth of October my brother-in-law – the Brigadier's older brother died. He'd been gaga for years. Martin was left some papers I knew nothing about. Martin never showed – anyway, somehow this made Martin terribly excited and then he became – oh, so secretive and strange. I couldn't understand it.' A crackling pause, a deep sigh. 'He always shared *everything* with me.'

Dinah almost felt sorry for Martin. No secrets, even his pockets ransacked.

'I haven't finished,' Mrs Crane went on. 'The reason I'm so worried – you see, Martin reminds me of how he was when he was thirteen and there was an – episode. We were staying in an old house in some village – in Suffolk, oddly enough – between postings. The Brigadier's last posting, it only lasted three months before he passed away. We stayed in this house only for a couple of weeks – and Martin was *sleepwalking* every night! And there were extraordinary noises – like explosions, and barrels being rolled around, things falling on the roof! Oh, we were glad to move again, I can tell you!'

'Did anyone try to explain the trouble?' Dinah felt a little giddy from the picture conjured by Martin's mother – and remembering the 'episode' on November the fifth.

'Well, we knew it was only for a short time so we just put up with it,' Rosemary Crane said. 'The old man next door did say that he thought that Martin was like a lightning conductor, and since October he's reminded me of that time.'

There was a heavy, troubled silence, then Mrs Crane continued, 'How funny – I've just remembered where that house was. A very pretty village – Coddenham. Is that near you at all? Martin was *very* interested in your house – funny name, Pooks Hall – he had the estate agents' particulars about it. I found them. Perhaps he was interested because Georgina would be living there. But, of course, she didn't.'

Dinah closed her eyes, wishing Martin's mother had never made the call.

'Dinah?' the voice said.

'I'm sorry, but I really don't think I can help.'

'I thought he might – ' Then a change of tone. 'Well, at least I tried. Goodbye, Dinah.'

After the call ended Dinah sat for a while. The log fire burned low. She recalled the way the flames had burst out into the room on November the fifth. She stood up and went to poke the logs. Slow sparks wandered up the wide chimney and ash settled as the wood disintegrated. She put a few small branches on to the fire.

'That was Mrs Crane on the phone,' Dinah said as she returned to the kitchen. Sam finished syphoning the last bottle of the present brewing and removed the plastic tubing from his mouth.

'What the hell did *she* want?'

'She's worried about Martin.' Dinah frowned. 'Thinks he's having some sort of breakdown, and wondered if we'd seen him around here. Poor old thing. . . . She did sound – perhaps I – '

'Dinah, you are not to feel guilty about Martin – not now, not ever, no matter how many breakdowns his mother thinks he's having!' Sam poured some of the clear pale wine for them to taste. 'What he ought to do is boot his mother out of his flat or get out himself – if it's not too late!'

During the week before Christmas Dinah took Simon on a visit to her parents in Bath. She risked the changeable weather conditions and drove, a day-long journey, trundling along in the Morris. Sam had wanted her to take his car but she was adamant, and both outward and return journeys were uneventful.

The visit was not a success. Both her parents had been extremely fond and indulgent of Georgina, and neither liked Simon very much. He, naturally, sensed this anew, and became taciturn and unattractive. Dinah could hardly contain her irritation and disappointment, the only mitigating factors of the trip being that Simon seemed to have forgotten Alice, and that Dinah's parents were genuinely pleased to see her and as genuinely disappointed that Sam was not with her. 'We do need to get to know him better, dear, though we'll always find it hard to understand how you could prefer him to Martin. Such a brilliant personality.'

Dinah cut the five days to three, and left in pouring rain and sleet, feeling almost lightheaded with relief.

On Christmas Eve Sam and Dinah gave a small party. Dinah had laid her completed rug, a present for Sam, on the smooth, warn pammets which tiled the sitting room floor. She had backed the rug with thick underfelt, as she had all their other rugs when she saw that the ground floor at Pooks Hall was brick or pammet throughout.

'It's so beautiful, I hardly like to *walk* on it.' Sam hugged Dinah yet again.

'You'll have to get used to it, or walk round it, then.' She kissed him back, and ran upstairs to change and to see if Simon was asleep.

The guilty scuffle as Dinah approached Simon's open door betrayed him. His 'stocking', one of Sam's socks, was not where it had been. Dinah grinned, thinking of the sock's pair, already stuffed with little parcels – in the foot the traditional apple, orange and nuts.

'Simon, I *know* you're awake.'

Gradually his head emerged and he lay looking at her, laughing, wriggling his toes under the covers.

'When's it morning? When's Christmas?'

'Morning'll be tomorrow – and tomorrow's Christmas.' Dinah stroked his pale hair. 'It'll come much more quickly if you go to sleep. It'll be ages coming if you stay awake – and you'll get awfully bored waiting.'

'Can I write in my book?' He paused, frowning. 'Alice can't write – isn't that silly? She's old and she can't write!'

Dinah drew in her breath. *I thought we'd got rid of her!*

'All right,' she said.

Simon's writing, apart from the wobbly letters of his name, consisted of lines of strange, runic characters in bright colours. As he laboriously made each 'word' he would describe a whole incident in the long and involved scenario he told himself – or Alice.

Dinah fetched his big book and the bag of crayons. She turned up the rheostat. 'I'll come back in half an hour – the party will have started by then – and if you go to sleep really quickly you'll make Christmas come in no time at all.'

'A very good party. I declare this house duly and thoroughly warmed,' Sam said after the last guests had left. 'Even though David and Jean couldn't come.'

He and Dinah cleared and washed up, nibbling at any food that was left, and drinking ice-cold lager.

'You know that legend about Christmas Eve?' Dinah folded the last of the drying-up cloths over the airer on its pulley above the Aga and made fast the cord. 'I wonder if we went out to the yard we'd find all the goats kneeling.'

Sam laughed. 'Want to bet? They kneel anyway to lie down so it'd be hard to differentiate.'

'Poor goats,' Dinah said. 'All the classic Nativity pictures you can think of, and not one goat among the other domestic beasts. Yet think how important goats were to the middle eastern people!'

'Still are,' Sam said. 'But it's the old pagan thing, the early Christian simply could not assimilate the goat – '

'Do you remember all the goats and the goats' heads in the Lurçat tapestries at Angers?'

Sam remembered, and it made him think of church, and tomorrow's service.

'How about church in the morning?' He asked. 'Matins is at eleven.'

Dinah's blank look might have been caused by weariness or forgetfulness, but Sam had the feeling that it was a deliberate device. *Damn it!* he thought. *Georgina wasn't even my daughter – but I'm prepared to put flowers on her grave at Christmas. It's supposed to be the children's festival!*

'Those flowers I brought home yesterday,' he reminded her, 'not the ones for the party – the other flowers, in those pails of water in the lobby. They're for Georgina. I want you and me to go to church tomorrow for Matins, and to put the flowers on Georgina's grave.'

Dinah stared, seeing in her mind's eye Martin standing across the stone from her, in his hands a circlet of bare, black branches. 'Martin,' she whispered, sitting down on the nearest chair.

'Darling, he'll be with his mother on Christmas Day – you mustn't let that phone call of hers prey on your mind!'

Dinah shook her head, dragging her fingers through her hair, then sat rubbing her hands up and down her thighs, feeling the textures of her silk brocade skirt, shivering in the thin silk gauze blouse in spite of the warmth of the kitchen.

'You go. I can't – '

'Dinah, she was *your* daughter! Yours, not mine. You can't just forget or ignore her because – because she's buried!'

Dinah stood up, crossing the kitchen to stand with her back against the rail of the Aga, her hands clenched on the metal bar, knuckles white. 'I wasn't there – ' She shook her head. 'Someone once said, if you don't see them dead or buried, you don't let them go, release them.'

'But you *know* that she's gone!'

'I know.' Dinah nodded sadly, and with a hand to her mouth, swiftly left the room.

Sam watched her go, a swift fleeing figure, delicate blouse the colour of her hair, neither blonde nor brown, and a flowing, gleaming waterfall of a skirt in richly gilded autumn colours.

Monks Hempstall church was gay with gold, bronze, yellow and pearl chrysanthemums, and greened with holly.

Simon behaved surprisingly well. He silently pushed a tiny tractor up and down the bookrest on the back of the pew in front of him during the prayers. And he la-la-ed the hymns and psalms with happy abandon in a high, sweet voice. Afterwards, Priscilla and Talbot took him back to the car, while Sam and Dinah unloaded the flowers and carried them across to the corner of the graveyard.

Dinah, ashen-faced, her hands growing numb from the cold, arranged the flowers in the containers as Sam placed and filled them with water.

Through her mind fled images of Georgina – in the garden and in the house at Pooks Hall – in places where Georgina could not actually have been. She tried to visualise what lay beneath this plain grey-white stone, now almost concealed by flowers, but her mind rebelled and slid away to other memories of Georgina. And all the time she expected Martin to arrive. She gave a start almost of terror when Sam spoke.

'We ought to put her name on it, and the dates, if nothing else.' He coughed, and Dinah saw that his eyes were filling with tears that had nothing to do with the cough. All she felt now was Sam's grief and his need. She stood up and put her arms round him, and was amazed to feel the warmth returning to her hands and body as she hugged Sam to comfort him as best she could.

After a while Sam loosened her grasp, keeping one of her arms round him, one of his round her. 'Come on. We'll freeze to the spot, and Simon's only had his stocking, yet. There's Christmas presents to open.'

Dinah walked with Sam back to the car, knowing that he was recalling last Christmas, and others before that, when Georgina had flamed like a candle with her excitement, able to light up the whole family.

Although Sam had known and dreaded how much he would miss Georgina today particularly, and although Dinah found herself thinking again and again of her daughter – and of Martin – the day was still a happy one, the climax being when they all went out to the yard and Sam wheeled out the scale-model, pedal-powered John Deere tractor.

Simon was once more speechless – but this time from wonder and delight, and the silence did not last long. After prowling round the tractor as though not believing it was real, stroking it gently, he suddenly yelled with glee and climbed in to the seat.

'Look! Look at me. I'm a real farmer on a real tractor!'

'Five go-old rings,' Dinah sang, almost in tune. 'Four collie-birds, Three French hens, Two turtle-doves – and a Part-er-idge in a pear tree'.

'Collie *dogs,* Mum – not *birds!'* Simon corrected her.

'Of course – whoever heard of collie-birds!' Dinah laughed, doing up the toggles of Simon's new duffel coat. 'On the Twelfth day of Christmas, our Simon went to school' she sang, putting out of her mind last year and Georgina setting off on her brand new bicycle, foxy hair flying, meeting her friends on the corner to swoop to school in a giggling group – bright woollen gloves and scarves cheering up the drab parkas they all seemed to wear. 'Come on, Si, we mustn't be late on your first full day.'

On the second school day Simon did not go.

Snow had come in the night and was still falling.

Simon and the collies romped like puppies. It was Sam's morning off from College, and he and Dinah joined in – running, sliding, throwing soft snowballs, making crazy tracks, and happily clowning in the silent, white world. They tried to build a snowman – ' And I can go walking in the air with him in the night' – Simon had been entranced by the film of Briggs' *The Snowman,* but the snow was too soft to bind and Sam said they would have to wait for the snowman until tomorrow.

When the blizzard ceased the wind suddenly dropped, and the stillness and silence were profound and magical.

Sam pointed to the house, white roofs now against a white sky. 'Just like the estate agents' photograph,' he said.

Dinah looked around at the house, the white expanse of the lawns, everything – the house, the farm buildings, the garden, the trees – all transformed, dressed overall in snow.

Although she had a strong feeling that the snow was obliterating all that had gone before, the feeling of something new approaching – which should have been a good, clean feeling – was chilling, like standing too long in the snow. She moved suddenly, turning to look behind her.

It was as though someone had called a warning to her.

Something not as white as the snow flicked out of sight under the darkness of the hedge. The old hawthorn held itself there, an almost perfect dome of snow on its umbrella-handle of trunk, and something was behind it – or someone.

Sam and Simon and the dogs were romping towards the east wing, where Priscilla was calling. They seemed to be miles away.

Dinah moved towards the hawthorn, and the hedge. There was movement at the shadowy edge of the woods. The dimly seen figure of the man raised an arm towards her: not beckoning, stopping her.

'Who are you? What do you want?' Dinah called softly, heart thumping as though to deafen her.

But he turned away, followed by the small off-white shape that appeared briefly again beneath the hedge and then was gone, like the man, into the woods.

Dinah felt choked by a deep and hopeless sadness. *William. . . . It was William Crane, I know. And so sad.* She stood until the cold ached through her feet and made her eyes water. Then she turned, and hurried to the house, the soft snow like the leaden-footed thrall of a nightmare.

Three days later the snow was cleared, mainly by gale force winds and torrential rain. After two days of this, the winter settled to days of raw wet wind, alternating with dry and frosty periods. Simon never got more than the base of his snowman but there were other things to do – such as driving his John Deere – and school, of course.

When Sam was at College and Simon at school, the house seemed too empty and Dinah was glad to feel that Priscilla and Talbot were not far away.

She spent her solitary hours working at her loom or her sketchbooks. Her work took up all her attention, but now, whenever she stopped, she would find that she was listening for voices, or turning quickly to see if a childish figure flicked out of sight round a corner or through a doorway. Out of doors she found herself looking for William and his little dog.

The voices still came to her at night, and Simon still talked to Alice.

Dinah, unable to stand it any longer, had put a curtain over the little window between her work room and the other. She felt guilty and ashamed of her fear – but once the curtain was over that small pane of glass she felt somewhat easier.

Dinah had hoped that once he was at school full-time Simon

would forget about his fantasy friend. Sam shrugged it off and said that maybe Simon would cling to Alice a while longer until he was more confident at school. It puzzled and irritated Dinah that Simon seemed so often to be quite hostile to Alice. *A bit like spooking yourself with your own invented terrors – maybe he gets it from me.* But what if they were not invented?

And Annabel? They had met, and the children had played together several times since Christmas and the New Year, but Annabel had now begun planning her research project for her higher degree, and was not so available.

Dinah could not help feeling that Annabel was reluctant to come to the house. It was as though both she and Sam considered that by ignoring what they knew of the Crane history at Pooks Hall, that history would cease to be – would become myth, and powerless. *They* heard no voices, so there were no voices to be heard.

Dinah grew more aware that the power was still there. Her work, however, was an opposing power, and had its restorative influence as she found the wall-hanging taking shape.

She wove a strange, bark-like, mossy, lower border, experimenting with new knots and loops and combinations of wool textures, weaving in shreds of tweed cut from an old autumn-coloured skirt, and sometimes a few glass beads.

Priscilla was spinning some especially selected wool from a parti-coloured Jacob's fleece. Dinah watched her one evening in the flickering light from fire and television screen. Sam was at a late class, Simon and Talbot watching the news: riots in Bangladesh, floods in Devon, a strike, some Royal lady alters the length of her skirt. It was time for Dinah to take Simon back to their part of the house and put him to bed, but she was reluctant to go outside.

'I wish we had a connecting door,' she said.

She was well aware that only months ago she would have angrily rejected such an idea.

'Easy enough to make one,' Talbot told her in his own way, as he switched off the television. 'Sam and I could do it.'

Priscilla was enthusiastic.

'I'll talk to Sam about it,' Dinah said, watching as Priscilla continued with her spinning, foot regular on treadle, her hands moving as though in a graceful dance. Those hands looked so delicate on the yarn, but Dinah knew that they were not delicate at all. Strong, and distorted from years of work, in the firelight they appeared as delicate and beautiful as moths.

Dinah sighed. 'Come on Simon, we must go.'

Talbot told Dinah that the dogs needed a run, so he would walk them back to their door.

The night was cold enough to make them gasp as they walked out into the almost solid chill of the air. Stars sparkled bitterly, high in the black gulf of sky, but near the ground was a pall of thick mist.

Dinah shivered. 'I don't like mist – I always find it horribly spooky!'

She stared out beyond the furry loom of the house lights – was William out there, keeping watch? Once again she felt a warning, and sudden fear snatched her breath away as the mist seemed to swirl and fold in on itself. She almost cried out when the two collies took off and raced across the short intervening space to vanish into dark and mist, barking furiously.

'What have they – ?' she squeaked, and Simon clutched at her hand and Talbot's.

Talbot laughed, and said that they often did that – and that they could hear things much further away than humans could.

'Foxes and things?' Simon looked up. 'Just foxes and badgers?'

Talbot nodded, and Dinah leaned forward and kissed him. 'Yes, foxes and badgers, that's all,' she said. 'Thank you for seeing us home — don't stay out too long in this cold.'

Suddenly there was silence. Dinah held her breath. What had happened to the dogs? Then she heard Talbot murmuring to them as Nimble and Quick returned, to be taken on round the house.

Dinah telephoned Annabel before Sam returned from College.

'I really was just about to call you,' Annabel said. 'I'm sorry I've been so much out of circulation lately – I think I've got myself better organised now, so that I won't neglect my friends! Dinah, would you like to do a bit of teaching?'

'Teaching?'

'Spinning and so on — dyeing, weaving, you know, all the processes. The girl who was doing it at the centre where I teach cookery is pregnant and they're looking for a replacement.'

'Priscilla's done more of that than I have – teaching, I mean. Come over, and we can talk about it.'

'Love to. When is Simon's birthday, by the way? It must be soon.'

'The third of next month – book the date for the girls.'

'Candlemas. No, the day after,' Annabel said, then: 'How are things?

'Oh, well, OK. I think I'd go bananas if I didn't have my work. I'd have to get out, take an outside job.' Dinah looked at the windows nearest to her. Out there was the mist, pressing against the glass out of the dark.

'Has anything been happening?'

'Well, no, except that Simon still has this wretched Alice in tow.' Her voice sounded brittle to her, false. How could she express how she really felt? Threatened. Haunted.

'Did you discuss any of it with Sam?'

'No.' Dinah glanced round. She thought she heard Simon, on the stairs. 'Hang on a second – I think Si is out of bed.'

He was sleeping soundly.

Dinah returned to the telephone. 'Sorry about that. Annabel, do come over – how about tomorrow? Bring the girls over for tea.'

Next day was dry, very cold, with the sun palely gleaming through a ceiling of high, white cloud.

'It's the moon,' Simon insisted, looking at the pale disc halfway down the western sky.

'Come on, Si.' Dinah bundled him into the car after school. 'Did you forget? Annabel and the girls are coming for tea.'

'I shall let Dumpling have a go at driving my John, dear – ' Simon's rendering of the tractor's name – 'but I don't think Charis and Mandy can'

'Oh, why not?'

'They're not proper farmers – they're just girls. It *is* the moon, Mum. I can look at it and I don't cry.'

Dinah laughed.

When Annabel arrived with the little girls, Simon immediately took them to see his tractor – and since there was also a small tricycle and also a go-cart that Talbot had made, the four children had enough wheels to keep them happy while the light lasted.

The cloud was clearing before a rising wind, like a carpet being rolled up. 'What a lovely evening.' Annabel drew a deep breath.

They took a walk round the garden and down the orchards. Dinah had been working hard all day and was glad of the air and exercise. Curiously, Annabel seemed to be drawn towards the dark fastnesses of Mongwodes, Dinah reluctantly following. Like Simon, she avoided this part of the property. She gave a violent start when a covey of partridges flew up from the rough grass almost at their feet, and whirred on busy wings away from the wood.

Annabel and Dinah watched them go.

A twig cracked loudly in the dusk of Mongwodes and both turned to stare, catching a fugitive glimpse of a figure fading into the shadows of the tangled wood.

'Who's there?' Dinah called loudly, emboldened by Annabel's presence, knowing that had she been alone she would have turned and bolted – although so far the figure she thought of as William had never made any sound. 'That's our wood, I wonder who . . . perhaps Steggles still has the shooting rights.'

'Either him, or a poacher perhaps.' Annabel stepped towards the hazel thicket bordering the wood.

Dinah glanced round anxiously. The atmosphere so near the wood seemed baleful and uneasy, though strangely Annabel did not seem affected. Indeed she pushed through the hazel stems and went quietly into the skirt of the wood.

In the wood it was curiously quiet, the brambles and the dead stalks of last year's nettles quite still, the dark green ivy leaves hanging limp in spite of the rising wind in the upper air winging through the tree tops. There was a sound like someone tripping over a fallen branch.

'Whoever it was tripped over a log, I think,' Annabel said, returning to Dinah. 'What's the matter? You look as though you've seen the proverbial ghost!'

Dinah grimaced. 'I thought – well, a ghost wouldn't fall over a log.' She laughed shakily. 'I just don't like the atmosphere down here – neither does Simon.'

'I don't feel anything – at the moment anyway.' Annabel shook her head and they started back towards the house.

Somewhere on the other side of the woods a car engine came to life, and the sound decreased and died in the distance.

'There goes our poacher – or your farmer,' Annabel laughed.

Later, when Sam had come home and joined them all at tea in the old dairy, Dinah asked if Steggles still had the shooting in their woods.

'I don't know. I think it was probably left that he could still shoot unless we wanted it for ourselves. Why?'

'Well, *he* wasn't shooting this afternoon, anyhow,' Priscilla said. 'He brought his old mother to see us – made me feel quite young!'

'It must have been a poacher we heard, then.' Dinah nodded at Annabel. 'Not shooting, just moving about in the Mongwodes – then we heard a car.'

'Maybe it was just someone out for country walk – you don't have "Keep Out" signs up, do you, Sam?' Annabel said.

'How odd!' Priscilla suddenly exclaimed. 'I've just remembered – the goats were terribly restless and nervy down in the orchards earlier this afternoon. I had to move them back towards the house, fussing about and bleating. They couldn't wait to get out of that far orchard.'

'You'd better take the dogs with you, Priscilla, when the goats are down there — do goats ever get rustled?'

'Oh, yes – but of course mine are all earmarked and identifiable.' She smiled at Sam. 'But you must remember that this place has been unoccupied for ages – it would be surprising if we *didn't* get people wandering in the grounds.'

'The odd poacher doesn't worry me,' Sam said, noticing that Dinah seemed particularly uneasy. 'One of my ambitions used to be to become a poacher – the romantic image, you know – moonlight, ferrets, lurchers, 'my delight on a shiny night' and all that. What do you think, Si?' He smiled at Simon and at Dinah.

Dinah, responding, said, 'Si saw the sun through cloud today and swore blind it was the moon.'

'I'm not blind!' Simon protested through a mouthful of cake. 'I saw it and it was the moon – I can't look at the sun!'

'Infant logic,' Sam laughed.

'What's logic?' Amanda Brooks asked, and her mother said 'Here we go – who's best at definitions?'

# *Part Four*

# Alice

Dinah was aware of the first blue of morning paling the dark sky at the windows. What had wakened her? Not Simon – and not one of the voices. Something more like a door slamming, but there was no wind. Sam also was awake.

'Did you hear anything?' Dinah asked.

'No, just woke up.'

'I thought – oh, never mind.' She lay down again. After a while Sam turned over and went back to sleep. Dinah lay awake, listening, and after a while there was a whispering of rain, nothing else.

Sam took Simon to school that morning, and after seeing them off, Dinah turned back towards the house and ran in out of the fine, flying rain. The trees looked black today, shiny with rain, branches and twigs like arms and hands, reaching towards the house. In the kitchen Dinah poured herself a third cup of coffee, having left both the previous cups to grow cold. She tidied the kitchen, throwing out the scraps for the birds.

After the washing machine was loaded and set in process, she went up to her workrooms.

Rain pattered on the window panes, blowing under the deep eaves against the walls of the house. It seemed to be blowing from all directions at once.

When she lit the oil stove and went to open the door into her second room so that the warmth could circulate, she stopped dead with a shocked little cry.

Her spinning wheel lay on its side.

For a moment the air in the room seemed to liquify. Dinah spun round towards the door as she heard a small, faraway laugh. She steadied herself, feeling giddy and nauseous. Nerves – she knew she was not pregnant, though not for want of trying – but had she really heard anything? And had the curtain over the tiny interior window moved?

'Don't be a fool,' she said out loud, peering about.

As she righted the spinning wheel, she thought: *One of the kids must have come up here when they were playing hide and seek – I told them not to come up here!* But she remembered being wakened this morning by a sound like a door slamming. Sam would say that the kids had been up here, tilted the spinning wheel – and it fell the rest of the way by itself.

She took the dustsheet off the loom, and stood for a time considering the weaving while her heartbeat steadied. At last the usual excitement began to take her over, the urge to continue, and yet she found herself this morning inventing distractions where none was offered from outside.

After her third unnecessary journey downstairs to check the washing machine she went into the sitting room and stopped half way across to the telephone. *But I wasn't thinking of calling anyone!* The wind whispered and nudged at the house, and the rain seemed to chatter at the windows. Dinah went to the telephone and dialled Annabel's number. No reply.

She had just moved away from it when the bell rang.

'Darling.' Sam's voice.

'Hello, are you all right?'

'Of course. Look, Di, about Simon's birthday the day after tomorrow – what have you got for him, apart from some new clothes?'

'Only a couple of books, so far.'

'Well – there's a trailer that goes with the John Deere tractor. I'll get him one, shall I?'

'That sounds absolutely perfect! But will it fit in your car? You'd better take the Traveller tomorrow.'

'It's a kit – prefabricated and packed flat – easy to transport and assemble. I'll bring it out today.' Sam paused, 'I have tomorrow afternoon off – a time-table re-shuffle – why don't we do something?'

'Like what?'

'I'll come home directly I'm through, we'll scoop up Simon

from school and go over to the seaside: lunch out, throw stones into the sea, take Priscilla and Talbot.'

When Sam got home Simon was in the kitchen finishing his tea, so it was easy enough to hide the large package upstairs under Dinah's and Sam's bed.

'I'll go round and tell the parents about tomorrow.' Sam returned to the kitchen and sneaked one of Simon's cheese pancakes. 'Or did you tell them?' he asked Dinah, noticing then how distracted she seemed. 'Work not going well today? What's the matter?'

She fussed with the kettle. 'Nothing really, just edgy. It'll be good to go out tomorrow – all of us together.'

'Like Cambridge. That was fun, wasn't it?' He touched her hair.

'Yes.' Dinah turned away, thinking of Martin. 'Yes, of course it was.'

'Di, are you sure you're all right? You're not – '

'No, I'm not pregnant again yet – neither am I at the moment pre-menstrual!' she snapped, then shook her head, rubbing her eyes. 'Oh, I'm sorry, Sam darling. It's the weather – I've had a twitchy day. Take Si with you – he's finished his tea now and he loves to go and sit with Talbot after tea, like two little old men!' She managed a laugh.

After father and son had gone out Dinah went to the telephone, thinking of the tension which had increased throughout the day – and it was nothing to do with the weather. It had to do with half-heard voices and half-seen shadows, distracting her and getting through to her even as she worked at her loom. Now she avoided looking at the windows, and was listening – always listening.

Pete answered the telephone. 'Ah, Dinah, I'll fetch her, he said. 'Bel's been expecting a call from you today.'

'Oh, Annabel!' Dinah's voice betrayed her anxiety. 'I'm scared – worried – I don't know – '

'I've been thinking about you. Has anything happened?'

'The kids must've knocked my spinning wheel when they were playing hide and seek – and it fell over by itself and woke me up early this morning.' She gave a shaky laugh. 'I suppose I let that spook me and it's been getting worse all day!'

'I'm not surprised!'

'I'm getting all speedy like I was before November the fifth. My skin's feeling all sensitive and *peeled* – I feel as though I've got nettle rash!' She paused. 'God, I must sound a wimp!'

'Dinah, just slow down! If you haven't any sedative in the house have a go at the gin bottle. I'd come over but I can't – it's my Group night.' Annabel paused. 'Is Simon OK?'

'He's fine. He gets a bit tired on school days, but he's fine.'

'Dinah, I know we'll see you on Saturday anyhow for Simon's birthday, but could I possibly come over tomorrow morning? Give me a ring. I could leave Dumpling with a friend on the way, so we won't be interrupted – though the afternoon would be easier as Pete is going to be at home working on some figures.'

'Oh yes, please. Do come!'

'I have my Group meeting this evening,' Annabel reminded her. 'We'll think of you. Don't forget.'

'Oh – er – no, thank you! You know, even talking to you now has made a difference – you've no idea!' Dinah felt her fingers and toes relaxing, though the veins were still up on her hands and her scalp felt too tight for her skull. 'I'll see you tomorrow, then.'

'Has Sam noticed anything?'

'He just thinks I'm stroppy. Oh, Annabel, how can we get this thing to go away? Make it go?'

'We'll talk about that tomorrow – I feel I should have more energy. The Group will tune in to you this evening,' Annabel said softly.

'What about the others? Won't they mind?'

'Of course not!'

'I mean, the others here?'

'Who, Sam and Simon?'

'No,' Dinah said, thinking: *William, and Alice – and Georgina.*

'Dinah?'

She gave a shaky laugh. 'I was thinking of – of William and Alice Crane – and Georgina. I must be going nuts! But I keep on feeling – that – well, something isn't allowing them to stay dead!'

'We'll talk tomorrow,' Annabel said.

Later, Simon in bed asleep and Sam's and her supper

finished and cleared away, Dinah went upstairs to her workrooms. She was determined to think only of the living. *It's the living who matter.* She knotted a few shreds of tweed into the weft of her fabric, also a watery ripple of pewter shiny lurex, then she made herself open the door to the other room, and forced herself to go past the spinning wheel and across to the window. Outside she could see only the rain flying on the night wind. She could hear the trees, out there, breathing in the wind and hiding their secret watcher.

The house itself seemed alive. The timbers creaked. Dinah remembered that not long after they had moved to Pooks Hall she had remarked on the fact that when a strong wind was blowing it was like being in a ship at sea instead of in a timber and clay built house. She had enjoyed it then, but now the noisy night was preventing her hearing any voices.

She returned to her loom and brooded over the design she had pinned to one of the uprights of the frame.

There was a strange lull in the wind, although the rain still slapped at the glass of the windows. Dinah looked up sharply towards the doorway into the other room. She had left one bulb burning in there. Now, though, the glow from the light showed not only in the doorway, but at the small window – which should still be curtained.

Dinah gasped. Her mouth dry and her palms tingled.

Her working lamps shining into the other room cast the shadow of her spinning wheel across the floor – *and the shadow was moving, slowing to a halt.*

Dinah's horrified gaze switched from the moving shadow quickly to the tiny window.

*Someone was staring at her through the glass.*

As though hypnotised Dinah crossed to the pane of glass dividing her brighter space from the other room. It was an aquarium situation – but who was the captive, in which tank? A dreamlike unworldliness clogged her mind, and Dinah whispered, as though hearing her own words would wake her to reality, 'I must tell someone that I know it's not Georgina after all. Simon is right.'

To be able to look through at Dinah the child had climbed on a stool. Now she stood balancing, a tiny hand on the window frame. She was a smaller girl than Georgina – smaller, but less childlike. She wore a rusty brown dress, and an obviously much laundered white linen cap. Her hair and eyes were exactly Georgina's colouring, but Alice's pale skin had not Georgina's healthy pink glow. Dinah saw her as pasty-faced and heavy-featured, even sullen. There was an adenoidal look about nose and mouth, and the eyelids were puffy from some vitamin deficiency. Alice's shoulders were a little hunched, and her attitude, first of curiousity – peeking through the window – was now defiant.

A flash of anger shook Dinah, and before her gasp of rage misted the glass she saw the child flinch.

This child had no business here, in the present, upsetting Simon – she had even ducked him under the water in the bath – and yet, as the pathetic entries in the Parish Register and other information came to mind, Dinah was overwhelmed with a deep sadness.

Then realisation of the situation hit her with stark terror.

Leaving lights and oil-stove burning, Dinah fled.

Sam was in the kitchen brooding over some students' notes, Irish music on the cassette player.

'Hey, steady on!' He looked up as Dinah came precipitately into the room. 'You sounded like a cavalry charge coming through the house – and not the *light* cavalry, either!'

'Have we got any whisky?' Dinah leaned against the Aga rail, struggling to steady her breath and the shaking of her limbs.

'Hey, sit down. You are in a state – I'll get you a drink!'

*What do I say to him?* Dinah sat at the big dining-table in the dairy, the light from the kitchen shining through between the oak studs. She drank almost half a tumbler of whisky in one swallow and held the glass out for a refill.

Sam looked so startled that Dinah almost laughed. But laughter, she knew, would tip over into hysteria.

She looked at the veins on her hands, trying to recall her conversation with Annabel. 'Tomorrow – ' she said, forcing her voice to sound normal – 'I don't think I'll go with you, Sam. It can be just you and Si and your parents for a change.' She saw puzzlement and disappointment in his face, but went on, 'I've so much to do here – I mean not only my work, but all the hundred and one things for Si's birthday and the party. He's asked me to make his cake in the shape of a tractor and I've never baked a John Deere before!'

She had finished her second drink and sat twirling the glass, her eyes febrile, as brightly glittering as the glass.

'Are you – what's up with you today, Di? Are you sure you're all right? I don't think we ought to leave you alone.' Sam moved towards her and put his hands on her shoulders. She trembled under his grasp. 'Dear God! If you were a rabbit your whiskers would be vibrating so fast they'd be invisible, and your eyes would be starting clear out of your little head! Dinah my darling, what is it?'

Sobs rose choking in her throat. Her chest hurt and her eyes stung. She twisted herself free of his hands and stood up, briefly hugged him, laid her cheek against his. 'Don't worry,' she forced herself to say.

It was hard for her to remain still and her gut felt knotted up with excitement. Her muscles twitched and jumped, and her skin crawled as though bitten by an army of red ants.

Suddenly she sat down again, looking in amazement at her hands. The ropy veins had smoothed away completely. She drew in a long sigh, closing her eyes, and saw clearly a vision of many hands joined in a circle – only hands, not faces – and by the flickering gentle light of candles she identified Annabel's hands. There was a soft humming sound in her ears.

She felt completely soothed, relaxed. She felt that, like a child, she could say to Sam: 'All better now!'

But he still awaited some sort of explanation for her previous mood – and a reason for her hurling herself down the stairs and downing two large whiskies in such rapid succession.

'I was looking out of my workroom window,' she lied smoothly. 'You remember Annabel and me seeing and hearing what we thought was a poacher? Well, in the light from the house I saw someone.' She paused. 'He stood so still I was scared. I suddenly couldn't bear to be up there alone!'

'That does it – we shan't leave you on your own tomorrow,' Sam said firmly. 'I'll find out whoever this person is!'

*Damn, I've blown it!* Dinah thought, but still amazingly relaxed, she said: 'Well, I'll see how much I get done in the morning.' But she was grateful to Sam for going upstairs to turn off her stove and lights.

In bed, waiting for him, Dinah lay in the dim light from the door open to the passage. The wind still leaned on the house, throwing patters of rain against the windows. Dinah was tired, and was drifting towards sleep when her eyes snapped open again, her heart-rate accelerating.

An adult voice, several rooms away, called out, and was joined by others, as though in altercation. Then there was a low, sustained cry, and silence for a while.

Dinah knew that Sam was in the sitting room now. Her intelligence said 'Late television' but the voice of fear said: 'It's them', and she could visualise, remember Alice now. *Alice Crane, why are you here now? What do you want? It's not Simon, because you and he don't get on all that well. . . .*

There was a child's laugh, then a sharp word from a man.

Dinah took Simon to school in the morning and arranged that he could have the afternoon out. Driving home, she was aware of the returning symptoms of rising tension and anxiety, that speeding feeling of impatience and panicky sensation of dread.

As she walked round the house to the east wing, the wind pushed her rudely, twigs and last year's leaves whirling up in spiralling spouts, and Priscilla's tea-towels tugged frantically at the pegs on the washing-line.

The trees were noisy, a rising clamour of wind carolling through their branches. Dinah felt naked in the wind, more than naked – flayed. She stared about, feeling observed. *William I'm sure. What is he trying to tell me?*

Dinah took Priscilla to Needham Market shopping, impatient because she had not had time to call Annabel.

'I'm so looking forward to this trip,' Priscilla said as they returned to Pooks Hall, 'so is Talbot – we both have happy memories of the Suffolk coast from the old days. It'll do you good, too, my dear.'

Sam brought Simon back from school and Dinah hurried him upstairs to change out of his school clothes, Sam calling after them: 'Don't be long, love. We'll have lunch at Woodbridge, and I thought Felixstowe would be fun this afternoon. It's so awful that it's nice! And there's plenty to amuse Si, even at this time of year. I've promised Priscilla and Dad an old-fashioned tea at that place down on the Front.'

Dinah had a memory of dark red carpets and white tablecloths, hot buttered toast and red jam. *What do I do? Shall I or shan't I go? Must 'phone Annabel. Why am I putting it off?*

Simon suddenly gave a strange whimper and held up his hands to her as they were leaving the bathroom.

Then he was sick – extremely sick. He wept miserably as his stomach spasmed and heaved and Dinah held his forehead as he doubled over the toilet bowl. 'It's all right, Si, darling, it'll soon finish.' *It must soon finish or he'd bring up his guts as well as their contents.* Dinah called out to Sam and he came running up the stairs.

'That's it, then,' Sam grimaced. 'No trip to the seaside for Si, poor little bugger. Is it something he ate, do you think?'

'I hope it's not some pox from school,' Dinah muttered, mopping Simon's flushed face with a damp cloth. 'Come on, sweetie, into bed with you.' She picked him up, limp and heavy. 'Sam, be an angel and get a hot-water bottle will you – and tell Priscilla we won't be coming?' Sam opened his mouth to protest and Dinah said, 'No, darling, you take them anyway they've been looking forward to it. I'll be OK here – I won't be alone.'

Priscilla brought the hot-water bottle.

'Schools are hotbeds of all sorts of germs,' she said. 'Too much central heating, and crowded classrooms.' She felt Simon's forehead with a practised hand. 'No fever, anyhow – that's good. Let him sleep it off. I'm sorry you won't get your little outing – are you sure you don't want us to stay?'

'You go and enjoy yourselves! I've a load of things to do.' Dinah smoothed Simon's hair, he was already almost asleep. 'You and Talbot wrap up well,' she said as they went downstairs. 'There's a big gale getting up, and it's always much colder on the coast.'

After hearing Sam and his parents drive off, Dinah went up to check on Simon who was still peacefully sleeping. She then went to the telephone. The Brooks' number was engaged.

Dinah waited a while and tried again, still unsuccessfully, and went into the kitchen to consider making the birthday cake. She made herself coffee, quite forgetting that she had had no lunch, and went to stare anxiously out of the windows

– each of the ground floor windows in turn. Only the wind was moving outside. Inside Simon slept, and the collies occasionally barked in the east wing flat.

In a way Dinah was glad of the dogs' alertness, but their barking also increased her fear – for what could they hear that she could not?

She quickly whisked up the basic mixture for the cake, filled three tins and put them in the oven. While they were cooking she went again to the telephone but Annabel's number was still engaged. Dinah rang the operator and asked him to try, but the number was not out of order, simply in use.

Perhaps it was the warm and delicious smell of the fresh cakes as Dinah took them out of the oven that drew Simon out of his sleep and downstairs.

'Mum, I'm hungry.'

*'Simon!* You startled me – I nearly jumped out of my skin!'

He giggled. He was bright-faced and rosy again, not sick at all, and carried a bundle of clean clothes.

Relief made Dinah temporarily forget her tension. 'You're really hungry?'

He nodded seriously. 'Really hungry.'

'What would you like to eat, then?'

'Toast and some cheese, yogurt and a egg,' he decided, and then added, 'Please. And then may I go out and play?'

'I suppose so.' Dinah frowned as she set the water on for the egg. 'Well, if you get through all this food you must be fit enough to go out and play!'

Simon topped up his lunch with an apple and a mug of goat's milk, and as Dinah saw that he was well wrapped up against the cold and the wind she told him that he must stay in the yard between the house and the farm steading – where there were no overhanging trees to shed branches, and where she could see him from the windows.

Now she felt a tightening of her scalp, and a sharp tingling of fear down her spine as a great gust of wind thundered in the chimneys and lashed the trees to a frenzied dance against the swiftly running stream of clouds. The wind tugged the door almost out of her grasp and Simon put out his arms and pretended to fly as he jumped down the steps to the yard.

He looked back up at her. 'It's my birthday tomorrow, isn't it, Mum? I'll be five – five what? What *is* five?'

'Five years old,' Dinah laughed, he looked so alive and happy. 'It means that you've been you, Simon, for five years – five Christmases.' She counted to five on her fingers.

'Oh, *that* five! I can count to five, Mum. I can count to twenty-thirty.'

She watched him go out into the wind, running to the garage to fetch his tractor.

The telephone rang.

Dinah slammed the door shut and ran through to the sitting room. She knocked into a chair, almost slipped on the new rug. *Slow down, slow down. Maybe a wrong number or the silent caller.*

'Dinah?' Annabel said.

She sat down, heart hammering. 'Yes. Oh, I tried to call you this morning,' she said, 'then Priscilla and I had to go shopping – I don't seem to know what I'm doing half the time – but thank you for last night. It did help!'

'It worked, I'm so pleased,' Annabel said softly. Then, 'Dinah, I feel awful about it but I can't come over this afternoon after all. Pete had to go out on an unscheduled job. His car is in dock so he took mine – and now my poor Dumpling has been sick as a dog. She's asleep now.'

After a short, stunned silence Dinah exclaimed: 'How extraordinary! So was Simon – I was just getting him ready to go out with the family on a trip to the seaside – he slept, too. Then he woke up hungry, so I fed him and he's now out playing.'

'They went out?' Annabel asked quickly.

'Yes, I didn't want this to spoil their day.' Dinah paused. 'Anyway, I was expecting you to – but neither of us can help our kids throwing up unexpectedly!'

'So are you and Simon alone?'

'The way I feel, I certainly would have been no sort of company,' Dinah said. 'And anyway Simon was asleep when they left. We'll be all right – I have plenty to keep me occupied. I hope Dumpling recovers as quickly as Si did. We'll see you tomorrow, anyway – if I haven't *burst* by then.' Dinah laughed, but tears were running down her cheeks.

'It's crazy, why today?' Annabel was saying, sounding almost angry. 'Pete having to take my car, Dumps and Simon both being suddenly sick – '

Dinah sniffled, shuddering. 'I must go and see if Simon's OK,' she muttered.

'Call me back if anything – if you want to talk.' Annabel sounded as distracted as Dinah felt.

Dinah could hear in the lulls in the wild wind's sound, Simon's voice as he manoeuvred his tractor about in the yard. She did not want to listen to what he was saying. He might have been talking and shouting to Alice – sulky-faced Alice, foxy hair blowing from beneath her cap. There was an occasional outbreak of bleating from the goats in the covered yard, and sometimes the barking of Nimble and Quick in the east wing.

Dinah went restlessly back to the kitchen and found the ingredients for the cake icing. Then instead of finishing the cake, she made a batch of pastry and put in the refrigerator, afterwards scrubbing the kitchen table. She was aware all the time that she was waiting, listening, fighting to control her excitement and filled with a dread that she could not understand.

She went to the door and opened it, then put on a coat and went out, hearing a renewed outburst of bleating from the goats. Buffeted and shoved about by the wind, Dinah crossed the yard, waving to Simon, and went to see if the goats were all right. They all had hay and water, and had not finished the feed in their buckets.

Nothing seemed amiss. When she took off her coat Dinah felt so electric that the lining of the coat crackled, and as it brushed the material of her blouse the skin of her arm felt dragged.

Then the house shook with a huge rattling crash.

Dinah felt weak with relief. Of course, thunder! Even in February. That was why she felt so tense and wound up – so electric. Maybe after all it had been thunder on November the fifth. *Rosemary Crane said Martin was like a lightning conductor! Why didn't he buy Pooks Hall himself if he was so interested in it? He could afford it.*

'Better get Simon in,' she said aloud, trying not to think of Martin. She put on her old leather coat again, and boots. The afternoon was darkening early with the storm. Slate-coloured and purple clouds were closing over the sky, racing fast on the wind.

Outside, she called, 'Simon, Simon – come in out of the storm' and felt the wind ram the words back into her open mouth.

The goats bleated in answer, but neither Simon nor his tractor were in sight.

The threatened rain still held off, and for the time being there was no more thunder, but the wind grew fiercer with each gust, tearing at the trees.

Angry with him, angry with herself, Dinah called again and again for Simon. She looked in the garage and all round the farm buildings. She ran round the house, the dogs barking excitedly as she came to the door of the flat. The door was shut – no tractor parked outside it – Simon had not gone to visit the collies.

Round the house again Dinah went, back to the yard. She shouted Simon's name, her voice shredding away on the wind, no more substantial than the faraway calling of the jackdaws tumbling and playing in the wild air, or the rooks wheeling over the tossing trees.

Dinah scanned the garden again, then trotted down the drive, bending against the wind, until she paused, panting, at the gate. No sign of Simon. She looked up and down the road, but she knew that he had not gone that way.

Back to the garden she ran in a flurry of hard, steely rain. She quickened her pace and felt herself duck as a peal of thunder boomed like a cannon overhead. Her voice became shrill as she called, edged with fear. There seemed to be a smell of sulphur on the wind, and something else – the hint of a familiar, unpleasant smell.

Dinah found herself in the walled kitchen garden. She walked warily across, and past the newly dug plots worked on by Talbot.

Simon's tractor stood halfway across to the gate into the orchards.

'Simon, come *on!* It's going to pour in a moment – where are you?'

She looked in the old sheds against the wall, in the greenhouses with their shattered panes. She looked in the little boiler room beneath the larger greenhouse, calling, calling. The wind rattled in the branches of the fruit trees, whined in the bramble thickets, hissed through the grass and roared in the woodland trees. Rain pattered a tattoo across the landscape.

Then across the rough grass of the orchard, Dinah saw something red.

She ran towards it, not believing what at first she was afraid it might be. She bent and picked up one of Simon's shiny red half-wellington boots.

The clouds were tearing away eastwards, and lemon pale sunshine streamed across the sky and through the trees, glittering and wet on twigs and grass.

'Simon!' Dinah's voice came out as a croak, echoed mockingly by the wind-tossed jackdaws above the woods.

Simon's woolly hat was caught on a hazel branch, between the orchard and the dark of Mongwodes. Dinah grabbed the hat, held that and the boot close. Something was very wrong. Simon would not have come here. *Si's scared of Mongwodes – so am I! He wouldn't have come here, not by himself . . .*

Dinah sobbed, thinking of him – five years old tomorrow – frightened, physically abused, in pain, murdered? She rammed a fist against her mouth to stifle the screams struggling in her throat as she recalled the figure she and Annabel had seen here, and the sound of the car beyond the wood.

She crashed through the hazel thicket and into the wood, Simon's woolly hat in one hand, his boot in the other.

She saw a broken branch and picked it up after stuffing the hat into a pocket. Peering down, Dinah saw what seemed to be a slightly worn path. Did she imagine it, or did the ground look recently trampled?

A shred of scarlet cloth was caught on a bramble. Simon's anorak. It was too high for Simon himself to have snagged it there. Someone had been carrying him.

For a moment Dinah stood in total disbelief. *This is not happening*. Then she stared wildly up at the bright, cold sky shining through the gale-wracked trees. 'Oh God, someone – *help me!'* she wailed.

She found herself running through the wood, a nightmare run. Then she came through a tangle of fallen branches and ivy to the edge of a dell.

There was a high bank facing Dinah across the depression in the ground. As she paused to gather breath, staring, there came another tearing explosion overhead, and a series of heavy, shorter bangs. Dinah gasped and her knees threatened to give way. She clutched a swaying ivy branch, dropping Simon's boot. Another explosion ripped away on the wind and Dinah cried out sharply.

The air seemed to hum and shimmer, and she saw a man with a spade, across the glade on the opposite bank.

He moved out of the trees and came down the bank at the side of the dell, to stand in the centre, the bank a little taller than he was, directly above him growing one of the tallest oaks in this part of Mongwodes.

For a moment it was as though dark clouds had covered the sky again and the sounds of the trees in the gale, the thunderous booming, were hollow and echoing. Dinah blinked, moistened her lips, and swallowed hard to clear her hearing. She took a step forward into the dell and the light cleared, the humming in her ears stopped.

She faced the man, and felt herself flooded by a hot red wave of anger which drove out even her fear for Simon's safety.

This was no ghost, this was not William Crane returned from the grave. Although he did carry a spade, this man wore no hat, nor was there at his feet a short-legged white dog with black ears.

'You! What the *hell* are you doing here?' Dinah was surprised at the strength of her voice.

Martin Crane stood smiling at her.

His bright red hair she saw was brindled with silver, blown by the wind. He was muddy and dishevelled. And his normally pale skin was ghostly white, tight-stretched.

'What about Simon?' Dinah demanded. 'You must have got him. Where is he?'

She moved forward then, staring past Martin at the bank.

Under the great roots of the tree which topped the bank were pieces of wood too straight to be roots, baulks and planks, timbers rotted and stuck with clay where they had been covered under the earth. A mound of earth and clay on the floor of the dell betrayed what had been done, and why Martin had a spade.

He had been excavating. But what, and why?

Angrily she snapped: 'And this is *our* property – mine and Sam's!'

As well as the smell of the newly dug earth which mingled with the normal woodland smells, rotten leaves and twigs, and damp vegetation, there was a strong, unpleasant and familiar smell – perhaps better described as stench. The words 'a stench of corruption' came into Dinah's mind.

Martin grinned amiably at her and lifted his spade towards the bank. She watched in fascinated horror as he prised open what was now recognisably a roughly-made and ancient door.

This fell outwards, its hinges at last giving way, and as a black cavity was revealed beneath the bank, the odour washed out in sickening waves.

'What is it? *What are you doing here?'* Dinah's mind was reeling, grappling with the apparently impossible. 'He's not – oh God, where's Simon? You haven't put him in – where *is* he?' Her voice rose to a cry echoed by the wind in the high branches.

He smiled now, a tense, bleak smile. 'Simon was just a decoy. He's of no account here. He's not a Crane.'

His tension and Dinah's connected, a crackling, tingling contact in the air between them.

*How strange he looks. Is he mad? A man like a lightning conductor, drawing down power.* 'But, Martin, where *is* Simon? Decoy or not, what have you done with him?' She tried to keep her voice low and steady.

Martin stared, and the smell seeped sickeningly out of the cavity behind him.

Then something cracked in Dinah and she ran at him, arms raised, brandishing her branch.

A great gust of wind swooped through the trees, tugging at the branch until Dinah, off-balance, let go. She felt Martin's thin, powerful hands binding her wrists, and she struggled, panting. 'What are you doing here – it's our wood – Simon's scared of it – where is he – what have – why – ' She twisted and kicked. 'Damn you, damn you. Will you let me sodding well *go!*'

'And have you scratch my eyes out?' He laughed.

She went limp. 'Oh god, please – I only want Simon! He's so little.'

'I'll show you what I am doing here, Dinah, and then you can have Simon – after you have done what I ask of you.'

'You've got no claim on me!'

'I have your son.'

Dinah moaned and twisted her wrists. Martin freed her and she stood rubbing the skin, breathing hard.

'Martin, he's scared of these woods! What have you done to him, bringing him here?'

'Georgina wasn't afraid of anything.' Martin dismissed Simon and his fear of the woods, and bent over a heap of sacking near the bank to pick up a powerful flashlight.

'Come here, then.' Gripping Dinah by the arm now, drawing her towards the cavity, the crude doorway – into the cave, the tomb. 'Maybe this made Simon afraid of the wood – maybe he felt the vibrations. Children are very sensitive.'

The smell was like an invisible barrier which had to be passed. Dinah pulled back against the hand which gripped tighter, hurting. She seemed to be swallowing solid lumps of smell. Outside, when she looked back, the wind lifted leaves and twigs off the ground and whirled them in a wild dance, and a sound like thunder cracked and echoed across the sky.

'Come on.' Martin almost hauled her off her feet. 'You have to see – '

Dinah cried out at a painful jerk of her arm. 'You *know* I hate caves!'

'Shut up whining, for fuck's sake! Just get in there and look!' He flashed the light beam about the cavity under Mongwodes, and monstrous shadows swelled and diminished.

Dinah stood within the chamber, shuddering with a deep chill – with revulsion, fear, loathing – and a sudden increase of excitement. Her skin felt electrified, her stomach curdled. Her scalp tingled and her heart pounded.

She searched desperately and in vain for Simon's small figure and silver-blond hair.

Under the bank a small, brick-groyned mausoleum had been built, shored up with massive timber joists set alongside the brick pillars, and with a rough herring-bone nogging of bricks between the timbers. Oak roots and probing bramble suckers tasselled the low ceiling.

Against one wall were rough wooden shelves, fallen at odd angles, and on them rested half a dozen coffins – little more than boxes of roughly nailed planks. In the wandering spot light of Martin's torch Dinah noted small details: the square-headed 'horseshoe nails' fastening the planks; a fold of greyish cloth; a hank of dark hair; growths of fungus; the place where a rat had gnawed through planking; mouldy paper labels on the box-lids. She saw another spade leaning against the far wall, and beside it on the floor an ancient, battered felt hat.

Martin now flashed the beam to the left, pushing Dinah forward, and she saw into a recess set back from the main chamber. Here were trestles on which planks lay to form a table.

It was not a coffin which rested on these boards.

Dinah saw the small delicate arm and leg bones, the birdlike little fans of the skeleton hands and feet, the pitiful empty arch of ribs.

The child's bones gleamed faintly amid the ruined rags of clothing — dark cloth, rusty with age, and as Dinah saw when she pulled her gaze slowly towards the head, the shredded remains of a plain white cap. She saw the foxy glint of the red hair – still such a lively colour – and she saw the terrible gaping space above the vanished eyes where the skull had been smashed like crushed eggshell.

Dinah shook her head from side to side, moaning, whispering, 'No – no.' From being tense and hyper-alert she was now so shocked, as to be almost completely numb. She felt, with a strangely resigned despair, how slowed down all her reactions were. She was even resigned to the smell.

'She's so like her, like Georgina, isn't she? Same colouring, same age.' Martin's voice was out of a nightmare – the words issuing from a face familiar and yet so strange as to seem quite alien.

'Georgina?' Dinah whispered, feeling as though her blood was at last beginning to circulate again. 'Oh no. Georgina was buried in the churchyard, there's a grave. Not here, not just *lying* here!' She experienced again that vibrant, humming sensation, and lights seemed to flash in pin-point patterns, shifting like dust-motes in the dark surrounding the pool of light still spilled on the child. Dinah whispered, '*Alice?*'

Tears filled her eyes. What had it been? It had to be murder, for had the child died in an accident she would have been buried. William's words seemed to hang in the air: 'God forgive mee – ' and 'Never bury deep enow – '.

'Yes, William, her father, killed her,' Martin said. 'Poor little girl – his Alice – murdered by a parent, just as my Georgina was.'

'No!'

He switched off the flashlight, and Dinah screamed.

Martin laughed, and suddenly her reflexes returned and she thrust past him into the daylight, the stormy daylight which was fading and full of noise and confusion in the gale. She leaned against the bank, sick and shaking.

Martin had followed and stood watching her. After a while Dinah faced him. She noticed that a tic twitched at his right eye, and as though in sympathy a nerve began to jump in her cheek. She dashed tears from her eyes and said, 'Simon was not in there. I know even you wouldn't do that to him. Now you've shown me – in there – where is Simon?'

Martin indicated the doorway behind him. 'This is where they put the ones who were – put out of their misery – or who put themselves out – a few that could not be buried anywhere else. And Alice, of course, she was the last one.' His voice was monotonous, and so quiet that Dinah had to strain her ears to hear each word. 'After he had – put Alice out of her pain, William closed it. He lived on – more than a little bit mad, hoping to die, but surviving *that* epidemic and afraid to take his own life. He died later of the small-pox, and was buried by the church. No-one knew about Alice – he set it about that she had gone into service over Cambridge way. Alice had small-pox. William couldn't bear for her to live on hideously disfigured, so he killed her – as you saw.'

Dinah felt awash with sadness, with William's misery at his

dilemma, his desperation – she even knew his love for his remaining kin, the red-haired girl, Alice. *Could I ever have loved a child like that? To do that to her?* Her sympathy went out to William, poor William. Dinah knew those moments of love that desire the loved object even to die, so that no more harm or pain can come to them. 'Poor, poor William – how he suffered,' she said softly.

'What do you care?' Martin stepped closer and Dinah moved away from the bank. 'You don't care about the dead or the living — just yourself. You didn't care about Georgina, even when you killed her!' The tic dragged at his eye in a travesty of a wink. 'William killed Alice – oh, yes – but he loved her, he was proud of her, thought her beautiful. It's all in his diaries – they were here! And I found out about this place from papers my uncle left me when he died. I'm a Crane, too, and so was Georgina – and she had to come back here – she came – *but you saw to it that after that one day she never came again!*' His voice was harsh now and accusing. 'But maybe I was like William, too, as much to blame as you. *I let you take her!* I let you have her and you destroyed her!'

A memory flashed across Dinah's mind – Georgina flying to meet her death – and superimposed upon it was the little heap of rags and bones and the hank of red hair that had been Alice.

'Why don't you say something?' Martin stepped closer and suddenly hit her across the face, quite lightly, but it shocked her and Dinah felt ringing in her bones the pain of her earlier injuries.

She bit her tongue and her ears sang. The trees roared and cracked in the wind and there was a flash and a sound like ripping cloth overhead. Dinah ducked involuntarily, and stumbled away from Martin who grabbed at her, but missed.

'I saw what you wanted to show me – I know what happened to William and Alice now.' Dinah touched her face where the skin still burned from the blow and the old bruises throbbed anew. 'Now, for God's sake, where is Simon?'

He shook his head. 'You haven't fulfilled your part of the bargain.'

'I *made* no bargain! What do you mean?' Dinah shouted over the roar of the wind.

Martin put the flashlight down and moved closer.

'She wants a body,' he said.

Dinah shook her head.

'*She wants a body.*'

'What?'

'She wants a body – *Alice,* of course,' Martin said. 'Don't you understand? Alice needs a body. *She wants to finish her life.* There *was* Georgina but then she died, murdered too! Good God, if I can understand it, why can't you?' He threw the last sentence at her with all the familiar impatience.

Dinah understood, denying that understanding. She glanced quickly about her for a way of escape – but she still didn't know where Simon was.

'Yes, Dinah, you will again supply Alice with the body she needs,' Martin said. 'It has to be a Crane, you see, so you and I must ensure that she can finish her life.'

The wind made a sound almost like laughter in the branches overhead, a hard and mocking sound.

Dinah clenched her hands tight under her chin – a Simon gesture – glaring at Martin.

He was laughing, like an echo of the wind, and it seemed that there were other voices laughing with him.

'I can't – I won't – ' Dinah gasped out. 'You're *mad!* All this digging in old graves – it's not good for you. You're obsessed with the past.'

He still laughed. 'A good try, Dinah, but not good enough. You want your precious little boy back?' Dinah made a movement as though to strike him. It was a mistake, for he grabbed her hands again. 'If you want Simon – well, my dear – you'll have to take the other as well.'

Once more Dinah had a sense of complete disbelief. Then the mood snapped and she began to fight. She tried to free her arms, to get a knee into Martin's groin. He put a foot behind hers and tripped her so that she fell on to the heap of sacking, where he held her down with an arm across her neck. Then he switched the flashlight on, directing the beam at her face.

Dinah still struggled, but the weight of the arm across her throat precluded much movement and Martin was now astride her. He laid the torch on the ground so that it still lit Dinah's face, and with his free hand wrenched at the waistband of her slacks – ignoring her flailing arms and desperate, clutching hands.

'If you hurt me,' Martin said, 'I swear I'll smash your head in and put you in the grave with the others!'

'Then she won't get a body,' Dinah hissed.

'And you'll never see Simon again!'

She moaned, twisting beneath his weight as he altered his position. Drops fell on Dinah's face, warm spittle, cold rain. She felt dizzy staring up past Martin's head at the sky so far away above the trees. They seemed to be whirling like the wind, round and round, while the sound of the storm grew louder, like the crashing waves of an angry sea and not the earth-bound complaints of a wind-torn wood.

Dinah began to cry, in a jerky, disjointed way. Martin hauled her slacks down, forced her knees apart with his, and at the same time clouted her across the head. Her ears rang with the blow, and she joined her hands together and pushed them beneath Martin's jaw, forcing his head back.

'You're mad – get off me – I don't want it – I don't want it – ' she yelled with all her strength.

'You didn't want Georgina either, but you're not going to kill this one!'

' – been killed – already – *just let them go* – ' Dinah's words spurted out fiercely as she struggled.

He was stonger than she remembered, with a mad strength, and Dinah stared now into the familiar face of a rapist. She screamed, arching her body under his weight, screaming and screaming, and the sounds tore out of her throat and mouth to tear like cobwebs in the wind.

Then somebody stood behind him, upside down to Dinah as she lay, dark and shadowy against the trees and the sky. *'Help me!'* Dinah cried, and a smaller figure was there, also.

As Martin positioned himself for the act Dinah saw the smaller figure move, to bend over Martin from behind, and she heard a man's voice above her calling, over the wind: *'Free us – now is the time!'*

Dinah felt hands, gentle hands, on her shoulders, holding her still where she lay panting from exertion and shock.

Martin had sat back on his heels, straddling Dinah's thighs, and now Dinah saw the little figure close in on him. Two tiny hands, childs' hands, slid round his skull to cover his shocked eyes. Martin swayed back a little, mouth open as though to cry out. Tumbling over his left shoulder the little figure came, embracing him now, letting him see her face which was then covered by the fall of bright red hair as she – after a triumphant aquamarine blue glance at Dinah – turned back to Martin and laid her open mouth on his.

The hands released her. There came a whisper in the sudden silence of the wind's halting: ''on't be coming n'more.' And Martin fell sideways off her.

Dinah scrambled to her feet, sobbing, dragging her slacks up and fastening them. She looked wildly round, but the dell was empty. There was no-one except herself and Martin. He lay on his back, staring up at her, the light playing on his face.

'Kissed me – who? Kissed – Georgina? Alice?' Then his eyes rolled from side to side and slid out of focus.

'Martin – Martin – listen to me, please!' Dinah bent over him. 'Where is Simon?'

'No Simon here – ever – ' Martin muttered, frowning, touching his face with his fingers. 'William – yes, two Williams, and Thomas and poor little Mary – oh, God help me, there was Alice – my own, my sweet, my pretty Alice!'

'Oh, my god!' Appalled at his words, Dinah knelt beside and shook him by the shoulders. 'You must tell me. Simon – where is he?'

But something was happening to Martin.

He was panting, tearing at the top button of his shirt. Sweat was starting out on his skin and his face was becoming deeply flushed, yet whitish round the mouth.

'Martin.' Dinah knelt beside him. 'Listen, just tell me where to find Simon and I'll go and get help for you – please.'

'No help – never no help now – no-one called Simon – ' he muttered in a hoarse whisper, eyes glittering up at her. 'Never – ' He moved his head from side to side. The sweat rolled down his face, drying there in the heat from his fever, and Dinah saw the flush deepen, the lips dry and crack. His breathing was shallow and noisy. Dinah could feel the heat from his body and she felt sickened as she saw his eyes become bloodshot and encrusted with matter.

'So quick,' she muttered in horror. What was wrong with him? She could not drag her gaze away, impelled to watch the man she had once known so well becoming a mad, sick stranger – removed from her knowledge by obsession, then violence, and now – what? Disease? A ghost's contagion?

Once Martin reached out and touched her face, and Dinah flinched back, scorched. He tossed and turned on the sacking and his features seemed to liquify, to blur and melt, running unrecognisably out of shape.

She watched in helpless horror as Martin's face became puffy and discoloured then by a spreading rash of inflamed spots of an even darker colour than the red of his suffused skin. He dragged at the neck of his shirt and Dinah saw the terrible rash on his chest also, on his hands and wrists – it must be everywhere!

Gradually, and yet so swiftly – *what had happened to time?* – the spots changed and became pustules which erupted, suppurating, everywhere: in his hair, on his eyelids and lips. The smell was nauseating – the smell of rotting life – a smell that had become sickeningly familiar. Dinah covered her mouth and nose – but she could not cover her eyes, she had to watch.

The man moaned, gasped, coughed. He vomited weakly, bloodstained and stinking, and Dinah could also smell urine and faeces.

The eyes, aquamarine chips between the grotesque lids, glittered damply at her.

'Elizabeth? My poor Elizabeth – forgive me – I killed her – save the suffering – God forgive me – forgive me! And Alice, too – forgive – ' The words appeared to have exhausted him. Then he began to squirm again. 'Dry – ' he moaned. 'Thirst – '

Dinah sat back on her heels. There was nothing she could do for whoever this was. He had called her Elizabeth, spoken of William, two Williams, Mary – and of course Alice. He had asked her forgiveness, taking her for Elizabeth.

'William?' Dinah whispered, kneeling up again towards him.

The pustules were drying now, drying and cracking. The fever still burned and Dinah could still feel the heat, though she was shaking from cold and shock.

'William?' she said again, and then, to her renewed horror and distress, he began to scratch.

He muttered and swore and Dinah watched as he tore with his nails at the shrinking, drying, cracking itch of the maddening rash. What comfort or relief could but ten fingers give to a body and its limbs covered all over with the intolerable itching? He tore at the irritation until the half-healed pustules shed their torturing, contracting scabs, and blood began to mingle freely with the pus, drying and flaking on the hot skin to produce yet more itching.

Once Dinah grabbed his arms to try and hold him from scratching, but something like a charge of electricity knocked her away from him, threw her back five or six feet, crying out in shock and terror.

*Like a lightning conductor. Perhaps if he dies they'll all be free to go.* Dinah crawled back to the agonised man and wept beside him, head bowed on hands, tears running between her fingers, sobbing: 'Poor William – poor – poor William – poor Alice – I'm so sorry – oh, Georgina – '

There came a gabble of voices, half heard beyond the wind, then only the wind. Dinah lowered her hands, wiping eyes and nose on her cuff, then fumbled in her pocket for tissues as she looked round.

Martin lay still and quiet. His skin had paled to an ashen hue, and he was perspiring lightly, the bright red of his grey-streaked hair soaked and dark. His lips were blueish, the cracked skin flaking. The puffiness was gone and his flesh had sunk in close to the fine bones – and over all the skin surface were the terrible craters of the small-pox scars, still fresh and tender.

Dinah cried out.

The man opened his eyes, shadowy, sunk far into their sockets. There was a flicker of life, almost of acceptance, a flare of recognition. Then a look of horrified wonder touched his face. 'Who – kissed – ?' a cracked whisper. As though peeled away like a mask the scarred skin disappeared, and Martin resembled himself again – or what seemed a sick wreck of himself. With an air almost of resignation, the eyeballs rolled upwards.

A series of mighty explosions brought Dinah trembling to

her feet again. She gazed helplessly round at the darkening woods, the wind-thrashed trees.

*What'll I do? He's dead!*

At the edge of the dell Dinah tripped, stumbled again to her feet and looked back. 'Oh, my god! He never told me,' she whimpered. 'Simon – oh, Simon!' Then louder, screaming, '*Martin – what have you done?*'

There was a heavy bang, and she felt herself hurled bodily backwards away from the dell.

Dinah was conscious of an extraordinary noise above the roar and crash of the wind – a groaning, straining sound. It filled her with a new terror and she turned and stumbled away from the dell, out towards the hazel thicket again, towards what remained of the wan and stormy light of the dying afternoon.

Behind her there was a rending, shrieking crash, and small branches and twigs rained upon her, seized her and raked at her hair, her shoulders and back. She screamed.

The void of hollowed space below and the battering of the gale above were too much at last. The oak tree leaned away from the wind as though in exhaustion. The tomb beneath its roots caved in. The tree fell.

It hit the ground in a shower of broken branches and twigs, from other trees as well as from itself. Then the great tree bounced.

As though in slow motion, the tree lifted gently into the air, twigs and branches and dead leaves too, all streaming upwards again with an infinite grace. Then it settled, debris pattering round Dinah as she stood in shocked indecision.

She must find out where Simon was, that was the only thought in her mind now as she struggled back into the fallen crown of the tree to clamber on to a branch and look along the trunk. She stared in amazement at the great mass of earth and roots which fanned up out of the mutilated bank above the dell, like a flattened bowl beneath the massive fallen tree.

Creeping along the tree trunk she saw the glimmer of the flashlight beam as it shone on the dead face where the trees broken limbs arched over Martin's body, not touching it.

The outing to Felixstowe ended amost as soon as it began. Sam drove into Old Felixstowe and down the short steep hill to the Front where he parked the car. The wind was blowing offshore and the waves were agitated and choppy, seemingly torn between obeying the shoreward pulling of the incoming tide and being pushed back by the westerly gale.

Gulls wheeled and cried, and Talbot, whose sight was still remarkably sound, pointed out a skein of geese following the shoreline northward across the river at Bawdsey. He identified the shapes of three ships, almost hull down and ghostly grey on the horizon.

They left the Promenade and forced their way against the wind towards the shops. Talbot and Priscilla hoped that Millars' Restaurant still existed. 'Of course it does,' Sam said. 'Felixstowe is halted in time, always just encapsulated as we remember it.' Then he suddenly stopped in the middle of the street.

Priscilla grabbed his arm, and a car swerved round them.

'Sorry!' Sam was startled. 'Do you mind – ?' He stared at his parents as though not really seeing them. 'Do you mind if we go home? I feel – '

'I know,' Priscilla said.

Talbot was already retracing his steps towards the Front and the car.

Dinah found that she was at the house.

She swayed in the wind. Her chest heaved, hurting, and she ached from bruises and smarted from scratches. Her last memory was of staring down the trunk of the fallen tree at the faraway dead face in the small spotlight of the flashlight.

With a feeling of total desolation she turned towards the house. She could hear the dogs barking in the east wing. 'Simon?' she called tentatively. Martin hadn't told her – she didn't know where Simon was! She called his name again, a loud despairing cry which set the goats bleating and the dogs barking afresh.

It was ended. The voices forever silent. Martin had been taken by Alice and William – all of them now released – and Martin had been the last of the line. But what was the point if she had lost Simon as well as Georgina? An aching sorrow for her little boy and her dead daughter crushed her thoughts, and she clutched her hands to her head, staggering.

Headlights suddenly pierced the dark, picked out the tossing turbulence of the trees and the bushes bordering the drive.

Two cars were approaching, came into sight, headlights shining blindingly into Dinah's streaming eyes as the cars swung into the forecourt to halt, like monsters, glaring at her. Dinah covered her eyes.

When Pete came home unexpectedly early, Annabel, after a hasty explanation, drove out to Monks Hempstall.

In her hurry she missed the usual Outwood Green turning, and doubled back along a by-road so narrow that she prayed that she should not meet another vehicle, or worse, come up with and have to follow a tractor or any other large farm machine.

Thinking of tractors made her think of Simon particularly – it was so odd that he and Dumpling had both been sick like that – stopping Annabel going to Pooks Hall earlier, and ensuring that Dinah remain at the house when Sam and his parents were out. She shuddered and hunched into her jacket. Flying twigs struck the car and she drove over a small fallen branch with a loud crack.

'What the *hell?*'

Annabel switched her lights to main beam to see better the small moving object on the road.

'Holy Christ! It's *Simon!*'

She pulled up and got out of the car into the gale. Her hair pulled loose from its knot and streamed like a banner in the wind. She called out, and he stumped towards her, limping in only one boot, scowling and muttering.

When he recognised her, Simon smiled through the mess of tears, mud and chocolate on his face.

'Hello, Annabel – please may I go home now? I want to go home – I left my tractor – ' He began to cry, holding up his hands to her.

She picked him up and took him to the car.

'Martin,' he sobbed. 'I left my John, dear, out in the rain – and he didn't come back.'

Annabel put him in one of the child seats in the back of her car and put a rug round him. She drove on, searching for a turning, a signpost, and then found herself on the Outwood Green road again coming from the wrong direction – but still on the right road.

'Nearly there,' she said, driving past a car parked in a gateway.

'That's his car – look! That's his car!' Simon cried.

'Whose car, darling?'

'Martin's – Georgie's daddy. But he didn't bring her back. He took me and told me to wait. I waited and waited and they didn't come.'

It didn't make sense.

Annabel drove on to Pooks Hall and turned into the drive directly behind Sam's car, which had come from the other direction. She began to see a glimmer of sense in Simon's story when by the house Dinah appeared, a demented figure, in the beam of the headlights.

Simon had become very bored, also cold and hungry.

At first he had enjoyed himself when Georgina's daddy Martin had come to visit. They had played together – with John, dear – all the way down the garden to the orchard.

Then it had changed and become frightening when Martin had grabbed him off the tractor and made him leave it behind. And Georgina's daddy had carried him to *that* wood, the wood where Simon could never bear to go because of something that he couldn't remember.

Simon lost a boot, and he lost his woolly hat, and he felt his anorak being torn by a bramble. Then Martin had told him to stop fighting and fussing, because he just might see Georgina. Simon became quiet then, because it would be nice to see Georgie again who was much more fun than Alice. Alice was too bossy, although he had a dim memory of Georgie being bossy and mean like Alice sometimes was, on the day she went away.

They soon came out of the wood to a path, and Martin put Simon in his car and drove along the bumpy muddy path in the wood until they came to a gateway on to a road. Martin stopped the car there and got out. He told Simon to wait. He found some peanuts and chocolate and gave them to Simon.

After eating the nuts and the chocolate Simon felt thirsty, but he couldn't find anything to drink in the car except something in a little flask. When he got the top off it was almost empty and anyway smelt of Dad's whisky. He wrinkled up his nose and screwed the stopper back on again.

The light faded and the wind buffeted the car, making awful noises in the trees, and once a big twig or a small branch struck the roof of the car with a clatter that made Simon jump. That made him think of his Mum saying she had nearly jumped out of her skin, and he began to feel lonely and scared, and he cried a little.

He wrapped himself in an old coat of Martin's, and wished he would come back with Georgie – he'd like to show her his tractor – but it was nearly dark and he'd left his John, dear in the orchard where it shouldn't be, and it would want to go into its garage for the night.

After what seemed like hours, and the cold and the boredom were too much, Simon stopped being obedient, unlocked one of the car doors, and got out.

Now he wished he had got out earlier while it was still light. He began to feel frightened again. Perhaps being bored waiting in the car would have been better than standing on the road in the dusk, not knowing where he was. He looked back at the car, and at the darkness of the bumpy path back to the woods.

Then, limping, the bootless foot soon becoming sodden and icy cold in its sock, Simon plodded away from the car along the road.

Afterwards, Simon told his story.

' – waiting for Georgie – ' ran like a refrain through the account. That and worrying about his tractor.

Dinah – relieved and grateful not only that Simon was restored to her, but also that he was remembering and talking about his sister at last – sat close to him and Sam. She was flushed from a hot bath, her hair damp still. Cuts and scratches showed on her face and hands, and once more the shadow of a bruise heralded a black eye.

'I went to look for him – I saw the tractor – the boot – his woolly hat like a trail drawing me to – that – ' but she wouldn't tell about that again, not in front of Simon, for at least Martin had not dragged him into that horror.

Sam and Annabel had listened earlier to Dinah as she tried disjointedly to explain what had happened. Knowing what they did about the Cranes at Pooks Hall, the story could not simply be discounted as a wild fantasy caused by Dinah's anxiety for her son, though neither really wanted to believe her.

When the three of them joined Priscilla and Talbot and Simon in the kitchen, Simon had eaten a good meal, was warm and dry again and cheered by Talbot's having been to the orchard to bring the tractor back to the garage. Simon seemed none the worse for his adventure, and was happy to tell his story now, sitting snugly and safe between his Mum and Dad.

After Simon's story was told, Sam turned to Dinah. 'So he doesn't know?'

She shook her head.

'And are you certain about Martin?'

Dinah closed her eyes, 'Yes – yes – it happened,' she breathed.

Sam and Talbot took flashlights and went out.

When they returned, both looked very shaken. They moved almost tentatively into the warmth and light of the kitchen as though reality were at risk, something fragile and not to be broken into by the horrors out there in the dark.

'I'm going to call Doctor Meadows,' Sam said.

'The Police?' Annabel looked up quickly, seeing from their faces that much of Dinah's story was true.

Sam nodded, sighing. 'I suppose so.'

Priscilla, who had not heard all of Dinah's story, looked a little bewildered, and Sam took her aside while Talbot, aware of a small child's 'insatiable curtiosity' as Kipling's *Elephant's Child* has it, took Simon out – well wrapped up against the wind – to say good night to his tractor in the garage.

The telephone calls had been made, and Priscilla had expressed for the whole family a wish that there should not be any publicity, when Talbot and Simon came back.

'Martin was quite well-known figure, of course,' she was saying, doubtfully.

'Why didn't he come back?' Simon asked. 'He told me to wait and he never came back. Where did he go?'

'He had to go away with Georgie, darling,' Dinah said gently.

'What about his car?' Simon's eyes were wide.

'I expect he has already come back to it and driven it away,' Dinah said, and stood up. She held out her arms to him and picked Simon up. 'I think you would go to sleep right away if I put you to bed now,' she said. 'Have you forgotten what day it is tomorrow?'

'My birthday. I'm going to be five.'

Simon's fears had been wiped away. His adventure had ended happily for him.

For the others, though, a new fear loomed, already hinted at by Priscilla – publicity.

There would be one inquest on the centuries-old bodies of certain inmates of Pooks Hall when it had been the Pest House, one of whom – a red-haired female child – had received a dire injury to her skull. An inquest must also be held on Martin Crane, possibly a descendant of a branch of the same Crane family as the seventeenth-century warden of the Pest House at Pooks Hall; Martin Crane, who had been found, dead, close to the fallen tree beneath whose roots the other bodies were found in a crude mausoleum. Martin Crane, dead from a cause as yet to be determined.

Here would be much grist for the mills of the popular press, particularly since Pooks Hall was now the home of Crane's ex-wife and her family – and more particularly since Crane and his ex-wife had lost a daugher, a red-haired girl of probably the same age as the child in the tomb.

Headlights flashed at the windows. The first of the official cars was heard drawing up outside the house.

Simon's birthday came and went. His cake didn't look much like a chocolate-iced tractor, but no-one minded.

The nine-days' wonder of the MONGWODES MAUSOLEUM came and went. Historians mingled with journalists and officials at the site and at the enquiries.

As was feared and expected the death of Georgina Crane was linked with that of her father – IS THERE A CURSE ON

THIS PLACE? – and with the long-ago death of that other red-haired child, Alice Crane. But the family closed ranks, with Annabel as well, and nothing was disclosed of anything which might be considered supernatural.

Simon never saw Alice again. When Dinah decided to ask him outright if he remembered her – like he remembered his sister Georgie – he frowned and said: 'Oh yes – she was here for a while, not like Georgie – but I didn't like her really.' His frown deepened for a moment, then cleared. 'Georgie was only horrid to me *once* – ' a sudden little shudder – 'that day – that day in the other car! But she never came back. Martin said he'd bring her, but they didn't come back.' He shrugged.

'I know. Sometimes people don't come back,' Dinah said, thinking: *And sometimes they do.* 'But we can always remember them, can't we?' She smiled, Simon also, and he nodded, turning away to play again with his dog – his own dog – chosen by himself. It was a small white terrier puppy, soft black ears perking over her bright eyes.

Later, the bodies from Mongwodes were interred in Monks Hempstall, and after that the interest faded, except for the publication of a few learned articles by local historians.

Alice Crane, at Dinah's insistence, was buried beside Georgina. On each flat stone was carved the name and the dates, in identical elegant script. On Alice's stone was asked the question: *'Is it well with the child?'*, and on Georgina's was carved: *'It is well.'*

*More Thrilling Fiction from Headline:*

**CRUELTY IS THE CURRENCY, CHILDREN THE MERCHANDISE IN**

# THE TRADE OF ANGELS

## DEREK PARKER

**'Readable, shapely, with a pleasantly evil denouement . . .'** ***She***

**As the last person to see little Jonny Brackenbury alive, illustrator John Opie is an obvious suspect when the boy disappears. And when a strange Greek dies practically in his arms, Opie realises he's mixed up in a very nasty business indeed.**

**Following his only clues – half a train ticket to Cornwall, a pornographic magazine and the muttered word 'Tiberius' on the dying man's lips – Opie sets out to clear his name. His first port of call is the fishing village of Polperro, his birthplace, where there is an unexpected Greek connection – and a brush with violence.**

**The trail leads to the ruggedly beautiful southern coast of Greece, but the deceptively idyllic setting cloaks a sinister vice ring of depraved and evil men whose deadly trade leads to innocence abused and an international network of corruption, torture . . . and murder.**

FICTION/THRILLER 0 7472 3245 8 £2.99

*More Crime Fiction from Headline:*

CAROLINE GRAHAM

# THE KILLINGS AT BADGER'S DRIFT

AN ENGLISH VILLAGE WHODUNNIT

"Characterisation first-rate, plotting likewise . . . Written with enormous relish. A very superior whodunnit . . ."
*The Literary Review*

Badger's Drift – a tranquil English village, home to Miss Emily Simpson, a kindly, well-liked spinster. But a gentle stroll in the woods near her home one day brings an abrupt end to her peaceful existence, for Miss Simpson sees something among the trees that she was never meant to see, and someone makes sure she will never reveal what it was . . .

To the village doctor, Miss Simpson's death looks natural enough, but her old friend Miss Lucy Bellringer is unconvinced and eventually drags the unwilling Detective Chief Inspector Barnaby into the case. His investigations reveal an unexpectedly seamy side to Badger's Drift – old rivalries, old loves, new scandals all come to light. And a second, horrifically gruesome killing shocks Barnaby into running the murderer to ground . . .

"An uncommonly appealing mystery . . . Graham makes her characters humanly believable in her witty and tragic novel, a real winner." *Publishers Weekly*

"Caroline Graham writes pungently, planting information with artful indirection, bringing baroque characters to life and death with equal aplomb, stretching the readers' wits and finally rewarding them."
*The Sunday Times*

**FICTION/CRIME 0 7472 3233 4 £2.99**